Some Kind of Comfort

Gary Clark

First published 2022 GCL Books.

Paperback ISBN: 978-1-8384010-4-7

www.garyclarkauthor.co.uk

SOME KIND OF COMFORT

GARY CLARK

Author's Note

Some Kind of Comfort touches on subjects that may be triggering or upsetting for some, including issues of bullying, sexual assault, self-harm, anxiety, PTSD, suicide and eating disorders. References and sources of support are provided in the back of this book for anyone who needs further information or guidance.

Mental health of young people is a more pressing concern today than ever in our history. The pressures to succeed, to look right and to fit in can be immense – compounded in times of uncertainty in the wake of the global pandemic. Now, more than ever, we need to look out for the well-being of our young people.

Some Kind of Comfort is a novel, with all characters, places and situations fictitious. However, the origins of the story lie in the author's journals of personal experience, which he wrote to help make sense of life during a difficult time for his family. The situations, illnesses and challenges faced by characters in the book, whilst purely fictitious, are rooted in the author's experience, and, he hopes, are written with sensitivity to the enormous pain of the many young people who suffer in similar ways to the characters in the book. If you are one of those such people, the author hopes you can find a sense of solidarity and optimism in the book; there are sources of support out there, and there are many people who care – hang in there.

For Ella.

Accept your superpower. Grow with it, shape it, and it will be your friend.

Part One
Death Dream

Chapter 1

12 days before I die

The air in the common room is humid and thick with silent anticipation. I turn to look at Ada and grit my teeth as I accidentally knock my guitar into my mic stand, releasing yet another pop and thud through the PA speakers. Even with her cut-down drum kit and using the smaller guitar amplifiers, the makeshift stage is only just big enough for the three of us, with Mia perched right at the front.

I try to catch Ada's eye, but she's already in the zone, playing through the beat in her head as we wait to start the first song – eyes down, hair flopped over her face. A bead of sweat tickles the side of my head as it makes for the floor. I need Ada to see me, need her reassuring expression, a nod of her head and that mischievous smile that tells me we'll be OK.

3

It was Mia's idea to play in front of year 11, and her natural persuasiveness has drawn a small crowd of almost twenty people, making this our biggest ever public performance. I steal a glance at the gathered faces.

Katherine and Matt, the school's alpha couple, are at the front, publicly draped over one another as if they're the main attraction. Katherine's presence alone tightens the knot in my stomach. There are smirks and the occasional quip, like we've opened ourselves up for criticism and they're not planning to hold back. My skin prickles.

I lower my head, focusing on my guitar strings. I shouldn't be here. Why did I think I could do this? Mia has already made it clear that she has no more patience for my mistakes. If I can't keep it together and get through this set, she'll flip out on me for sure. She's invested everything into this band, and the auditions for the Arena gig.

The Arena competition is *the* band competition: the pinnacle of the unsigned showcases outside of London, and the only redeeming feature of our dead-end town. It's run every year by the London Academy, my target college for the singer-songwriter course. The finalists get to play on stage at the summer's Arena gig, supporting some A-list band with a capacity audience. But, more than that, the winners get a place at the

Academy, and that's my best, if not only chance of getting there.

I shuffle back from the front of the stage. My hands are wet with sweat. I hold so tight to my plectrum for fear of dropping it that my fingers go numb and it slips onto the floor. My vision blurs with the panic, and for a moment I can't see it. Perspiration drips from my forehead as I lean down to retrieve the little red plastic triangle.

I straighten, take a deep breath, and try to settle. The anxiety I'm feeling is *not* a rising panic, *not* the beginnings of an attack – it is merely the expected and normal adrenaline response to the situation, on stage in front of all these people. It will pass, and I will do this right. People will see.

Mia glances at me and the tangles in my head tighten. 'Get on with it!' I urge under my breath. I look at Ada and at last she meets my gaze. And there it is – that nod and confident smile that tells me we might just make it through this. She reads my desperation to get going and immediately counts us in with four clicks of her drum sticks. I take in a deep breath on the third click and, at last, I let loose.

I hammer on the strings of my guitar, channelling the built-up adrenaline through my hands. Mia says something into the mic – an introduction – that I don't catch, and then she joins in, her bass guitar punctuating the rhythm. Her smooth voice slices through the room, as cool as ice. I spit backing vocals through gritted teeth. The clean, electric sound of my guitar explodes from the speaker system and bounces around the walls of the common room. In less than a minute, my head is clear and I'm flying.

Ada pounds on the drums, mouthing the rhythm and flinging her sweat-dampened blonde hair around as she crashes out the beat. Mia is calm, almost static in comparison. The natural, rich tone of her vocals speaks for itself. When we play and *click* together like this, the music is everything, and it reminds me of how it used to be: me, Ada, Mia, together, jamming, writing songs. The summer before last we did the four-week residential masterclass at the Academy – a taster of the full time course. We were never closer than we were that summer.

As the last chord rings out, I pluck up the courage to look up. Danny is at the back of the room. His presence sends a ripple of warmth through the room. In the short time I've known him, since his transfer here from some school up north, he's shown kindness and understanding I forgot existed. He nods his head at me. As much as he likes to melt into the background, with his height, his olive skin and floppy hair, he can't help but stand out from this crowd. He gives me a half-smile and I look away, back to my guitar strings, my comfort zone.

The first two songs go down well. People actually clap after the second one. The third is our least rehearsed. But, still, it should be a walk in the park. We're halfway through and I'm just starting to relax when things start to go wrong.

The problem is that third song requires the least of me. No backing vocals, and little more than a three-chord acoustic sequence on the guitar. The problem is: There's space for my mind to wander. I'm suddenly conscious of the feelings around my body – the lightness in my head that could mean I'm about to faint; the slight wobble in my legs that reinforces this possibility; the numbness in my cheeks that means... something; I can't remember what. I try to think where I am on my anxiety scale, the scale of one to ten introduced by my old counsellor, Terry. I must be heading up to a six.

Breathe. In for three... out for five.

The numbness spreads to my chest, my arms. I'm going to lose my balance. My fingers tingle and begin to numb. I fumble the picking of the strings, and my glaring incompetence is amplified through the room. Mia is looking at me. I can feel it. I avoid her glance. My heart thumps in my chest and I hold back tears. I want to curl up into a ball.

Breathe. In for three... out for five.

I drop my plectrum. Everyone is looking. My hands shake and the strings become impossible to distinguish from one another. The fumbled notes ring loud and I grind to an excruciating halt. A mix of embarrassment and anger is etched onto Mia's face. I look at Ada. 'Sorry,' I say, in little more than a whisper. The room closes in and it's like I slowly sink into a vat of treacle. It fills my ears. The background noise fades. Katherine laughs and says something to Matt that I can't decipher.

Why did I think I could do this?

My head spins and my stomach churns. I know this feeling, and I can't stop it now. There is only one way this ever ends.

I search the room for Danny but can't see him.

The head spin accelerates and I need to get out. I desperately yank at my guitar strap to release myself. My breathing shallow and frantic, I squirm to get free and drop the guitar to the floor. I stagger across the stage and fall through the door into the back room. The door closes behind me and the noise of chatter abates as I slide helplessly onto a chair. I lean over, my head between my knees, sweat dripping from my forehead and my pulse thumping in my ears. I am useless. Why can't I get a hold on these panic attacks? I feel sick.

The door flings open and Mia and Ada pile into

the back room. Mia's mouth is open but no sound emerges, just a fish gulping for air.

'What happened?' Ada asks, looking at me.

'I'm sorry,' I croak, my throat sore and mouth sucked of all moisture.

'Sorry?' Mia parrots back at me, her voice rising. 'This was supposed to be our moment, our chance to get people on side. The influential ones. Katherine was there!'

I shake my head, the panic now subsiding and leaving me with the shivers.

Ada crouches next to me, sympathy in her eyes. 'Panic attack?'

I nod. 'Sorry,' I say again.

Ada is about to speak, but Mia interrupts. 'Sorry doesn't cut it, Charley! Not now. Not at this stage. We have a few weeks until the deadline for demo recordings, and then it's straight into the auditions, and we are nowhere.' Her face flushes red. 'What if this happens when it really matters?'

She sits down on a table and nods for Ada to join her. They look like twins with their long, straightened hair and identical skirts hitched up above the knee. I shiver again.

'It was rubbish,' Mia says, pulling her hair around her neck and over one shoulder like a scarf, stroking it gently.

'It wasn't that bad...' Ada says.

'Not *just* Charley's freak-out. It's the songs. We need something new, something fresh. Someone needs to finish that song Charley started.' She nods towards me but keeps her eyes trained on Ada.

There's a knock on the door and it opens a crack. Danny's face appears and I straighten, aching for him to come in.

'Piss off!' Mia shouts.

Danny hesitates, glancing at me for confirmation. I give him a gentle nod that tells him I'll catch up with him later and he slides back from view, the door closing behind him.

'What is with him?' Mia says, scowling at me.

'He's–' I start, but my throat is too dry and the words break up. Mia huffs and waves away my noises.

She looks past me, as if by allowing her eyes to rest on me she'd be admitting some level of compassion. 'This has got to be right if we want to get through to the Arena audition,' she says.

My thoughts rush around in my head but won't settle. This is what happens when Mia is like this. Too many thoughts, all at once. What does she want? What can I say? Will I be able to get hold of my panic? How will I ever get on stage? Streams of thought collide, twist around each other and then tangle. After that, I can't think straight. The thought tangles have me, and , like a straight-jacket, the more I try to break free, the more they tighten. Why has she become so cold? What have I done wrong?

Ada looks at me. 'Can you finish off writing the new song?' Her tone is soft.

I start to reply but Mia dismisses me again with a wave of her hand. She jumps off the table and makes for the door, saying something about having to see Mrs Franks. 'Get it finished,' she says, 'and get it together, Charley, or we'll find someone else.' She links arms with Ada and drags her out the door with her.

I am alone.

I stay a while.

My anxiety lingers at a level four out of ten from its earlier peak at about eight.

At level four, it's OK. It's manageable.

WHEN I GET HOME from school, I switch off my phone, not sure if I can take any more from Mia today. I've no appetite, and the smell of Mum's cooking turns my stomach. I tell her I have homework and head up to my room early, but I can't focus on work, so I curl up in bed.

Dad pokes his head around my door on his way to bed. 'Goodnight,' he whispers.

'Night, Dad,' I say.

With the confirmation that I'm awake, he comes in and flops down on the bed next to me like he often does.

'Long day? Out saving the world again?' I ask, sleepily hoping for one of his infamous make-believe stories, something to take me into a fantasy for a few minutes – anywhere but the real world of Mia and Arena competitions.

'Tough one today,' he says. 'I flew to Greenland.' I smile into the darkness and lean into him as he shuffles around at my side, getting comfortable on his back. 'With the ice caps shrinking, those polar bears are getting squeezed. We got a tip-off on a real bad'n we've been after for a while, so it was a rush job to get me over there. I used the PM's private jet.'

'Fancy,' I say, smiling again, my eyes closing and head resting on his shoulder. I only catch snippets of the rest of the story; disconnected feats of incredible bravery – a crash-landing on an ice lake, an avalanche, arm-to-arm combat with a polar bear.

Chapter 2

11 days before I die

The grey of the morning seeps into my room. I roll over and pull back the curtains.

I need to burn some calories so I message Danny and tell him I'm heading out for a run. Usual route. I'll take the steep path up the east slope of Butser Hill. He'll take the longer, steadier climb to the top. I get no reply, and I know he'll be scrabbling around to get ready and out of the house. He's faster than me but I'm nearer the hill, so if I don't waste too much time I can beat him. It's always a competition with Danny.

I crouch on the landing to tie the laces of my running shoes. The noise of Lucas's online gaming seeps from his room, all machine guns and shouting. I smile at the image of him at his console, synced up with his friends, headset on, consuming sugar and storming the battlefields.

I pause in the kitchen to roll a cigarette from Mum's tobacco, my ears open and tuned to any approaching footsteps. I stuff the roll-up and Mum's lighter into my sock just as she comes into the room, pushing her hair back with her glasses and perching them on top of her head. She smiles, scanning my face. She's worried about me. Always worried. Every day, questions, probing, monitoring.

She puts the kettle on. 'Breakfast?'

'Later,' I say.

'Everything OK?'

Her words make me prickle. I tell her I'm fine and head for the door, the fleeting sense of guilt for fobbing her off pushed away by competing thought tangles. She needs me to be OK. She's still talking as I step outside. I look up towards the hill and draw a deep lungful of fresh air. Mist rises like steam off the fields. It looks kind of magical. I start to run.

I keep a steady pace, pushing through the pain when I hit the steeper section of the hill: the timing of my strides, the uniformity, driving forward like a metronome. The summit comes into view and the going is good, energy levels high. Danny will struggle to keep pace with me today. At the top, I catch my breath and take in the view of the old oak that stands

managed to keep a hold on it for long enough to at least make it out back without passing out.'

He hands me the cigarette. I look at it for a moment, then push away the thought of contamination. If I can't share a cigarette with Danny, then what's the point?

'How are you feeling now?' he says.

'Still up there at a level four. I can't seem to shake it off.'

He puts a hand on my arm and my muscles tense for a moment, then I relax. He pulls away. 'Up to the point you freaked,' he says, 'it was good. Seriously. I've not heard you that tight before.'

'Ada was on top form,' I say, smiling at the thought of her pounding the drums: all arms, hair and sweat. 'And Mia was...well, you heard her. That girl can sing.'

Danny looks sideways at me. '*You've* got the voice too.'

'I couldn't do what Mia does, couldn't deal with that level of scrutiny. I can't even keep it together at the back of the stage.'

Danny nods, kicking out at the leaves at his feet. 'I'd like to hear you sing, you know, not just backing vocals. Something you've written.'

I choose not to respond. I've only known Danny for a few weeks, since he only recently joined from a different school up north. We don't see much of each other at school. We only ever talk when we're on a run together, but there's something about him that puts me at ease more than anyone else. He gets my connection with the music. He can see it. I can tell. 'Mia was in a right mood afterwards,' I say.

'I saw her,' Danny says.

'She did that thing where she pulls her hair over her shoulder like a scarf and strokes it, like that James Bond villain with the cat.' I force a smile for Danny. I'm drifting from Mia's favour. It's obvious. She usually tolerates me, probably for the band, but it was different this time. She wouldn't even look at me.

'The evil mastermind. Sounds about right,' Danny says. 'I hear that she's entered the Arena band competition.' He exhales a plume of smoke.

I shift my position against the tree to ease the numbness in my shoulder. 'Already? She told you that?'

'Ada put something on Insta last night. Did you not see it?'

I shake my head. 'They've entered without me?'

He shrugs. 'Don't see how they can do it without you.'

Mia is freezing me out, and Ada's going along with it. I wouldn't put it past Mia to find someone else for the guitar, even if it meant they weren't as good as a band. 'Maybe it's for the best,' I say.

Danny snorts. 'Defeatist.'

'I'm kidding myself anyway. I can't even play the year eleven common room. I'm never getting on a stage in front of thousands.'

'That competition comes with added incentives, though,' Danny says, giving me a sideways glance.

'She'd love to win that, with a place at the Academy up for grabs,' I say, looking up into the trees. A pair of starlings shout to each other across the clearing from their perches above our heads. I hand the cigarette back to Danny.

'Not just one place...' Danny pauses as he takes a drag. 'A place for *each* band member, irrespective of your exam results.'

'How do you know so much about it?'

'Used to follow it when I was up in Sheffield. Renowned institution, the Academy.' Danny smiles. He knows I have my heart set on a place there, and the Arena gig has always been a possible route in, if a long shot. Getting through to the auditions is tough enough, and it's a lottery from there. Even if I did get through with Mia and Ada, I'm not convinced I'd ever make it on stage without ending up in a shivering mess of a panic attack. Maybe they've done me a favour – made the decision for me.

I fold my arms against the cool air on my sweat-dampened body. 'I'll just have to take my chances with the traditional application route.'

'Speak to Mia.'

I shake my head. 'I think she'd rather I were dead in a ditch right now.'

'They need you. You're the soul of that band,' he says with a serious tone.

I think of the Martin D18 guitar I got for my sixteenth birthday. My most precious possession, with tones that blend so well with my voice. 'She just needs someone she can manipulate to help make her shine,' I say. 'In any case, that competition is the sheer definition of long shot. Do you know how many bands enter that thing?'

'From all over,' Danny says. 'Hundreds of demo entries. Maybe thousands?'

We are quiet for a minute. The breeze from the south brings the cabbage-like scent of the rapeseed fields that I always connect with the beginning of the summer. I think of the striking, homogenous yellow you see from the perimeter at the south end of the woods. Danny and I rarely get that far, preferring to stop and talk here before heading back.

'Right, tosser.' He leans into an exaggerated lunge, limbering up. 'Back via the summit again, or around the bottom?'

'You think I'm running anywhere with you looking

like that?' I smile as Danny pulls a ridiculous geek-face and hikes up his running shorts, jogging on the spot.

'Your shoelace is undone,' I say, crouching to help him. 'Let's go the flat route back, see if you can keep up with me.'

Danny laughs. 'Yeah, you're funny, Charley.'

I finish tying his laces together and spring up and away, heading for the path out of the woods. I look back over my shoulder. He jerks after me and stumbles forward, face-first into the carpet of leaves. I stop and watch as he scuffles, sits up and swings his legs in front of him. He gives me one of his full-on grins, a rare smile on both sides of his face. I turn and run.

By the time I hit the foot of Butser Hill I'm sprinting. I slam into my back door and double over, gulping for air. Danny reaches me a few seconds later. Another hundred metres and he'd have caught me for sure.

'Good work, Danny,' I say when I catch my breath.

'You got me this time,' he says, between gasps for air.

I give him a smile. 'Later, then?'

'Later,' he says as he walks away, backwards.

He turns and heads towards the foot of Butser Hill, where he'll take the path round to the Maudsley Estate. His mum and little sister will be waiting for him.

'Hey!' I shout after him. 'Thanks.'

'What for?' he shouts back.

'I don't know...' What am I thanking him for? For just being there? Someone to talk to who doesn't judge? I don't know.

'Any time, Charley,' he says with a half-smile.

The kitchen is quiet when I push through the back door. There are pancakes on the side, and the sweet smell of maple syrup in the air. I don't feel like I've burned any calories. I return Mum's lighter to the table and scrape the pancakes into the bin, pushing them down, out of sight.

Chapter 3
10 days before I die

Something hits the back of my head and a scrunched-up bit of paper drops to the floor. I look around.

'Play us a tune, Charley.'

Katherine, the ultimate alpha female and Mia's idol, smiles at one of her vacuous clones, one of the same-face-same-hair crew. Katherine is most dangerous when her boyfriend Matt isn't around. At least Matt seems to rein her in a bit. She's the archetypal bitch, the mould for the rest of the copycats, the stem cell for the brainless clone army. I have this recurring daydream in which I turn around and punch her pouty face. Then the beautiful Matt ends up breaking up with her and falling in love with me for being so rock hard.

The bell sounds, and people start to move. Mia and

Ada pack quickly, link arms and leave without a glance in my direction. They've barely spoken to me since the gig, and still no mention of the competition. I'm not sure I blame them. Anyway, my focus right now is on keeping my thought tangles under control so I don't spin out.

I stop to lighten the load of books from my bag into my locker on my way outside. My energy is waning. As I close the locker door and turn the key, Katherine and Matt walk past, not noticing me. Matt is nice-looking. He has short hair, longer on top. There's something about him that calms me: a flick of his eyes in my direction, a covert, supportive word in a debate in class, or something more subtle. I don't know what. Just a feeling. His parents own one of the nice houses on Highfield Road.

They pause in the corridor. Matt is right up in Katherine's face with two inches between their noses, her height matching his. She leans back against the wall and Matt stares, his expression menacing, his jaw tight. The spell breaks and Matt relaxes. He takes Katherine's hand and they walk on as if the weird exchange had never happened. I scrunch my eyes and look again to check I'm not imagining it, but there they are, turning the corner at the end of the corridor as if everything's normal.

Outside, French-plaits-Ellie gives me a fleeting

sideways glance and skilfully shuffles her feet to edge me out of Mia's circle. I slide over to Ada and give her a gentle nudge. She flicks me a smile and makes a gap. No one else seems to notice me.

Inside the circle, I start to feel dizzy. I bite my lip, squeezing my teeth together until I taste blood. I shift my feet to steady myself and shake my head clear. I feel sick. Fear gathers. Familiar sensations, yet different somehow. Every time is different, so it's impossible to tell if it's panic or real sickness coming. I lose the thread of the conversation and look down at the ground to avoid catching anyone's eye. I'm thinking it must be a stomach bug. I sway and hold on to Ada's arm to stop myself from stumbling. She looks at me, asks if I'm OK, saying I look pale. Thought tangles are coming fast now. My mind races and the mantra fizzes around my head: *the only thing to fear is fear itself...*

I instinctively look around for Danny. Despite knowing him for just a few weeks, he's the only one in school who understands my panic attacks. He hasn't said as much, but I'm sure he has suffered too, in the past. I imagine his hand on my arm. 'In for three,' he'd say. 'Hold... then out for five.'

Mia is still talking and holding her audience. Her expression is determined, like she's working hard to maintain her queen bee persona. But it's the dimples in her cheeks as she smiles that give her away. Beneath the kick-ass bitch facade, she's no different to me or Ada. We've been friends for as long as I can remember, and those dimples just remind me of the giggling fits we used to have – the sleepless sleepovers and the hours of make-believe games in her parents' outhouse. And now her survival strategy seems to include my condemnation.

Sweat on my forehead cools me and I shiver. Ada glances at me, then turns back to Mia. The counsellor's voice scratches around in my mind, fighting to be heard through my stream of thoughts and images.

'What's the worst that can happen?' he says.

'I'll be sick,' I reply.

'Is that the worse thing?'

'Yes.'

'Worse than dying?'

'I'd rather die than be sick.'

'Why?'

'Because, Terry, being sick is the worst thing ever. I have a sick phobia, remember?'

'What's the bit that makes you so scared?'

'Not knowing when it will start or stop, getting up in the morning, going to school then feeling sick and not being able to get home, to the toilet. Feeling sick on the bus, or the train. Not knowing how often I will be sick or for how long. Being sick in public, the waves of nausea, the retching, stomach cramps... Shall I go on?'

'How many times have you been sick?'

'Loads...'

'I mean on how many separate occasions?'

'One. When I was seven.'

'And remind me how old you are now?'

'Sixteen.'

'So once in sixteen years and nothing since you were seven. That's not bad odds.'

'If it's once every seven years, then I'm overdue and I'd better be careful,' I said. 'You know I haven't been sick for that long because I *am* careful.' I paused. 'I'm clean. I eliminate the risk.'

Mia drones on and I covertly check the temperature of my forehead with the back of my hand. It's warm and sweaty. I'm at a level seven and fast approaching an eight on the anxiety scale, a tiny step from an irretrievable nine.

In for three... hold... out for five.

Something pulls me back. A subconscious image. A feeling, or a thought. My breathing steadies and I drag myself further back into calm.

In for three... hold... out for five.

Ada is laughing with Mia, glancing briefly at me from time to time. Tension begins to seep from me, and it's as though it's taking my strength with it.

In for three... hold... out for five.

I run my fingers up and down over the soft, raised

bits of the scars on the inside of my arm, under the sleeve of my top. The touch of them gives me perspective. The tension continues to drain from me like water from a barrel. Then comes the bitter residual. The post-panic hangover.

I hear my grannie's voice in my head: 'I want you to think of it as a gift, Charley.'

I could never conceive of the chaos in my head as a *gift*.

'I have a few years on you,' she said, 'and one of the things I've learned is that people like me and you, we go a little deeper than most. We dig that bit further down and really *feel* people. What affects them. What makes them sad, happy, scared. How they might feel if we reach out to them – touch them, or don't touch them.'

My grannie could read me. She understood the thought tangles, the OCD, my phobia. She suffered too, though she never talked about the details. I wish I'd asked her about it, before it was too late.

But she was wrong. My thought tangles are anything but a gift. They are an indicator of my selfishness. It's all about me. Me, me, me. Every thought, every second of every day in my own head, my own problems and worries. Sick of it.

Chapter 4
9 days before I die

The days are becoming more challenging. Just making it through school is sapping the little energy I have. I treat myself and bypass Mia and the girls at lunchtime and go straight to the music department. I tell myself I'm going there to do some work on the new song, which is kind of true. I head for the solace of the soundproofed recording room where the outside ceases to exist when the heavy door thumps closed.

On the other side of the glass vision panel that forms the wall between the studio and the 64-channel sound desk, to my surprise Danny is inside, playing a guitar with headphones on. He's hunched over his guitar, concentrating on his finger positioning on the fretboard.

I've never heard him play before. Our friendship

has been short. I knew he played, but I've never considered whether he is any good. I always thought his skills lay more in sound engineering than in performance.

Red lights race up and down on the sound desk and I flick the switch so that Danny's guitar comes over the monitors: clean acoustic arpeggio, competent and practised.

I suddenly feel guilty for eavesdropping and reach over the desk to flick off the sound. I pause with my finger over the switch when his vocal drifts in. His Sheffield accent is clear in his singing voice. As he lifts his head up to the microphone, he catches sight of me. I flick off the sound and duck out of sight, cringing. I feel stupid for hiding and come back into view. He mouths something and points at the desk. I switch the sound back on.

'Hey, Charley? Are you OK? Can you hear me? Were you listening to that?' he asks. I nod, with a brief smile. 'I could do with someone to help me finish it off,' he says, looking hopeful. I shrug then lean over the desk to activate the intercom so he can hear me.

'You want me to help?' I say. He jumps, almost falling off his chair; the volume of the intercom is way too high. I laugh and then I slide the volume fader down a bit.

'What do you need?' I say.

'Bit of polishing, and some vocals.'

'OK, let's do it next week, in here?'

'Awesome,' he says.

'Let me know then.'

'Awesome,' he says again. I motion that I need to go and he nods with one of his characteristic half-smiles.

AN AFTERNOON in double maths passes quicker than usual as I spend much of it ruminating on Danny's music and the possibilities for us to hook up, to create some stuff together.

As I come out of school to head home, he is just ahead of me. I smile, watching him for a moment as he plods along carrying his guitar case. He's hunched, in a thick parka coat with a fluffy hood.

My phone pings and I pull it out of my pocket. A message from Mia.

Mia: Where'd you go?

I start to reply but can't think of what to say.

Mia: You done that song yet?

Me: Nearly.

Mia: ...

If she's asking about the song, then maybe she is including me in the band competition after all. I turn my phone on silent and slip it back into my pocket as I fall into step with Danny. 'Hey, how's it going?' I say.

He says hi as he flicks his hair away from his deep blue eyes and smiles. We are quiet as we amble down my street of identical terraced houses, each with its own postage-stamp-sized front garden, lovingly personalised. The silence is a little awkward.

I wonder what Mia's response was. It digs at me and I resist the urge to look at my phone.

'Nice shoes,' Danny says, breaking the tension, a little humour in his tone.

'What's wrong with them?' I say.

'Nothing, I said they were nice.' He gives me one of his lopsided smiles.

'Yours too,' I say, with a smirk of my own. 'Even if they are a bit...'

'What?' He laughs.

'I don't know, a bit... you know.'

'What?'

'A bit... mature? I think my dad has the same ones.' I smile up at him.

'Oh, that's nice,' he says. 'Any other fashion tips?' I sense him looking sideways at me.

'I'll let you know,' I say, without catching his eye. 'How long have you had that thing?' I nod at his guitar.

'A year maybe,' he says, looking up at the sky.

'You kept that quiet.'

'Yeah, I started playing around the same time as...'

'What?'

'Nothing, too much information.'

'Go on,' I say.

He sighs. 'I got this guitar around the time I was trying to stay out of the way of my dad. It was a good distraction for me. He left in the end, but before that, he was a nightmare. Aggressive. He was fucked up, really.'

'Sorry.'

'We're better for it. It's just the three of us now.'

'How's your little sister?'

'Katie? She's OK.' He looks over his shoulder as if expecting to see her. 'She's got some after-school club today.' He pauses. 'I'm a bit worried about her. She gets anxious.'

'Oh no,' I say. That might explain why Danny is so intuitive about my anxiety. 'I know how that feels. Do you want me to talk to her?'

Danny smiles. 'Thanks. No, it's OK. But I appreciate the offer. Might take you up on it at some point.'

'Any time,' I say.

We get to my house and he stops at the end of the path as I continue to my front door. I open it and my dog BB greets me, then jumps up at Danny, trying her best to wash every bit of his exposed skin. He leans down and gives her some attention.

'Jesus, your breath smells,' he says, leaning his head away from her and looking up at me.

'Thanks,' I say.

'Not you. No human can have breath as bad as this,' he says, just as BB lands a smacker of a lick right on his mouth. He leans away, grimacing and wiping his lips with the back of his hand.

'True love,' I say, then call BB away.

Danny raises a hand and turns to walk away towards the Maudsley Estate. I call him back. 'Hey. You want to jam something? We could work on your song?' I surprise myself with the confidence in my voice. He's never been in my house before.

He looks around as if I could be talking to someone else. 'Why not,' he says, stepping back towards me.

Mum is in the kitchen, still in her work clothes, her smart-casual gear that gives the air of relaxed authority. She's worked her way up to a senior position in a women's charity. She says she's not at the sharp end anymore and I know she misses the day-to-day contact with the women in the shelters. Any excuse to get out of the office and she's straight back on the street.

'Hey, Mum.'

She smiles at me. Her eyes turn to Danny. 'Hi. And who's this?'

Danny towers above her by a good six inches. He reaches out his hand and Mum takes it, her smile broadening. 'Danny,' he says. 'Charley and I are in some classes together.'

'Sheffield?' Mum says, then looks at me with a wry smile. 'Solid northern roots.'

Danny nods. 'We moved down just last year.'

'I like a—' Mum starts.

'We've got work to do,' I say, interrupting. 'Music.' I motion for Danny to follow me out of the kitchen before Mum locks him in to a full-on discussion on the blessings of being a northerner.

'Nice to meet you,' Danny says as I usher him out of the room.

'You too, Danny,' Mum calls after us. 'I'm making some food later if you want to stay?'

'No, Mum. He's not staying.' I roll my eyes and Danny laughs.

'She seems nice.'

'Yeah, well, you don't have to live with her.' I pick my acoustic guitar from its stand in the corner of the lounge and hand it to Danny as he takes a seat on the sofa. 'Try that for size. I'll make tea. You want one?'

Danny nods as he inspects the guitar, gently handling it as if it were supremely delicate. 'Beautiful...'

'Sugar?' I ask.

'Two,' he says, not taking his eyes off the guitar.

In the kitchen, Mum is leaning back against the side with a smirk, watching me as I fill the kettle.

'What?' I say, managing to keep my smile hidden.

'Nice boy.'

'He's a *friend*, Mum.'

'Where's he from? He's nice looking.'

'Sheffield. He told you that.'

'I mean originally? His family?'

'His mum is from Indonesia, I think,' I say. Danny hadn't told me this but a few weeks back, before we really knew each other, we were in a geography class and the teacher asked Danny all this stuff about the Indonesian islands. There are over 17,000 tropical islands apparently, most of which are uninhabited. I remember thinking that it sounded like a place I could get used to, somewhere Mia couldn't get to me. Then the teacher said something about the Sumatran tiger and I went off the idea a little.

'And is there something—' Mum starts.

'*Friends*,' I say, my tone tightening. I stir sugar into Danny's tea and pick up both mugs to head back to the lounge. Mum gives me a wink.

She's wrong. I don't think of Danny like that. The last thing I need is someone else who Mia could target. She's already made comments about Danny, and how she thinks he's stalking me, and that I should see him as a threat. Yes, I see him when we go running, but that's it. And the music... I don't know about the music yet. He kind of took me by surprise in the studio today.

'This is a sweet guitar,' Danny says as I place his

tea on the table next to him. He strokes a few chords. It's nice to hear my guitar from a distance for a change, in someone else's hands. The tone is beautiful, a perfect balance between the solid bass end and the crisp treble. 'Here.' He hands it back to me and unzips his own guitar case to slide out his Takamine G-Series. A decent guitar, and well worn in by the looks of it. 'This is my old friend.'

'Looks older than a year,' I say.

'It was second hand when I picked It up. Nicely run in. Matured.' He picks at the strings. He's right. For a G-Series the sound is remarkable. I watch his fingers slide between the different fret positions as he works through a sequence. His technique is interesting – not technically brilliant, but he has something else, something raw and natural. He transitions between chords like he was born to play – the guitar is like an extension of his arms, part of him and flowing with his energy.

I get myself in sync and follow his lead, gently accompanying his arpeggio with a simple chord sequence, careful not to overpower his sound with my clunky playing style. I'm used to thrashing out the chords just to be loud enough to reach a level with Ada's drums and Mia's bass. This is different, this is a marrying of two sounds, not a competition for space in the soundscape. 'That's beautiful. Is that what you were playing in the studio earlier?'

Danny nods. 'I wrote it a while ago, but I can't get the vocal to sit right. I have half an idea that you might give it a go for me?'

My heart thumps in my chest at Danny's suggestion, a reaction I wasn't expecting. The thought of Danny handing me the responsibility to take a lead vocal on *his* song both excites and terrifies me. I love to sing. Any opportunity. Even on stage if I can keep a hold on the anxiety. But this is his tune. 'I can help. But it's your song. The lead has to come from you. Why don't you sing it through, and I'll pick up the backing, see if we can work out a combination vocal line with some harmonies to give it whatever you think is missing?'

Danny smiles and starts to play, working through a sequence of intro chords. I'm waiting for the right time to come in. He starts to sing and his deep tone fills the room. It takes me a moment to get a hold of myself to accompany him rather than just stare. I brush some chords, following his lead.

At the second chorus I pluck up the courage to add a harmony, accenting his melody and trying my best to bring out the energy in the words. As I sing, he looks up at me and his eyes sparkle in appreciation. He gives me the confidence to stretch my vocal, to dig a little deeper. As he strokes the final chord, there's a lone round of applause at the doorway and I look up to see Mum grinning at us.

'Mum! Seriously?'

'Sorry. I couldn't help it. That was beautiful. Your voices together, and the two guitars...'

'OK, thanks, now close the door behind you.'

Danny laughs as Mum retreats from the room humming the melody of his tune. She leaves the door ajar. Mum is almost as passionate about music as I am. She has a beautiful voice herself, and an ear for music like no one else I know. From as young as I can remember we have sung together, without any instruments, just singing around the house. I think I knew every word to Springsteen's 'Thunder Road' before I'd even heard the original version. Mum says that my very first words, before my second birthday, were from The Beatles classic 'Eleanor Rigby'.

'She's right,' Danny says. 'Those harmonies were spot on.'

'It's a great song,' I say, returning my guitar to its stand and cradling my tea.

We exchange small talk for a minute, but it feels a little strained and I can't shake the feeling that I need to go for a run. The closeness of the four walls, the intimacy and Mum just the other side of the door seem to take something away from the simplicity of what

Danny and I have together – the freshness of our friendship, the authenticity.

I absently slide my hand up my sleeve to feel the scars – most of them old, some not so. I can mostly resist the urge to self-harm, but sometimes it's all there is.

Regret bubbles though my body. I shouldn't have invited him into the house, should've kept it simple. It was working: we run, we talk out of school and it's real, it's the *only* thing that's real. Now I've made it something else. 'I need to... er. I need to...' I say, standing.

Danny puts his tea down. 'Sure. Of course. Sorry.' He slots his guitar back into its case and slings it over his shoulder. I avoid eye contact.

'Thanks, then,' he says, turning for the door.

'I'll see you.'

'Yeah,' he says, closing the front door behind him.

It leaves me feeling empty, like I had something for a minute there, in my hands, something good, but it scared me and I let it go.

Chapter 5
7 days before I die

Yesterday's experience with Danny brings mixed feelings that I can't yet decipher. It's like I need to back off for fear of screwing everything up, but I can't help feeling a little optimism. There's nothing romantic there. It's just the sense of companionship that I miss. Something real.

'Hey, dreamer,' Mia says, nudging me. 'Who's that I saw you with yesterday?' she asks as we stand waiting to be served in the school canteen.

My heart pounds as I slip into defence mode. 'When?'

'After school. That boy?'

'Oh, that was Danny,' I say. Ada steals a glance at me, one eyebrow raised.

'Thought so,' Mia says, placing a sandwich and a

bottle of water on her tray and shuffling towards the till. 'He looks weird,' she adds.

What does she mean by *weird*? I decide to leave it. 'We go running sometimes. He lives on the estate near me.'

Her gaze lingers on me for a moment. Eventually she says, 'Sorry about the other day.'

'What for?' I ask, knowing very well what Mia should apologise for. She was harsh after my panic attack, and she knows it.

'I was a bit stressed out at the common room gig. I didn't mean to snap at you.'

'Hey, no worries,' I say.

'What are you having?' she asks. 'I'll get it.'

'Just this,' I hold up a bottle of water, half expecting her to laugh and tell me to piss off and buy my own water. Today's Mia doesn't do stuff like this. Today's Mia is more likely to insist that I pay for *her* lunch.

'You need to eat,' she says, taking my water and placing it on her tray. I don't respond. She huffs and moves to the till.

We sit at the only remaining empty table over by the windows. Maybe Mia has come around – realised that she's been blocking me out, and that our friendship might be worth something. There's an unfamiliar fizz though my body, a glimmer of hope. Ada smiles and says, 'What's he like? Danny?'

'It's not like that. He's a friend. To be honest, I don't really know him that well. We just bumped into each other when we were out running.'

'He's pretty,' Ada says.

Mia shakes her head and screws up her nose. 'What would you know?' she says to Ada. 'He's not exactly your type.'

'I'm gay. I'm not blind.' Ada rolls her eyes.

Mia laughs and looks at me. I smile, and for a moment it feels like it used to. Me, Ada and Mia, laughing. Us against the world.

She looks past me and her expression changes to one I can't read. She straightens and averts her gaze. I turn to see Katherine and Matt take a seat at the end of our table. Katherine glances over and gives a slight upwards nod to Mia, ignoring me and Ada. Matt gives me a smile, and that's enough to counter the coolness from the self-appointed head girl.

Katherine is tall and skinny, her breasts too big for the rest of her body. Boys can't walk past her in the corridor without their jaws dropping open. She's been with Matt for months, but there's something missing between them. It's like they're an old married couple who have lost their spark. Their public displays of affection seem forced. They're the trophy couple.

'What's up, Mia?' Katherine asks. 'This a band meeting or something? Don't let us interrupt.' She smirks at Matt, reminding me of my embarrassing display in front of most of year eleven.

'No, it's fine. We're just—'

'I was kidding,' Katherine interrupts. 'From what I saw the other day I don't think there's much chance of you guys being called a *band*.' She looks directly at me. 'Can't take the pace up there, Charley?' She laughs, but Matt's expression is stern.

'I thought it was good,' he says, looking at Mia. She forces a smile, tentatively eying Katherine, who remains quiet. Katherine is always full of it until Matt speaks, then she turns submissive.

'Thanks,' Ada says, breaking the tension a little. 'Especially the drums, eh?'

'Pretty good,' Matt says.

Mia seems to tense up. 'We could do without the meltdowns, eh Charley?'

I look at her but can't formulate any words. Her tone is far from light or humorous. She's serious.

Katherine laughs again.

Mia continues, 'You play guitar, Matt?'

He nods. 'Not really your style, though,' he says, glancing at me.

'Maybe we should mix things up a bit. I've seen you play,' Mia says.

Katherine stands, pushing her tray away from her. 'Let's go, eh Matt?'

Matt looks from Mia to Katherine. He rolls his eyes and follows Katherine from the room. He glances at me as he leaves. Is that sympathy in his expression? I'm unsure of him. We watch after them in silence until they're out of sight and Ada says, 'What the fuck, Mia. Charley's our guitarist. What are you trying to do?'

Mia looks sheepish. 'Just trying to get those two on side. I didn't mean anything by it.' Ada sighs and looks at me, but I say nothing. I'm deflated after the whole interaction with Matt and Katherine. I don't have the energy to argue with Mia. Ada is about to say something more when Katherine appears at the door to the canteen, striding towards us.

'What the...' Ada says under her breath as Katherine reaches our table, her eyes fixed firmly on Mia. She slaps her hands down on the table and leans in so that her face is just inches from Mia's. Mia leans back but Katherine stays with her.

'If I think you are making a play for Matt, you'll be sorry.'

Mia whimpers.

'Hey,' I start, but Katherine stops me with a glare.

'And I mean it. If I even get a sense that you're trying something... You know what I mean?'

Mia nods. Katherine screws up her face. She looks kind of weird, like she's trying to look evil or something. I almost laugh but every cell in my body is screaming with anxiety. Then, she lifts a hand and flicks Mia on the underside of her nose, like really hard. Mia yelps and holds her nose. 'You've been warned,' Katherine says. She straightens and walks away.

When Mia looks up, her eyes are watering and Katherine is already out the door. Mia looks at Ada, an expression of fear and exasperation turning to one of anger and humiliation. She pushes her chair back and stands, taking Ada by the arm and storming from the canteen without looking back.

Chapter 6
5 days before I die

The air is clear and fresh as we head up Butser Hill in the fading Sunday afternoon light. A solitary grey cloud rushes across the sky. Lucas runs ahead with BB and I link my arm with Dad's, resting my head against his shoulder. I rub my hands together, feeling the roughness over my knuckles. If I clench my fists, I can crack the skin.

The sun has dropped below the top of the hill so we can't see the source of the orange glow rippling through the sky. We walk in silence, conserving energy for the climb and concentrating to avoid twisting an ankle on the uneven ground.

The skin on my shoulders prickles. This morning, in the shower, the urge to turn up the heat was strong. My habit of pushing up the shower temperature started as a way to make sure I was clean, and to get rid of as much contamination as I could. But the feeling brought more than a relief to my OCD – it brought a rush, and a release of tension. It became akin to self-harm. I turned the temperature up to the maximum and pushed through for as long as I could, until I could hardly breathe, and then pushed a bit more. If I relented too soon, then I'd have to go again before I could allow myself the cooler water. I don't mind the pain; the more it hurts, the bigger the rush. It's like when I go running, it's good pain. The afterwards is confusing, though. The immediate rush is soon clouded in melancholy.

'You seem distracted,' Dad says, tightening his grip on me and pulling me from my thoughts.

'Mia's being a pain in the arse again,' I say.

He sighs. 'What's she up to now?' There is resignation in his voice.

'Nothing really,' I say, allowing him to drag me along, helping me up the steepening, grassy slope. I breathe heavily.

'What is it?' Dad says, stopping so he can look me in the eye. I say that it's nothing and continue walking, a few steps ahead.

He catches me up and we link arms again. 'How are those polar bears?' I say.

He laughs. 'Proving elusive. Just when we think we

have them cornered, they find a way out. Then they regroup and come at us again.'

'I thought their territory was getting squeezed? Things should be getting tougher for them?'

'You'd think. The thing is, they can be nasty when cornered. If we give them no way out, then I don't know what might happen.'

'You might need to bring in the big guns.'

'Resources are limited over in Greenland. It's heading for a vicious head-to-head, I reckon.'

'You need me to fly in? Reinforcements?'

Dad pulls me close. 'I think I do. You might be just what we need.'

We rest at the top of the hill and I perch in my favourite spot at the base of an old silver birch. I lean with my back to the white, tiger-striped trunk and look out over the ridge to where the sun is just touching the top of the treeline. A sprawling oak in the field in the middle distance casts a scattered shadow of twisted branches.

I relax, and my thoughts of Mia, and school, drift to Danny. The picture of him in my mind brings a smile to my lips. Then a sinking feeling returns as a blanket of confusion descends once again. I need to figure out what Danny is to me and where he fits into my messed-up world.

I'm released from my thoughts for a moment as

Dad and Lucas double up laughing about something. BB is excited, jumping up at them. They're like three kids together, Dad in his old grey-black T-shirt and his flared jeans that he insists will come back into fashion.

'Lucas, look at this sunset,' he says and opens out his arm to receive Lucas in a side-by-side hug. I feel a momentary pang of sadness. I've not been able to hug Lucas like that for as long as I can remember, for fear of germs and contamination. Lucas stands with Dad and they lean in to each other, comfortably locked together. Lucas looks like a work-in-progress version of Dad with his scrawny frame and black Minecraft T-shirt. I look back at the horizon, the sun now half submerged in the trees and the shadows over the field merging with the darkness.

At least I have *them*, I think to myself, looking at Dad and Lucas. They are my constant, with Mum too. Whatever happens at school, I have my family.

'Let's make tracks,' Dad says, 'before we can't see anything and disappear down a rabbit hole.' He drags his eyes away from the fading, orange glow in the sky and starts to move. I tell him I'll catch them up, not breaking my gaze over the therapeutic landscape, feeling a rare sense of freedom.

When I rejoin them, I link my arm with Dad's as we walk. He looks at my hand and strokes his thumb over the dry sores on my knuckles. He tries to catch my eye but I keep looking ahead, at Lucas and BB racing down the hill.

Chapter 7
4 days before I die

At lunch on Monday, I stand at the entrance to the canteen, trying to think of a reason to go in, or a reason not to. I scan the sea of faces. The clatter of knives sends spikes of pain through my head and I cover my ears with my hands. The smell of hot food is confusing: I'm hungry, but I feel sick. I buy a bottle of water from the vending machine in the corridor and head outside, eventually gravitating to the group gathered around Mia. I can't see Ada anywhere.

When Mia spots me, she stops mid-sentence and then looks away to avoid my eye. I have no energy to fight. I edge back from the circle as it closes in like an organism rejecting a foreign body. I squat with my back to the wall of the science lab, out of sight. My head is pounding. I can still hear Mia's voice: indecipherable words and laughter. I push myself up off the floor and stride towards the school entrance. I need to get away, out of the poisonous atmosphere, somewhere I can breathe.

I sit down on the voyeur's bench opposite the school gate, shaded from the sun by the six-foot wall behind me. I put my water down and tug my headphones from my bag.

'Hey, Charley,' comes Matt's voice. I look up and he's standing with his rucksack on his back, his athletic upper body less than a foot from me. His hair is crafted like it always is. He's almost perfect.

'What's up?' I say, trying to be cool. In truth I'm a little apprehensive. He's a nice guy, but he's *Katherine's* nice guy, and Katherine takes no prisoners.

'Heading home for lunch. I have to let my dog out. He's just a pup, and Mum's at work. Why are *you* out here?'

'Getting away for a bit, you know.' I study his face, my cheeks warming. He's undeniably good to look at. He has a dimple in his chin and stubble that makes him look older than most of the boys in our year. He's buff, fit from rugby.

'You want to walk with me? I live just over there,' he says, pointing in such a way as to provide no useful information. I hesitate. He offers me a Marlboro Light.

'Screw it, why not?' I stand and take the cigarette.

'So what's the deal with you and Katherine?' I ask as we walk.

'Oh, that's pretty much run its course. What about you? Who's that bloke you're with?' he says, glancing briefly in my direction.

'There's no one at the moment.' I don't want to appear too sad and lonely. I feel a twinge of guilt for Danny – even though there is nothing like that between us. Matt casts a more lingering look down and sideways at me, but I avoid it, keeping my head facing forward. He is smiling to himself when I do look a few seconds later.

'Here we are.' Matt flicks his cigarette away and jumps over a low wall around the perimeter of a small, tidy front garden. He disappears into the house and I stand for a second, twisting the ball of my foot into the remains of my discarded cigarette. I'm about to turn back when Matt pops his head around the door and smiles. 'Come on, come and see Oscar,' he says, then disappears again.

I walk up the path and a German shepherd puppy greets me at the door, jumping to lick my face. Matt calls him off, eventually having to physically pull him away. We walk through to his kitchen, a small space just wide enough for one person to pass, with a table at the far end. There's a lingering smell of burnt cooking oil, and dishes litter the worktop. He apologises for the mess and lets Oscar out into the back garden through a door at the end of the kitchen. It's a well-loved outside space: full flower beds frame a tended lawn.

Matt hands me a glass of water and pours one for himself. 'How's the band thing going?'

I take a sip and place the glass on the worktop. 'Fine. Most of the time.'

'I meant what I said yesterday. I thought you guys were good.'

'I was a fuck-up,' I say.

'Don't be too hard on yourself. It takes a lot to put yourself out there.'

I smile and turn to look out over the back garden. What am I doing here with Matt? Am I flirting? Maybe I should make an excuse to leave.

I sense Matt approach me from behind. Before I can turn around, he slips his arms around my waist. My heart races as his hands move up my torso and he kisses the back of my neck. I twist around.

'Matt?' I push him gently away and he steps back. I think about kissing him. But – what about germ transfer? But it would be so nice...

'What's wrong? You're single, I'm kinda single, empty house, why not?' He moves towards me again, smiling and drawing me in. He smells sweet. He kisses me and I kiss him back. I melt into him and my head swims. His hands move from the back of my head to my back and stray down to my arse. I pull away slightly.

'Hey,' I say, light-hearted, moving in to kiss him again. His hands stray once more and I pull away again, further this time.

'What?' he says. There's fire in his eyes now.

'I said, no.'

'Fuck, Charley, that's what you came here for.' His raised voice scares me. He has an obnoxious, macho swagger about him that I haven't seen before. 'Don't blow it, Charley. There are plenty of other girls in our year who would take your place right now.'

My mouth drops open, but before I can say anything he moves towards me again and I have to step backwards.

The atmosphere changes. He moves at me and uses his strength to spin me around, twisting and holding my arm behind my back. The immediate, shooting pain through my shoulder is blinding, and I let out an involuntary screech as I lean forward to move away from him.

Adrenaline surges and my heart pounds. He pushes me further down. He has a tight grip on my arm behind my back. He moves his other hand to the back of my head and shoves me forwards, over the kitchen table with a clatter of crockery. He's strong, moving in short, quick jerks.

He pins me to the table with his pelvis and pushes himself on me from behind. I struggle to twist my head to the side to catch a breath. I manage only a muffled, desperate plea for him to get off me. I can't move. My face is squashed onto the table. He's laughing.

'See, you like that, Charley. Come on, you like that.' He's pushing, rhythmically. I can't catch my breath. Can't scream. I feel faint and I pray that I don't pass out. There's pain in my shoulder then, just pain, nothing else.

He releases his hand from the back of my head and starts to fiddle with his belt. My panic escalates as I realise what he's planning. His other hand is still holding my arm. With a fresh burst of adrenaline, I twist to try to get loose, but he reacts by pushing my arm up higher. The pain through my elbow and my shoulder is absolute. My head spins.

I catch a glimpse of his face through my darkening, blurred vision. Saliva is foaming in the corners of his mouth and his greasy hair has flopped over his forehead.

He turns his attention from his belt to my skirt. As he does so, he releases some pressure and I take my chance. I twist around hard, blanking the pain, twisting further so that I spin around towards him. He's off balance and I manage to wriggle free, pushing him back. My elbow swings around hard and catches his face with a satisfying crunch. He stumbles, cradling his nose, with his trousers around his knees. I run, hoping I've smashed his nose hard enough to disable him.

As I clatter through the kitchen doorway and into the hall, I glance back. He's struggling to pull up his trousers. He spits obscenities, and I continue my run, unable to stop before I hit his front door with some force, pain shooting through my tender shoulder. My heart thumps as I fiddle with the latch. I need to get out before he comes at me again. He spills into the corridor from the kitchen, fastening his belt. My heart leaps once more as I scrabble at the door.

'Hey, what? It's OK, I'm just messing. Come on, Charley. Let's just have some fun.' His words are innocent enough but the subtext is menacing. I work at the latch. My fingers can't get a grip. Matt's dog is barking in the kitchen and my head is pounding. 'Charley.' His voice is pleading. 'Don't make this into something it's not. Don't overreact.' He takes a step towards me, hand outstretched.

Finally, the latch gives. I twist it and swing the door open in a single move. Matt lurches towards me as the door slams against the inside wall. I slip through and I'm running.

'You fucking whore! You stupid fucking whore! That's the best offer you'll ever get!' he shouts at me as I run down the road, back towards school.

I run through the school gate, not stopping until I get to the music department, where I duck straight into the girls' toilets. I stand in a cubicle with sweat and tears pouring down my face, breathing heavily and swaying gently. The smell makes me retch. I carefully position myself, not touching the walls or the door. Germs disperse into the air around me, passing from molecule to molecule and settling on my clothes, my skin. Nausea comes in waves. Matt's contorted face. The pain in my shoulder.

I can't get hold of the panic. I'm too far gone. I push open the cubicle door with my foot and look out into the room. I try to focus on the white porcelain basins, but they rush and blur. My throat constricts. When I try to move, the floor slips away. My face slides down the white cubicle wall and I catch the strong smell of piss before knocking my head on the side of the toilet.

Asleep.

Dad is close.

Mum too. I can smell her perfume.

She's keeping an eye on us both.

Grannie is up there.

Dad moves as he sighs. He whispers.

'We shouldn't have just stormed in there.'

'What?' I reach down and hold on to his thumb
and he wiggles it inside my fist.
'The bears. We underestimated them.'
'I thought you had them?'
'We did, Charley... and... I don't know... I
thought...'
'Shh, Dad, ease down.'

My head thumps with pain to the beat of the
pulse in my neck.

'Everyone thinks these bears are stupid, easy to
manipulate. They think we can keep them
locked up behind fences and walls. But we
can't. The pressure is building. We can't ignore
them – pretend they don't exist.'

Dad is quiet again, and I sense him drift away.
'Dad?'

'Charley?'
My eyes crack open. I'm lying on my back. Mrs
Franks is leaning over me, her face way too close to
mine. I can smell lunch on her breath. Two girls,
maybe a couple of years below me, peer around her to
look at me.
'Charley, it looks like you've hit your head. Can

you tell me where you are?' It takes a minute for me to gather my thoughts. I remember sliding onto the floor, and I recoil at the thought of where I am, what I'm touching, and the germs. I pull my head off the filthy floor. Images of Matt pulsate in my vision as my head pounds.

'Can you stand up? I need to get you to the nurse's office.' She pulls back my hair on the side of my head to look at the damage.

'I'm fine.' The last person I need to see is Maggie.

'We'll let the nurse decide that.'

'I'll be fine.' I wince with the pain in my head as I stand. Mrs Franks holds my arm to steady me and signals for the two girls to leave.

Mrs Franks leaves me in Maggie's office. I feel dirty from being on the floor of the toilets. Maggie tries to sit me down but I refuse to settle until I've washed my hands, so she lets me use the staff bathroom. When I return, she gives me a look of 'What took so long?'. I shrug and look away.

She dresses my head wound while probing, relent-lessly. When she's done with my head, I stand to leave.

'Just sit there, Charley. I'll make us a cup of tea and you rest. Don't move.' She holds her hands up to me as if using the Force to keep me here.

'Green tea!' I call after her. I'm thankful to be alone. I look around at the clutter: a noticeboard rammed with pinned leaflets, a desk with none of its surface visible under the papers, books and stationery. I try in vain to look at nothing. I don't want to close my eyes for fear of spinning out, but I need to clear my mind, make use of the solitary minute I have to recharge. The floor is the only place that isn't streaming clutter and unwanted information into my brain, so I look down, cup my eyes to shield my peripheral vision and try to clear my head. Matt digs at my consciousness.

Maggie returns with the tea. My skin is prickly and my jaw aches from clenching my teeth. She sits on a chair facing mine. She's young, somewhere in her thirties with shoulder-length straight brown hair and an athletic physique. I guess that she plays a sport: hockey or netball; football, maybe. How the fuck she got the job as school counsellor is beyond me.

'Talk to me, Charley.' She sips her tea. 'What happened?'

Matt is in my head but only as a confused blur, a mush of conflicting feelings. He assaulted me. He tried to... But, before, he'd been a kind of ally, a friend. He kissed me. He's always been nice to me. I should tell Maggie.

'Is everything OK with your friends?'

'What friends?' I look her in the eye and she tilts her head, presenting her cheek, inviting a slap.

'Mia, Ada, Ellie,' she says.

They are the last thing on my mind. All my focus is now on keeping Matt's face out of my head – the sickening sight of him, saliva in the corners of his mouth. I look down at the floor again. 'I can't do this,' I say, more to myself than to Maggie.

'Perhaps we need to...'

'I can't do this, Maggie,' I say again. I stand and we stare at each other for a moment before the bell sounds to signal the end of the day. I reach for the door.

'I need to talk to your parents. Shall we talk tomorrow, then?' Maggie says.

I pause at the open door. 'Let's not bother,' I say, closing the door behind me.

Chapter 8
1 day before I die

It's taken me three days to get it together. In that time, neither Ada nor Mia contacted me. Not even once. Only Danny messaged to ask where I was, if I was OK, and I couldn't bring myself to message him back.

I leave for school and take a detour up the hill. I choose the longer, parallel path that Danny uses, with the gentle gradient, where the south-facing slope is already sun-dried of morning dew. Save for a few early joggers and dog walkers, the hill is all mine.

At the viewpoint, I bend my knees and fold myself to the floor in my favourite spot for headspace, leaning back against the scratchy, layered skin of the silver birch. Lighting last night's half-smoked roll-up, I close my eyes, inhale and slowly breathe out, allowing my shoulders to drop and the tension to ease a little.

He's dangerous. I need to tell someone. I need to tell Mum. But tell her what? What *really* happened? I *wanted* to kiss him. I rest my head on my knees and rub my chin over the rough nylon of my skirt. It has a clean, washing-powder smell. It's Mum's smell. I can't seem to make sense of it all.

Bruises on my forearms peek from my sleeves. I cover them and turn to peer out over the ridge, wincing a little at the pain in my shoulder. The old oak stands alone in the middle distance, stretching out its twisted limbs. I look back towards my house. The pull to bury myself under my covers and shut out the world is strong. I turn back to the hill. The treeline is dark and rigid, an army in waiting. I finish my cigarette and force myself up. I *can* do school. I'll talk to Maggie, figure this out. I won't let Matt drive me away.

When I hit the main road and the hill has disappeared behind a row of houses, I'm already up at anxiety level six. I'm alert, the kind of alert you feel when you've had no sleep and adrenaline pushes you on. But the closer I get to school, the more I shrivel on the inside. I stumble through the school gates, and I'm trembling, creeping up to a level seven or eight.

In the corridor, I feel detached from reality. I turn to check my reflection in the window. My face is pale. It looks drained and podgy, a bloated corpse just pulled from a lake.

I half walk and half lean on the white walls of the corridor, dragging myself along and adding to the scuff marks at shoulder height. The floor looks wet, but I can't be sure. My body shrinks under the surface, my skin folding over itself.

People blur past me in both directions. Then I see *him*. He's with *her* again, walking towards me. I stiffen. Fear stabs at me and I scan for an escape path, a door, anything between him and me. I drop my gaze, glancing just once to see them laughing together, not looking in my direction. I hunch and tighten, trying to make myself small, squeezing up against the wall. They pass without a look. He almost brushes my shoulder. I feel a sharp slap on my arse. I jerk my head around and see his smug, sickening smile. He winks and turns back to Katherine and they slide around the corner.

I bend double and gag, then steady myself with a hand on the shiny white-gloss windowsill. The world moves in circles around me and the fabric of my life unravels, as if I'm coming apart at the seams.

I leave the school grounds and stumble home in a daze. In my room, Matt is in my head. The sound of his laughter is in my ears, and his smell in my nose. Darkness closes around me. My body is numb. I need to feel something real, something I can control.

I find a razor in Dad's drawer in his bedroom and

sit back on my bed. I use a pair of scissors to dig at the razor-head, releasing one of its three thin slivers, which I hold carefully between my thumb and forefinger.

I pause a moment. A flash of uncertainty passes through my body as I question myself. But this isn't a choice I'm able to make. There are no other pathways. This is the only release, and I have no idea where it will lead.

Chapter 9
Death day

In the morning, I pull myself up to sitting on the side of my bed. My arm is a mess. In the night, blood has seeped through the layers of Mum's bandage and a red blotch has spread from its dark centre in imperfect, concentric circles. I feel disconnected from myself, like I'm looking at someone else's arm.

When Mum came in last night, she was so controlled, detached almost. She's had to deal with my self-harm more than once before. Through my tears, I could see the determined expression on her face and I sensed her resolve to make me OK. She cleaned me up, applied a dressing and a bandage to keep things in place. By the time she'd finished I'd stopped sobbing and the adrenaline levels had returned to normal, leaving space for the feelings of shame and worthlessness. I had no words.

Music leaking from the discarded earphones on my bed brings me around. They're still plugged into my iPhone. I yank at the earphone jack to silence it and then force myself to stand, steadying myself with a hand on the windowsill. The dizziness is worse than usual. I hold still for a moment and rub the back of my neck. The pain in my shoulder has spread through to my jaw and it's making me feel sick. I look into the mirror on my bedroom wall. It's merciless. My heart sinks at the sight of myself. I force my fingers through my tangled hair, sick of the way it hangs, lank over my wide shoulders. I look down at my body with disgust and catch the metallic, cloying aroma of blood and sleep.

Mum said last night that the cut probably wouldn't need stitches, but we'd need to see the doctor this morning. She was upset. I sobbed so hard. I wanted to explain the relentless panic, how bad it is at school, what Matt had done. I wanted to say how I can't understand what's going on in my head. Words wouldn't come.

I drift down the stairs and into the kitchen, only to be knocked back by the nauseating smell of toast and the wall of noise. Pins and needles spread across my cheeks. Mum scurries around, collecting Lucas's things for school, making tea, eating toast. Lucas stares at his laptop screen at the kitchen table with dubstep leaking from his headphones as he watches YouTube images of a blocky *Minecraft* landscape. BB is manic, sniffing around the floor for scraps.

I slump onto a chair at the table. I have an over-whelming compulsion to lie down. A bitter, metallic taste seeps into the back of my mouth and the pain in my jaw intensifies. Mum looks over at me.

'I can't get a doctor's appointment, Charley. I'll have a look at your arm in a minute.' There was a pause.

'Charley?' Mum's voice is muffled, trailing off as if I'm being submerged in water. Her lips move but she makes no sound. My chest is tight as I try to breathe. The pain is now in my arm as well as my jaw. My head spins: fast, faster. My body shakes.

Then nothing.

Just blackness.

~

There's a girl.

She has a fuzzy irritation in her left calf. She needs to stretch out her leg, but she can't move.

And she can't see.

Sound is muffled, as if she has headphones on
but there's no music.

Faint smell of lavender.

She concentrates, trying to tense her left calf
muscle, but feels nothing. She tries again, and
it tenses this time, then relaxes. Then she tries
again and gets nothing. She drifts away.

Someone's touching her hand. She tries to
close her fingers around theirs, but her fingers
won't move.
Now the hand is gone.

She might be dead.

She throws up, a snake being pulled out of her
stomach and through her mouth.

Lights flicker behind her eyes.
She chases them.

Part Two
Limbo

Chapter 10
Limbo Week 1

The girl is me.

Pain. Everywhere. Daylight the other side of my closed eyelids. The smell of sticking plasters is in my nose and I think of Mum. People mill around. I sense them, though I can't hear them. My mouth is dry. I taste blood. I have ulcers on the insides of my cheeks, and a stinging pain in my constricted throat.

I open my eyes, just a crack. Light floods in and screams around the inside of my skull.

I can see now. I'm in a hospital bed. As my eyes adjust to the light, I watch a nurse moving between beds, then stopping at the one opposite mine, checking the drip and talking to the patient, a girl, a bit younger than me. The nurse turns and catches my eye.

'Good morning. How are you feeling?' She checks

my drip and pulls a digital thermometer from her top pocket. I try to ask her what happened to me but I only manage an incomprehensible croak before the thermometer is shoved into my ear.

'It's OK. Your throat might be a bit sore from the tube we had in there. Do you feel up to a sip of water?' She reads the thermometer and doesn't look concerned.

'Can I get some tea?'

'Let's start with the water.'

'What happened?' I whisper.

'The doctor will be around to speak to you. He'll fill you in.' She hurries away, and as she crosses my field of vision I catch sight of Mum and Dad, apologetically weaving around a nurse and heading towards me. Mum's face is drawn, her skin grey.

'How are you, baby?' Mum whispers through a smile, her eyes glassy. 'They told us you'd be waking up about now.'

'What happened? How long have I been in here?'

'Has the doctor been around yet?' she asks, just as a gaggle of medical people congregate at the end of my bed. There are four or five of them, all with white coats and tired faces. A tall man with glasses comes to the front and picks up my chart.

'How are you feeling this morning, Charlotte?'

'Charley,' Mum says.

'I'm Doctor Smart,' he says. 'Do you know why you are here?'

'How long have I been here?'

'It's Monday today, you came in on Friday...' The rest of his words fade as I count up the loss of three days.

'I don't remember...' I say.

'No.' The doctor looks at me over his glasses. 'We think you had a mild heart attack.' He pauses to allow his words to take effect. 'Malnutrition can cause loss of heart muscle.' He pauses again. 'We see this sometimes in cases of anorexia nervosa, where the heart walls can thin and weaken.' Dad flinches at his words.

The doctor looks down at his clipboard, as if reading from notes.

'The loss of mass from your heart and other organs is relatively minor, so we expect a good recovery.'

My head spins, trying to take in what this doctor is saying. A heart attack is fucking extreme. Memories coalesce in my head and I see Matt, and the blood on my arm. I look down. There's no dressing, just an angry-looking scab, warm to the touch. 'We need to get you strong again. You'll be in for a couple more days and then you can go home, on a structured feeding plan. We also have CAMHS due to schedule an appointment for when you get home.'

'CAMHS?' I say.

'Child and Adolescent Mental Health Services,' the doctor says and moves on with his trail of assistants before I can ask any more questions.

'Charley, talk to us. How long has this been going on?' Mum says. 'You've not been eating, sweetie.'

'I *have* been eating.'

'Not enough, Charley, for f—' Dad spits out the words. I look away from him. I have been eating. There's no way that my diet has caused a heart attack, whatever they say.

'Your body weight is so low that your organs started to shut down,' Dad pushes. I try to ignore his words, let them pass over me. 'Not just your heart: your liver, kidneys,' he says. I look at my hands. I'm careful with my food intake, I follow the advice.

'Charley.' Mum's tone is gentle now. 'Talk to us.'

'I'm just watching what I eat, Mum, to keep slim...' I trail off as I try to figure what's happened. My head is still thumping, it's hard to think.

Mum says, 'Charley, if you don't eat, you'll die. It's as simple as that.'

I look at them both, their faces pale and creased. Dad looks wasted. I know I have to eat, I *do* eat, just not too much. They won't get that. I pull myself to a sitting position. I need to get them to chill out.

I tell Mum that maybe I've been restricting too

much, maybe I need to be a bit more careful. 'I'll do their feeding plan thing, Mum, like the doctor said.'

Mum sits on the side of the bed. Her grey skin is drawn and heavy. I place my hand on hers and she smiles, reluctantly. 'I'll do the plan,' I say. 'Don't worry, please don't worry, it's fine. I'll be fine.'

Dad places his hand on top of mine.

I MUST HAVE DOZED OFF. When I wake, there's no sign of Dad, and Mum is asleep in the chair next to my bed. She looks old. The bags under her eyes are accentuated by the harsh light. The ward is quiet. No other visitors.

A woman hobbles past on her way back to her bed, and I think of my grannie. I recall the time I was helping her with the washing up. I was miles away in my own thoughts when she said, 'It's hard work, isn't it? Exhausting. The OCD.' I stared at her, thinking that there was no way she'd have known that I had OCD. She just smiled at me. 'You've got good at hiding it. I remember your tapping rituals from when you were little.' She was talking about how I would tap objects a certain number of times as I counted through to numbers that felt right. Always multiples of three.

'But...' My mouth hung open.

She stopped washing up and rested her hands on the edge of the sink, suds sliding into the basin. 'I had it too, you see. Well, I *have* it. It never really goes away, but it's something you can learn to control, to manage. You must have known I have it too?'

I shook my head, still unable to speak.

'I have a mix of things,' she said. 'OCD is in there somewhere and there might be other labels, but let's just say I understand some of what you experience.'

'Mum never said...'

'It's not so easy to explain to people who don't have it, as you know. Especially now. Everyone seems to say they have *a little bit of OCD*,' she said with air quotes, giving me a sideways glance and a smile.

It was like we'd revealed our membership of a secret club. And it felt good. I felt a wave of relief wash away some of my loneliness. I had an ally.

'Those people,' she said, 'who say they are a bit OCD, they don't quite get it, do they?' She motioned towards the kitchen table and we sat opposite each other. That's when she said her thing about it being a gift.

I must have looked incredulous because she gave me an amused smile. 'We go a little deeper,' she said. 'I remember when your Grandad proposed to me. I didn't even know what was wrong with me back then. I just thought I was...' She paused. 'I don't know what I thought. Anyway, Grandad gushed out all these feelings he had for me.' She smiled. 'You remember what he was like, the old sop. He said that what he loved about me most was my "sense of things". We talked about it over the years, and what he really meant was what he thought of as my depth of empathy, of understanding, and the way I would mine people's emotional core, to get into their hearts and their souls. Not for my benefit, but so I could understand *them*, and be a good person for *them*.' She paused then to gauge my reaction, which continued to be one of incredulity. 'You have that too,' she said. 'I've seen it in you.'

'Hey.' Mum drags me from my thoughts. 'You're miles away.'

Her eyes are all red and it looks like she's been crying.

'I was thinking about Grannie.' I sit myself up a little higher in the bed and the effort takes all of my energy. 'I miss her,' I say.

Mum looks at me as if to say something then looks away.

'What?' I ask.

'I don't know. Your grannie would have been so sad to see you like this,' she says, looking down.

Two years ago she left us, and it feels like two weeks. Mum said it was old age. She died of *old age*. Whatever that means.

'I still talk to her sometimes,' I say. Mum laughs and says that she does the same.

'You know she had OCD, like me?'

Mum nods. 'Of course. But we never really talked about it. That's one of my few regrets, not talking to her about things.' She looks at me pointedly. Me and Mum have always been so open about my mental health. She understands my OCD, and how it is rooted in my fear of being sick. It's complicated, and I'm sure she doesn't understand all of it, but she tries. The look she's giving me now is a challenge. She thinks I'm not being honest with her. She thinks there's something else, something to do with the eating.

'I'm tired, Mum,' I say. She puts a hand on my arm. I turn over and snuggle down, my body aching with every movement.

THE NEXT TIME I WAKE, I rub my eyes and see that Dad is sat in the chair next to my bed. He's reading a book. Mum is standing over me, watching, making sure I'm still breathing, like she says she used to do when I was a baby. She sees I'm awake and adjusts my pillows. I straighten up, sitting back against the headboard.

'Any news from GCHQ, Dad?' I smile at him. He lowers his book and smiles back.

'It's all gone mad.' He sighs.

'The Russians?' I say.

'No, it's Greenland.'

'Not more problems with the polar bears?'

'Yep.' He looks from side to side with exaggerated seriousness, leaning towards me and lowering his voice to a whisper. 'They've brought in reinforcements. A second battalion. We've been staking them out. And they're training them,' he says.

'Shit, Dad, what for?' I try to look serious but I can't help a smile. Mum rolls her eyes and pats down my bedclothes, then passes me the cup of water left by the nurse. I take two small sips that sting my throat as they go down.

I look at Dad. 'What for?'

'We're not sure yet. Maybe suicide-bomb missions,' he says, deadpan. I almost spit the water out with a laugh. Mum finally breaks a smile and Dad beams at me.

Chapter 11
Limbo Week 2

I need to go for a run.

I haven't been for over a week, since before I was in hospital. There's no way Mum will let me go running again, not until I can prove I'm eating enough. How the fuck she expects me to prove it – like I need to take pictures or something. She won't believe me when I say I've eaten.

In my room, I lean my head against the hard PVC window frame. A blanket of fog is settling over the field. Mum is with me, watching me as she sifts through my clean washing, folding and sorting it into neat piles while pinging stupid questions at me.

Matt gets in my head sometimes, but I know he can't do anything to me, and I'm not scared of him. I'm not sure how I'll be when I go back into school.

I lean over and crack open my window to release

the musty, lifeless air. I sit cross-legged in my big leather armchair so that my head is level with the window opening and I can feel the fresh air on my face. I think of Danny. I miss him. I've not spoken with him for ages. He's messaged me a few times but I never know what to say.

Mum won't let me run, but she'll let me take the dog out. I can easily kill some calories on the hill. 'I might take BB and Lucas up the hill to wear them both out a bit,' I say to Mum.

I message Danny.

BB BOUNDS TOWARDS THE SUMMIT, her ears flapping with each stride like she's trying to take off. Lucas tries in vain to keep up and I maintain a good steady pace, blanking the pain in my leg muscles and pushing on to break a sweat. With my head down to keep a watch on my footing, I smile to myself at the sight of Mum's pink welly boots, hastily squeezed on to my feet when I left the house.

We climb through a thick layer of fog, not emerging into blue skies until we reach the summit. From there, we look out over the blanket of mist draped over the landscape.

'Wow.' I breathe out the word. Lucas sits on the

viewpoint bench. His head is down, he's already distracted and watching his own foot draw a shape in the dusty ground in front of him. I look back to the moving landscape. The pristine, white, foggy dunes are spoiled only by a smattering of taller trees stretching through its surface from below.

'Nice, eh?' comes a familiar Sheffield accent. Danny is stood behind the bench with a guitar case slung over his shoulder and his half-smile in place. He's blocking out the sun so that his head has a strange orange glow. His eyes are clear, reflecting the tone and shade of the slate-blue sky.

'Who are you?' Lucas asks, and Danny laughs.

'He's a friend from school.'

'Boyfriend?' Lucas retorts with a smile.

I give Lucas a nudge and look away.

'It's not that beautiful, anyway,' Lucas says, nodding towards the fog. 'You can't see anything.'

'It's peaceful,' Danny says. 'Less cluttered.'

'You got my message, then?' I say.

'I was taking the long route home from school, anyway, so I was already on my way up here.'

'Bit late to be in school?'

'I was in the music room.'

We are silent for a while, looking out over the clouds. Lucas is restless and soon stands to head back down.

What must Danny be thinking? I don't know how much he knows about why I was in hospital, or if he knows anything about what happened with Matt.

'When are you coming back?' he asks.

'Soon.'

'Are you recovered?'

'I guess,' I say, and I turn and start down the hill. 'You can head home this way if you want some company.'

Danny moves to catch me up, and we walk side by side as I strain to keep my eyes on Lucas and BB in the gloom ahead of us. 'How's the song?' I ask.

'Nearly there. It could still do with a bit of Charley input, though.'

'Really? Not sure my input is worth much right now.'

He shrugs. 'You didn't answer any of my messages.'

'I was ill, sorry. I didn't have a phone, and Mum's been keeping me wrapped in cotton wool.'

'Sounds bad. What was—'

'Nothing,' I interrupt. 'I'd rather forget about it for now.' Danny looks at the floor.

'Next week, Wednesday lunchtime?' I say.

'What for?'

'Music, recording. I'll help.'

'It's a date,' Danny says.

We are silent again, and we walk deeper into the

thick fog as we approach the foot of the hill. For a moment, we are entirely alone. Our surroundings have faded, and Lucas and BB are invisible ahead of us. The wind drops and there's a hush. It feels intimate, almost embarrassing. I need to say something.

'My granddad was from Sheffield,' I say, then cringe at how immature I sound, as if I'm trying to exaggerate some tenuous common ground. 'Your accent, it's really similar to how I remember his.'

'That explains it. You've got northern roots. I knew there was something about you that I liked,' he says with no awkwardness.

We are quiet for a while.

'Have you spoken to the others? Mia and Ada?' he says as we get to the part of the hill where the fog starts to thin, gradually revealing more of our surroundings.

I shake my head. 'Not much. There's a bit of friction. Girlie stuff. Mia is a bit of a diva, but she's OK.'

'I don't know how you deal with it.' Danny looks at me as we negotiate the steepest bit of the hill. I feel the tightness in my thighs.

'No choice.' I look up at him. 'What else do you do?' I shrug.

'You can opt out. There are better things to be doing than nursing egos.'

'It's not that simple. It's a fragile equilibrium. You

have to be careful. Pull at a thread and the whole thing unravels.'

He looks at me again and shrugs. He sees it as so binary – as easy as in or out. 'What would happen if you pulled at some of those threads, let it unravel? You should give it a try.'

'Is that what you do?'

'I can't be doing with any of it,' he says.

I smile to myself at his self-confidence. 'If I did that, opted out, none of them would talk to me. I'd be on my own.'

'That sounds like a result...'

'I can't just not have friends,' I blurt.

'I'm just exploring, Charley. I can see what Mia and her lot are like. Then there's Katherine and her harem and I think, shit, where do you go for some respite?'

'Where do *you* go?' I ask.

'Here.' He points to his head. 'And here.' He turns around and presents Butser Hill. 'The boys at school are mostly OK, though, compared to the girls. More *Big Bang Theory* than your *One Tree Hill*.' He laughs at his own joke, making me smile. We are interrupted by Lucas shouting from a distance that he'll see me at home. I wave him off and call BB to stay with me.

Danny and I pause awkwardly for a moment at the

point where our paths diverge. He breaks the spell by taking the first steps, walking tentatively backwards.

He stops. 'I hear Mia is scouting for a new guitarist.'

I look at the ground and try to stop the thought tangles from tightening. My head is confused. 'Yeah, not sure it's my thing anymore,' I say, without conviction. Danny frowns and I think about the Academy, whether I'm going to get the grades I need to even compete for a place. Whether I'd cope if I did get in. The competition could be a way in, but for that I'd have to work closely with Mia.

'If there's anything I've come across since I've been down south that's *your thing*, it's this,' Danny says, starting to move backwards again. 'See you at school then, Charley. Come find me if the evil ones are getting too much.' He makes a mock terror face, then smiles as he looks down at my feet. 'Can't take you seriously in those!' he shouts, then turns and continues on his way.

He walks off with his characteristic stoop and confident bounce. I look down at my feet and smile at the sight of Mum's pink boots.

MY GUITAR STRAPPED to my back, I walk down the white lines in the middle of the quiet road that leads up to the school, in the space between the parked cars on either side. I can see more clearly from here. I can see if there's anyone approaching me from any direction.

Up ahead is little Toby, a sweet boy in year seven. I sometimes walk with him to school if we bump into each other. I'd rather be alone today so I slow down a bit. The terraced houses bear down on me from both sides of the road. I wonder if anyone in them has a mental head like mine. I wonder if there's a girl skipping breakfast. Or someone blaming herself for being too drunk last night. Maybe she got what she deserved, what she was asking for.

As I approach the school gates, Danny is walking with his beautiful little sister, Katie. She is slight, delicate, with a darker complexion than Danny's. She says something and beams up at him, as if waiting for a response. Danny is deep in thought and I try to guess what she asked him. His music, his love life, his friends? He looks back at her and answers with a guarded smile, making her laugh and nudge him. He slings his arm around her shoulder as they walk through the main gate and I feel a pang of envy for their closeness.

I reach class and pause at the door. People scurry around, finding their seats.

'Charley, sit down, dear.' Mrs Davies's voice is firm but not unkind. With everyone seated, I'm exposed. All eyes are on me as I move towards a space near the front, next to Kian. A stream of mucus edges its way down his top lip, and he eyes me with distrust, shuffling his chair away as I sit down.

Mrs Davies calls my name and I jump a little in my seat, causing a laugh to ripple through the class. 'Are you OK?' she says gently. I tell her I'm fine, quickly looking away, terrified that she might press me further or ask me to stay back after the lesson. The effort in class to keep from spiralling is immense. When the bell finally releases me, I let out a breath, slump forward over my desk and wipe the sweat from my forehead with my sleeve.

I consider heading straight home, but force myself to go to the music room. Danny is at the mixing desk. 'Hey, Charley, I wasn't sure you were coming,' he says without looking up. I shed my coat and bag as he adjusts the channel sliders, then taps each microphone in turn, checking the mixing desk for a signal. He looks at me. 'You look spaced.' His expression is one of confusion. 'Play some chords and we can get the levels,' he says, turning back to the blinking red LEDs.

My mind drifts as I strum chords and Danny fiddles with the recording desk. My guitar digs into my thigh and pushes against my tummy, making me uncomfortable. I'm bloated from yesterday's food that Mum and Dad forced on me. They think they know more than I do about nutrition. Not many people know more than me about calories, and what I should and shouldn't be eating. I need to get a bit smarter about managing meal times so that they back off a bit. I'll cook tonight, get on top of it and make sure I give myself the right amount.

'Charley?' Danny is raising his eyebrows at me.

'I'm ready,' I say with mock annoyance. 'Let's do it.'

'You remember the chords?'

'Remind me.' I smile at him and he pulls some papers from his bag.

We jam the song for half an hour, and I add backing vocals. We try a couple of recordings but there are still mistakes until the third take, which Danny is pleased with. He's animated in the music studio, not his usual laid-back self.

'What do you think?' he says, slumping in his chair. He has downloaded the completed track to his phone. I nod my approval. It's a good track. 'First time I've put one of my own songs down. The lyrics, they're quite personal.'

'If you're not revealing your inner self and giving up something personal, then you might as well keep quiet. As the famous saying goes.'

'Bollocks.'

'It's something like that. Like, what's the point in writing a song that doesn't mean anything to you? You have to be authentic.'

He smiles at me then, and turns to unplug his phone from the recording desk.

'Tell me about Sheffield,' I say.

'Northern post-industrial city with a population of about half a million—'

'Funny,' I interrupt. He looks at me with a satisfied smile, then draws breath and tells me a bit about his family. His grandparents on his mum's side are both Indonesian, but his mum was born in England. His dad is Sheffield born and bred.

He tells me about his old school. His friends turned on him for no good reason that he can recall: an argument that escalated beyond the point of no return. It wasn't long after he'd split with his girlfriend, so it was doubly difficult. He says it got worse from then on, and music was his outlet. 'I've learned to keep my head down, stay out of the firing line.'

The lunch bell sounds and I ask him if he wants to hang in the studio and play some more music.

'I need to find my sister and sit with her. She's not doing so great.' He looks at his watch and speeds up the packing of his bag. I try not to look disappointed. My mind switches to the challenge of what to do now, how to get through lunch.

'Thanks, Charley,' he says on his way out. 'It sounds great. It'll get me through this coursework.' He smiles and the door closes behind him with a slow, heavy clump.

Alone in the studio, my own breathing is the only sound in the room. It falters, and I have to focus to keep the air sliding in. I count to three, hold for two, then a long breath out for five. My ears are ringing now with the rising anxiety, like tinnitus. The more I notice it, the louder it gets.

Chapter 12
Limbo Week 3

Dad is fussing around the kitchen, like a jolly frickin' TV chef, preparing a precisely measured meal. I sip at my water.

'One hundred grams of pasta, one hundred grams of meat-based accompaniment, forty-five grams of sauce.' His upbeat commentary makes me feel sick, so I try not to listen.

He dishes up and I check to see if Mum is coming. Tension rising: level five then quickly through to six and seven.

'What's up?' Dad beckons me to the table. I can't move from the sofa. 'Charley, you need to follow the plan, come and sit down.' When I make no signs of moving, he steps over to me and holds me by the arm. He half drags, half guides me to the table. I sit, but I'm not planning to voluntarily lift food to my mouth.

The tubes of white, swollen pasta look obese.

I can't touch my cutlery.

Mum is here now and she picks up my fork, spears some pasta and lifts it. I close my mouth. The pasta falls back to the plate, but she persists, refilling and raising the fork again. I close my eyes. I can't look. I can't open my mouth.

Mum gently encourages.

Dad huffs and sighs.

I can't listen to them anymore. My head is full of tangled shit; nothing makes any sense. I put my fingers in my ears, squeeze my eyes shut and keep my mouth closed.

Mum jabs the fork at my lips. Food drips down my chin onto my lap. She pauses for a moment, then tries again, pushing the fork at me. It hurts.

I drift away and into my head. My breathing is quick and shallow, accelerating the spin and numbing my thoughts.

I'm not here. *This isn't me.*

The girl starts to cry.

She opens her mouth a crack as she sobs, and

her mum pushes the fork in with its creamy,

flabby pasta.

The girl gives way.
She's weaker than she thinks she is.
Tears stream down her cheeks as she chews
and swallows, food mixing with salty tears and
mucus. Her mum keeps going, pushing in the
food. The girl isn't willing; she's being forced.
This isn't her fault, but she's weak.

Her mum is crying now. Her dad takes over
and picks up the pace, fork after fork until it's...

done.

It's all in.
It's done.

IT's Friday and there's a weird atmosphere in the house, as if we are going on a trip, to a wedding or a funeral or something, rather than an appointment with CAMHS. Mum gets dressed out of her night clothes for the first time in days and I'm half expecting Dad to make a flask of coffee for the occasion.

My phone pings. Another message from Mia to fix up some dates for rehearsals for the Academy competition. We need to create a demo tape for the first round to see if we can get through to the live auditions. My enthusiasm is waning, but Danny keeps nudging me forward.

The air in the car is thick with tension. There's an expectation from Mum and Dad, as if something's going to change from just one more appointment. They think I'm getting fixed. Or they're hoping at least to hand over responsibility to someone else. I know that Mum's head is zapped because she forgets her seat belt until the car objects with an increasingly high-pitched beeping.

I'm relieved when Dad finally reverses into a parking space at the front of the clinic. I get out and lean up against the side of the car, looking around at the tired, single-storey building that I've visited so many times.

The CAMHS reception is signposted to the right as we get inside, handwritten on a piece of card with a drawing of a block-arrow underneath. To the left is the sexual health clinic, which has a proper sign with big letters shouting the way to the waiting room.

Mum checks us in as Dad puts a ticket on the car. I wait in the no-frills waiting room. It's empty but for me. It has hard plastic chairs, stood against the walls like boys at a primary school disco. Orange carpet. Tea stains.

A tall, skinny man approaches us, probably

younger than suggested by his bald head and glasses. He's jittery, either naturally highly strung or overloaded with coffee. He's clutching a blue document wallet with papers poking out of the edges.

'Charley,' he says.

'Yes,' Mum says, on my behalf, 'we're just waiting for my husband.' We all turn at the same time to see Dad hurrying towards us from the direction of the sexual health clinic.

We file in to a therapy room where two women sit in lounge chairs around a low, circular coffee table. They smile as we enter. I sit down, unable to muster any kind of smile in return. I need to wash my hands. I clamp them together and try not to touch the chair with them.

The bald man does some introductions. The names pass me by, but I get that the women are a psychologist and a psychiatrist. The man is called Luke. He takes me into a side room for some basic observations: weight, height, pulse and blood pressure. I've lost track of how many surfaces I've had to touch, and can't remember if I've then touched my face or my clothes. Tension in me rises.

'So,' Luke says, settling into his seat when we get back in the room, pausing for a moment too long, as if he's forgotten what he was going to say. 'Perhaps you can tell us what led you to the hospital episode earlier this month?'

'I crashed.'

'In what way?'

'I probably undershot my calorie target.'

'And what was that target?' Luke asks, putting pen to paper.

'Six hundred.'

'Calories?' Luke pauses and peers at me over the top of his glasses.

'Yes.'

'You've been working to a target of six hundred calories a day?'

'Yes.'

'OK,' he says slowly, finally writing something on his pad. 'Is that what you think you need?'

'That's what I thought, yes. To maintain but not add any weight,' I say. Six hundred actually allows me to gradually *lose* a little weight, to keep me on course.

He closes his pad and pushes his glasses on to the top of his smooth head. 'Let me explain something.' He speaks slowly and leans forward in his chair. 'You need about five hundred calories a day just for normal brain function.' He pauses. 'Then, you need about a thousand to help keep your bodily functions going, so that's your organs, muscles and such like, quite important things. And that's for when you are at rest, no physical exercise.' He pauses again, for longer this time, then continues.

'So that's fifteen hundred for the really basic stuff. Then we need about another thousand to account for the normal daily exertions, like walking to school, bit of exercise or whatever.' He tries to catch my eye.

'At first, a target of six hundred will mean that your body starts to break down muscle and other tissues to re-direct energy to maintain vital organ function. When did your menstruation stop?' Luke says.

'A few months ago.' I glance at Mum then back at the tango-coloured carpet.

'Where did you get the idea of the six hundred target?' he says.

'Something I read,' I say. 'On the internet.' I follow the joints in the carpet tiles, as if I'm working my way out of a maze.

He makes notes for a moment and no one speaks. 'Charley's obs show that she's significantly below normal weight. She's a measure of seventy three percent of her normal range. Her temperature is low, as is her blood pressure, a little, and her heart rate.' He looks up, scanning our faces. Mum and Dad glare at each other, then at me. The anguish on Mum's face cuts into me and tears fill my eyes.

The psychiatrist speaks then. She has a soft Scottish accent. She talks about medication to help manage the anxiety. The other woman talks about the option of inpatient treatment at a specialist hospital.

Inpatient.

The word hangs.

'A psychiatric ward?' I say, looking at the psychiatrist.

'The behaviour that you've been displaying has been shown to be difficult to resolve in a home environment, and a change might be needed to break that cycle.'

I reel. Discussions bounce around the room, none of them sinking in: options, medication, hospital.

'Is she being sectioned?' Mum asks, panic in her face.

'Inpatient treatment is the option we recommend,' Luke says. Mum and Dad glance at each other again before Luke continues. 'Hillside House,' he says, addressing me specifically, 'is an excellent facility.'

'I don't need a psychiatric hospital?' It comes out as more of a question than a statement. A tingling feeling fizzes through my body as my fear mixes with a sense of... something... *validation* of my pain.

The doctors remain silent. They were talking like admission is an *option*. The way they look now, it doesn't appear like there's an alternative.

So, I *am* ill?

These people are saying that I need help. That the

feelings and thoughts I live with every day are not normal, and that there might be a way to help me.

Validation.

I'm making a fuss.

I'm not ill. Not like other people with real mental health problems.

The thought of being somewhere taking up a bed in a ward brings feelings of guilt flowing through my veins like poison.

I want to curl up in bed and never come out. I want to shrink to a tiny sliver so that no one can see me.

I want to feel better, but I can't imagine anything that could change what I am feeling right now. What could possibly change what goes on in my head? Why am I here? In this room? In this world?

I look at Mum to see if I can read what she's thinking.

'How long for?' I ask, no more than a whisper.

'Six, maybe eight weeks as a start, depending on how you go,' says the psychologist.

'I'M SORRY,' I say to Mum and Dad as we get back in the car. 'For being like this.' Dad starts to protest but I interrupt him, needing to get some words out. 'My head is so messed up. I'm so *fucking* anxious the whole time I can't think straight. The thoughts are so bad I can't think about anything but the routines.' Tears stream, but I have to continue. 'I can't *think* any more, I'm so tired. I can't tell what's OCD and what's real.'

Mum puts her hand on my arm. 'It's not too late,' she says, 'to fix things...' She smiles and wipes away my tears with her sleeve.

I think about my grannie.

This is rock bottom, I think. Ground zero.

It starts here.

Part Three
Hillside

Chapter 13
Day 1 in Hillside

I open the car door and the tranquillity hits me. The only sound is the twittering of birds.

A blonde girl, younger than me with clothes two sizes too big, ambles in the twilight from the car park to the main building of the Hillside psychiatric unit, her parents trailing close behind. Luke, the CAMHS nurse, arrives in his silver Ford, there to *support my transition* to inpatient. The hospital itself is a haphazard assortment of brick buildings nestling into the trees and bushes.

I am numb. I am apprehensive about what is to come. My hopes for progress are not high. There's no quick fix for the anxiety, the OCD and the more sinister elements that flow from those roots. But there's a splinter of light amongst the darkness. Surely, this place at least offers a possibility of a pathway to something better.

I look at my bags stacked in the car and realise I don't have my guitar. Would I even be allowed a guitar? I wonder about the music competition, and my chances of getting through to music college after all this. The realisation of being away from home filters into my mind, and it makes me miss my little brother. Lucas is a tonic for the pressure of everyday. He grounds me.

The woman at reception smiles and offers tea and coffee while we wait. Mum says no but means yes. Dad says he'll have one. Probably he'll put sugar in it so he can share with Mum.

Luke approaches us and keeps up the small talk as we wait to be called in. I edge away from them, pretending to read the information on the staff notice-board but taking little of it in: something about car parking, an advert for a training course. My eyes glaze over and my vision blurs as I take a minute to shut down and recharge. I think of Danny. I should have messaged him. But what was I supposed to say?

The waiting area is smaller than it looks in the photos on the website. The walls are cluttered in real life, with info-posters and notices, leaflets and artwork.

A small woman in a knee-length cardigan strides confidently towards us, her two companions trailing

'You might have left a germ that can make you ill, is that it?'

'Yes.' I think for a minute about the logic of my thought processes when I'm inside the OCD. There used to be connections between the rituals and the outcomes, but most of them have been lost with time.

'What else might go wrong?'

'Anything. Something with my friends, maybe. Or my work.'

Dr Gilani leans forward in her seat. 'Like what?'

'I don't know,' I say, too firmly. She does the silent thing again. I stay quiet.

'Give me an example of what might go wrong with your friends if you don't do the hand wash routine right.'

She's trying to open up my wounds, to expose my vulnerabilities. Maybe she's trying to catch me out? She thinks I'm being a drama queen. I've been through these things so many times. 'They might freeze me out. Or humiliate me or something, anything. Or I might screw up my exams and piss away any chance of getting in to the Academy.'

'And, has any of that happened?'

I almost spit the word, 'Yes.'

She pauses for a second. 'Is that how the routines grow? When something goes wrong you have to step it up a bit?' Her voice is calm and measured.

'Maybe,' I say. But they also grow sometimes when things go right. There's no logic. I guess that's her point. I never said it was rational.

'Let's move on.' She pauses. 'We have zero tolerance to self-harm in Hillside. Do you understand that? Do you think you can comply with this rule?'

I nod and look over at Mum, who forces a smile then looks away.

Dr Gilani talks about Hillside House, what they expect of the young people, the *contract* for my time here.

Sandra, the eating disorder specialist, says that there are a high number of patients with eating disorders. She says that Hillside is aware of the potential for negative interactions, how vulnerable I could be and that they would be monitoring the situation.

'Monitoring?' I say.

'Yes, we need to be sure that what we are doing here is helping you in the right direction. Sometimes the high concentration of people with similar eating disorders can result in worsening conditions as the young people react to each other.'

'So what happens then?'

Sandra looks at Dr Gilani, then says, 'If that happens, or if you're not making the progress we need to see, then we have no choice but to send you home.'

'Then what?' I ask. Surely they must have a process for helping people beyond inpatient treatment.

Sandra looks confused. 'What do you mean, dear?'

'What happens then? If we have to go home. If this place isn't helping?'

'Well...' Sandra stumbles and looks again at Dr Gilani. 'Nothing.'

Mum sits up straight. 'Nothing?' she says. 'You can't mean nothing?'

Sandra makes to speak, but Dr Gilani raises a hand. 'We just mean that if Hillside is not right for Charley, then we will have no choice but to discharge her back to the care of CAMHS. At least until she turns eighteen.'

Mum is spooked now. 'Then what?'

'Let's not get too far ahead of—' Dr Gilani starts.

'Then what?' Mum repeats, her voice more stern.

'Post-eighteen, care is provided by the adult psychiatric care sector.'

My skin tingles with anxiety. Despite all I've experienced about the inadequacies of resources in the mental health care system for children, the system for adults looks to me a whole lot more scary. It's like I've been set an ultimatum – play by the rules and make progress, or we kick you out to the mercy of the system outside. Then when you turn eighteen we will throw you into a loony bin and that's it. But they don't say how I'm supposed to untangle the mess in my head. I don't even know what those rules are.

Back in reception, Mum and I embrace. She holds me tight for a moment, wipes a tear from her cheek and then gently wipes away one of mine.

'I don't have my guitar,' I say.

'We'll bring it in, when we visit,' Dad says. His eyes are big and wide, like he's trying to take in as much of me as he can before he goes.

I watch them leave. The automated barrier closes behind their car like a prison gate. An empty feeling spreads from my stomach to my chest.

I am alone.

Opposite the hand basin in my small rectangular room, there's a narrow single bed pushed into the corner, its head end up against the back wall. It's neatly made with a white pillow and beige bedspread tucked in tight, and folded back at the top with a white sheet. It feels clinical. I wonder about making it more homely. This messes with the thought tangles: If I make it homely, then it will be a nicer place to be, which means I want to be here, which implies that this is all my choice, my fault.

When Mum and Dad left, Dr Gilani handed me

over to a nurse, Simon, who checked through my stuff to make sure everything was approved as safe. Simon must be in his thirties, with short, prematurely greying hair. The lanyard hanging around his neck was too long so his ID card swung around the level of his belt, making him look even smaller, like a kid pretending to be a grown-up. Everything was OK but he kept hold of my moisturiser. Apparently they dispense moisturiser if and when required, from the medication centre.

I shove my case into the bottom of the oversized, white melamine wardrobe standing against the end wall of my room, the case filling just a fraction of its space. My eyes are drawn to the big window in the back wall. I switch off the light and move closer to it, then twist the handle and push it open until it stops with a jolt on its restricting latch. A welcome rush of cool air pours in and I take a lungful. It feels like the first breath I've taken since I arrived.

I pick my tobacco from my pocket and sit down on the bed to roll a cigarette, sinking into the mattress so that my knees end up higher than my hips.

After Simon's checks, I followed him through the corridors to my room. He pointed out the landmarks: the dispensary, the games room and the girls' lounge. The last place he showed me on the ground floor was the secure unit. He called it a 'special place' or something like that. I'd read about it before I came in. It's where we go if we're considered a danger to ourselves or others, a separate flat with space for a twenty-four-hour nurse and facilities for force-feeding – which makes me think of tubes, sedatives and restraints.

I kneel near the opening of the window in my room so I can blow out my smoke. I have a line of sight through the trees to the hill opposite. In the gathering darkness, I can still make out the features of the land-scape. The woodland falls away sharply from the hospital grounds into a river valley, and then up again on the far side to a peak that's at around the same elevation as the hospital.

I finish the cigarette and flick the butt so that it spins in an arc and clears the tall hedge opposite my room. A solitary tree stands on the crown of the hill opposite, stretching into the sky and backlit by the setting sun. A flash of light at the foot of the tree catches my eye. The fading sunlight must have momentarily reflected off something – a discarded bottle maybe. The likeness of the view to that from Butser Hill is undeniable, and it calms me.

'Small but functional,' Simon had said as he led me into my room. 'A shared shower and toilet down the corridor,' he added, and it crossed my mind that my irrational half-plan that I might not have to leave my room was already dead. The idea of a shared bathroom space hit my chest and raised my anxiety. I had to push the thoughts away to deal with later, or I'd have spiralled.

The darkness closes in. All I can see in my window is my own reflection, lit by the light seeping from the cracks around the door. I don't look like me. I have no idea what I'm doing. I don't even know if I really understand what I've signed up to by coming here. Will I be able to eat?

SIMON IS at the bottom of the circular stairwell, waiting to escort me to the dining room. Other patients flow around him, glancing up at me as they pass. Most are expressionless. I wonder if they're dosed up on something. Others are laughing and nudging into each other as if this is any other school or college.

The dining room is full of big round tables. Some are empty and some have just one patient, with their nurse. One table is full, and the girls' laughter takes me back to the school playground, making my stomach lurch. I check them out, half expecting to see faces I recognise. One of the girls is centre stage, telling a story. The others lean in to listen and then all rock back in their seats, laughing.

The table nearest me has just one girl. She's pretty, with blonde hair tucked behind her ears, and she has her head down. Her nurse is quietly encouraging her to eat. Simon leads me to a separate table, empty but for a plate of pasta, with mince and a red sauce. Next to the plate is a small plastic cup of water and a second one with lemon squash. I pick up and examine the name plate with 'Charley' written in colourful, artistic lettering.

'The young people here make the place names,' Simon says, pulling out a chair for me. I smile at the thoughtful, decorative lettering. Simon sits two chairs away from me at my table. Every little element of Hillside feels carefully planned, managed and practised. I look around the room. The blonde girl is refusing to even look at her food.

'One step at a time, Charley,' Simon encourages gently. I push the pasta around my plate until the white shells have all turned orange in the sauce. The blonde girl stares at her plate with tears rolling down her face. She lifts a hand and forks in a mouthful in one sweeping move, then drops the fork back onto her plate and twists her head away from her food, as if she can't bear to look at what she's done.

'Concentrate on your own food, Charley,' Simon says, almost whispering. I look down at my plate for a second and back to the girl as she winds herself up for some more. I pick up my own fork. A mouthful goes in easy, too easy. I'm giving in to food with no fight. The intrusive thought grows and morphs into disgust, multiplying like bacteria. Food is mandatory, I remind myself. It's non-negotiable.

When I finish, I feel bloated and guilt-ridden. I look back over at the sad blonde girl who has also finished and is staggering to her feet. She looks defeated, and I feel her sense of failure.

Chapter 14
First night in Hillside

I shield my eyes from the light from the doorway, squinting to see who's there. Still half asleep, I'm disorientated and grasping at evasive memories. 'Mum?' I call out.

A whispered female voice says, 'Just checking in on you, Charley. Go back to sleep.' The door clicks shut and I strain my eyes to make out the details of the room around me. Memories seep back in and a knot tightens in my stomach.

I'm on an hourly watch for my first night in Hillside, because I'm new, an unknown quantity at an 'uncertain level of risk', they said. They know that I have trouble with self-harm, and the strict rule on self-harm in Hillside is apparently not always enough to stop it happening. I retreat under my covers, a tortoise into its shell.

By the time I've had four checks, I'm wide awake. I study the ceiling of my room, scanning the joins between the rows of ceiling paper, slightly lifting in places.

After the meal last night, Simon led me to the girls' lounge. It was full and noisy with activity. I saw some of the girls from the dining room, the redhead that had been commanding attention on the happy table, and the blonde girl, still looking beaten. I must have looked uneasy at the doorway because Simon suggested we rest somewhere quieter. The boys' lounge was empty. There are no boys in Hillside.

Staring up at the ceiling, I think of home. The knot in my stomach tightens. I'm in a box room on the side of a hill, in the middle of nowhere. With no music. How did it get so bad?

Chapter 15
Day 2 in Hillside

After breakfast the next day, a hush comes over the girls' lounge when I walk in behind nurse Simon. He takes advantage of the quiet and introduces me.

The redhead is Max. She's around my age, maybe a bit older, around seventeen or eighteen, shorter than me but heavier. She has dark-rimmed glasses and short, beetroot-red hair in tight curls. With some effort I force a smile at her. She burps at me, like a dog barking. She turns back to the TV. A couple of the others laugh and Simon rolls his eyes.

Violet is younger, fourteen or fifteen. Her straight, brown, shoulder-length hair hangs over her face as she looks down at her hands. She's fiddling with something, concentrating hard. When Simon introduces us, she looks up at me through her hair without a smile and quickly turns her attention back to her hands.

I sit down on a two-seater sofa where I can see the TV. Violet glances at me but I keep my eyes forward. Old feelings of being trapped, judged and frozen out by Mia and the girls at school flow into my head and push out at my skin.

The other nurse gives me a broad smile and introduces herself as Lisa. She has a gentle expression. She's wearing a long woollen cardigan stretched tight around her chest. Her style reminds me of Mum.

My mind races, struggling to process the events of just two days: from home to a psychiatric ward, feeding myself for the first time in days.

I see out of the corner of my eye that Violet is still shooting me glances, but I'm too scared to look up. 'This is funny,' she says and nods at the TV as the opening credits of a programme come onto the screen. She has a quiet voice with a slight northern accent, probably softened from time spent in the south. In those three words, and a look, she exuded warmth. I sigh with relief. She has a melancholy sense about her. Not sad, particularly, but resigned, as if this is as good as it gets.

'What is it?' I ask, as friendly and unthreatening as can be.

'*Doctors*. It's just people with weird illnesses and

doctors sorting them out,' she says, looking at me again with a smile. Her movements are slow, as if she's conserving energy. 'It's addictive. Can't not watch it,' she says. The redhead, Max, lets out a derisive grunt as if she's pissed off with everything.

'How long have you been in here?' I ask Violet, not sure if it's an allowable inquiry.

'Forever,' she says. 'Feels like that, anyway. It's more like a few months, but I can't see an end to it. Seems like a continuous cycle of trying some concoction of pills, getting it wrong, me feeling like shit, and repeat.'

'Sorry,' I say.

We watch the TV in silence for a minute. She looks at me again. 'You'll settle in,' she says, as if she knows what I'm feeling.

A small bundle of bits of metal sits in her lap. 'What's that?'

'My lock-picking kit,' she whispers. 'I'm practising on this padlock.' A smile lights up her face.

'Can we play pool yet, Simon?' Max asks. She makes me nervous. Simon looks at his watch and says we can disperse if we like, or we can hang and watch the TV. Max jumps up, nudging Violet to follow, but Violet nods at the TV and says she's going to watch the end of the programme. Max looks pissed off and mumbles something I can't hear as she slopes out. The other girls follow, leaving me and Violet with Lisa.

Violet sinks deeper into her armchair, half watching the TV and half working on the padlock with two metal pins. Lisa seems to relax too when the others have left. She has a soothing and personal manner about her, as if she wants to get to know me, us, all of us. I figure she's sizing us up for all the right reasons, figuring out how we tick.

Chapter 16
Day 3 in Hillside

Max lines up a winning shot on the black ball. It hits the centre of the pocket. She turns sideways, leans against the table and grins. She knocks the butt of her cue on the floor. 'Any of you think you can take on the master?' She looks at Violet.

Max doesn't unnerve me like she did when I first got here. I've been trying to keep to myself as much as I can. Interactions with any of them are confusing, and Max gives me a sense that she could flip at any moment. She's unpredictable. I gravitate towards Violet. She doesn't say much. Even when I talk to her, she doesn't always respond.

'Not me,' Violet says to Max across the pool table. She walks over to Willow, who's standing at the window. Max's disapproving gaze follows her then returns to me, a single, beetroot-red eyebrow raised.

'I'm in,' I say, feeling brave. I pick out a cue and hold it up at the thick end to check if it's straight. I put it back and choose a better one. Max watches me and pulls a 'whatever' face. She racks up the balls, moves some around in the black plastic triangle and nods at the table, signalling for me to break.

I'm pretty good at pool. I got good from all the tournaments at the campsite on our family holidays. It nearly always rained, and Lucas and I would end up in the so-called sports room, playing pool and table tennis. I can hold my own against anyone at the pool table.

I pick out the white ball and place it in the 'D', then lean back and push my whole bodyweight into the break, pocketing two red balls. I sink two more reds before playing safe, leaving Max a tricky shot to stay in the game.

She's good. Her first visit to the table matches mine and the next few minutes has Max and me sinking balls in equal measure, leaving it down to a black ball finish. Max is at the table but the pocket is not on. She can play safe or go for a double into the top corner. I figure she'll take a chance. She goes for it but the ball stops short, over the pocket. Her face drops. I step up and clear the black, trying not to look smug.

Max snorts a laugh. 'Nice,' she says. 'Hey!' she

shouts to the others, 'Charley's a hustler. I've been here three months and she's the first one to give me a decent game.' Violet and Willow turn towards us and Violet cheers. Max racks up the balls again.

We play another six or seven games. Willow heads back to her room. Violet stays with us but shows no interest in picking up a cue. Max and I are on a roll, evenly matched. I learn from Max that she's in Hillside for a combination of post-traumatic stress disorder, depression and anxiety. There is some incident that's the root cause of the PTSD but she doesn't offer it, and I don't ask. I also figure out from Violet that Max's dad has never been around, and her mum is 'flaky', as Violet puts it. She says that Max's mum would not normally turn up for the Wednesday visiting times, then some-times she'd roll up the next day when visitors weren't allowed, usually making a bit of a scene.

Simon comes into the games room at around half past nine, suggesting we finish up and head to our rooms.

'Enjoy yourselves?' he says, looking at me.

'We had a good battle,' I say.

'I took it easy on her,' Max says to Simon, smiling as we follow him towards the residential wing. Other girls mill around the corridors, heading back to their rooms.

'Night then, girls,' Violet says as she veers off to her

room. Max comes alongside me as we walk behind Simon up the stairs.

'You're settling, then,' she says, not a question. 'It can be dull in here, so we have to make our own entertainment. Like winding these idiots up.' She nods at Simon in front of us.

'You heard about Elsie yet?' she says with a smile as she stops at her door.

'Elsie?' I say.

'Yeah, Elsie Fisher. You must have heard the story?'

'No.'

'I'll tell you about it. Remind me.' She disappears into her room.

Simon continues on his circuit and I step into my room. I leave the light off and walk over to open my window. I stand looking out over the fields while I brush my teeth. The hill is still visible, the tree silhouetted by the white light of a half-moon. The intricate tangle of branches takes me back to Butser Hill, with my family, with BB. Thick clouds pass in front of the moon, pulling a dark blanket over the hills.

Chapter 17
Day 4 in Hillside

When I get the eight o'clock wake-up call, I feel as though I've hardly slept. My eyes are dry and grainy and my body is empty with fatigue. My window is still open and the sound of twittering birds fills my room.

I open my eyes a crack. There's a clear, blue sky above the trees outside my window. A single cloud hangs motionless. I soak it up for a moment, comfortable in the peacefulness.

I dig around in my clothes for some leggings and my favourite jumper. I look in the mirror on my way out of the room and pull my hair back into a ponytail, looking away before being dragged into negative thoughts. I step out of the room, right foot first over the threshold and into the corridor where the sun is bursting into the building through the wall of glass.

Outside, a portly man repeatedly swipes his staff pass at the main entrance without success. A woman approaches the door and pulls it open without swiping any pass, then skips through, flashing him a smile.

The smell of toast and the sound of clashing crockery drifting up from the staircase makes me uneasy. At the bottom of the stairs, there are others heading to the dining room. I catch their glances, attempting a smile at any who hang around.

As I enter the dining hall, the blonde nurse with the severe fringe, Laura, motions for me to sit at her table, which turns out to be *my* table. My lonely name plate and breakfast are laid out for me. Weetabix, two bits of toast, two drinks. In Hillside, it's always more than I would eat for breakfast at home, even before I got bad. It always looks like too much.

'Has it increased?' I ask Laura, nodding at my food.

'Same as always, Charley. You're on the maintenance plan, you know that. Sleep OK?' She takes a seat opposite me and places a folded newspaper on the table. I shrug and push the Weetabix around in its creamy milk. Others are settling at their tables.

'Let's get going shall we, Charley,' she says and turns her attention back to her newspaper. I take a mouthful of cereal. The milk tastes like cream, immediately heavy in my stomach.

Max and Violet are with another girl on the same

table with two nurses. The non-eating-disorder table. Max is mucking about, the centre of attention. She's making everyone laugh and I can't help but smile. Violet looks lost. The cloud has come in again. Her head is down and she's staring at her toast.

The table across from mine has a nurse with a girl of about my age, long black hair tucked behind both ears. She has dark make-up and piercings in her nose and all up the top edges of both ears. She stares into space, away from her plate, a familiar expression of defiance. Willow comes in, flanked by two nurses like prison warders. Her beauty is muted by a pale and sickly complexion, and the red blotches around her eyes stand out.

I get through my cereal, finally pushing the empty bowl towards the middle of the table and looking up at Laura in minor triumph. She glances up and nods towards my toast before settling her eyes back on her newspaper. No fanfare anymore for finishing a bowl of cereal. I nibble the butter-soaked toast. Laura doesn't look at me.

I take another bite and then cram the whole thing in my mouth to get it done. Like a pig. Some of the others in the room are clearly struggling and I'm shovelling it in. It feels wrong. I feel guilty again for being here, as if I'm a fraud. People here are ill. More ill than me.

The girls' lounge is full and noisy with conversation. As I walk in, Max burps the two syllables of my name. Violet has her knees drawn up to her chest and head resting down. I find a seat in front of the TV.

'She's on a bad one,' Max says without shifting her gaze from the TV. 'But she'll come out of it.'

One of the nurses, Susie, is crouched on the floor next to the sofa trying to engage Violet.

People start to move, getting ready to leave for the school classes. Max stands and gives me a short salute, leaving with the others. The room empties and Susie heads over to me. Her shoulder-length brown hair has a fringe just long enough to get in her eyes.

'We need to run through some OT plans,' she says. I must look confused because she clarifies: 'Occupational therapy. I'll talk you through it. Violet will be coming to the OT room with us today.' She glances over her shoulder. 'OK?'

'Sure, fine.' I look over at Violet. Her dark hair is flopped over her face and her gaze fixed on the floor.

THE OPEN-PLAN OT room takes up the whole first floor of the school building. It has an art section, a mini-gym and a yoga zone. Violet joins a small group doing some craft work, and Susie leads me to a separate area next to the computer zone with a table and two wooden chairs. She opens a folder and looks at me across the table. 'Charley.' She leans forward and brushes her fringe out of her eyes. 'OT is going to help you. Think of it as one of the limbs of your recovery. You'll need to work hard, but it will be worth it.' She takes me through some of the planned activities.

When she's done, she leaves me with some forms to fill in. I look around for Violet. She's drawing, while the others in the group are creating something with bits of paper and glue. Susie is perched on the edge of a table next to the wall, talking to another nurse.

I finish my forms and walk over to Violet.

'Hi, Charley,' she says as I approach, glancing at me and then returning to her pencil drawing. I must have looked surprised that she was talking because she quickly explains that she's OK. She's feeling OK.

'Which one's you?' I ask, looking at her picture of four figures, a mum and dad with two children. She taps her pencil on the smallest figure. I point at the next biggest one. 'Is that your sister? How old is she?' Violet is silent for a minute, then looks at me as if deciding whether or not to talk about it.

'Older than me. I don't see her much anymore,' she says. 'She's my sister by blood but I live with adoptive parents now and she lives somewhere else.'

'You must miss her.' Violet quietly adds curls to her sister's shoulder-length pencil-hair. 'How old are you?'

'Fourteen.' She smiles and her face lights up. 'What about you?'

'Sixteen.'

She pulls a hard plastic segmented toy out of her pocket and twists it, changing its shape. 'My stress snake,' she says, holding it up. It's so worn that the colours have faded from what was probably a bright, striped pattern to a single smear of faded oranges. She twists it to demonstrate, then hands it to me. I try it. Violet watches with amusement at my lack of dexterity. 'It gives my hands a focus, same as my lock picking. It distracts me and keeps my head from going funny.'

'It's cool,' I say, fiddling a while longer before handing it back. 'It looks well used.'

'My sister gave it to me.'

'Hey, you two,' Susie says, sliding over to us. She addresses Violet: 'Everything OK?'

'Good, thanks,' says Violet. Susie seems relieved. She tells us to head to the dining room and Violet perks up. She looks at me with a smile, turns to fold her picture in two and shoves it into her back pocket.

Chapter 18
Day 8 in Hillside

After the evening meal, as I head to the girls' lounge from the dining room to find the others, Nurse Simon pulls me aside. 'You have some post,' he says, handing me a white envelope that has clearly been opened.

'A good read?' I say.

'We have to check. You know that. Especially post like this with something in there.' He nods at the envelope in my hand, which I can feel has something heavy as well as a note.

'What is it?' I ask, peering into the envelope.

'Some kind of MP3 player.'

I guess it's from my parents but the writing looks unfamiliar. I pull the letter out far enough to see that it's signed from Danny. My heart sinks a little for reasons I can't quite figure. I haven't yet connected this new world with the old life and the people outside. I'm not yet sure what I think about the two worlds co-existing. I close the envelope and divert from the lounge towards my room.

I open my curtains and push open the window, then drop onto my bed and tip the envelope onto my duvet. Leaving the little blue MP3 player, I open the single sheet of paper and read Danny's spidery handwriting.

Hey Charley,
Your mum gave me the hospital address. She
didn't want to say where you were but I kind of
made her, so don't blame her.
I know you can't have your normal phone or
anything so I thought I should send you some
music to keep you going. There's a whole album
on there by Matthew & The Atlas. Sorry about
that but they are awesome and you need
educating in their awesomeness. Then there's a
load of random stuff that I think you will like.
If you can, then let me know that you're ok. Do
you need anything? I can come to see you?
I'll work on the next set of tunes to send you
Danny x

I pick up the MP3 player and turn it over in my

hand. I hadn't planned on Danny knowing I was here, but now he knows, I feel OK with it.

I'm one week in to my time in this institution already. The words of Susan and Dr Gilani repeat in my head. Their warning about making progress rings loud. I don't know what progress is for me yet, the direction in which I need to move. It's like I've only just arrived. I've had no psychology yet. I've not started in the schooling sessions that everyone else goes to. I need to hurry up and find my feet, get on with getting on. Whatever that means. The alternative is too scary to imagine. It's like this place is my last chance, my final hope of getting meaningful help. If Hillside can't drag me forward, then what's the point?

I pick my earphones out of my drawer and plug them into the MP3 player, pressing start and lying back on my bed. I smile up at the ceiling as Springsteen's 'Thunder Road' fills my ears and rocks me to sleep.

The polar bears fly at me through the mist,
their teeth gnashing, dripping with blood. I
look back over my shoulder as I run across the
ice, my feet sliding, slipping, struggling to gain
traction. The bears bound towards me at

incredible speed. They barely seem to notice they're on the ice, their feet sticky like snow shoes.

They gain on me.
I search the horizon for signs of Dad.

Nothing.

Snow falls hard, thin and cold, and coming at me from all angles. The ice opens out in a wide expanse before me and it's clear I have no chance of getting to the other side of the frozen lake before the polar bears reach me. More bears now, piling onto the ice from all sides, cutting off my escape route, filling my field of vision. My legs slow as the futility of running becomes obvious. The bears maintain speed, as if desperate to reach me – like I'm food, and their first meal for an eternity.

Chapter 19
Day 9 in Hillside

Izzy is late.

I've been waiting outside her therapy room for twenty minutes. I'm not leaving. If I leave, I don't know how long it will be before I get another appointment.

Without getting up from my plastic chair, I tap on Izzy's door again. I wait.

No answer.

I saw her for, like, five minutes when I'd been in Hillside for a couple of days — I wouldn't call that a psychology session. It was more like an introduction, a welcome meeting. I've had sessions with the nurses, and with OT, but it's the psychology I need to get me on track.

A noise comes from inside the room, like a closing of a drawer or a cupboard. Then nothing.

She'll come soon, and we can kick off on my plan. When I saw her before, she said something about a tailored plan – a pathway for me through the therapy and treatment at Hillside. This is what I need, something I can grab onto and pull myself through. A guide. A lifeline.

I push one of my earbuds back in, keeping the other ear free in case Izzy calls me in. Having Danny's music in my head helps me. I think. It's a bit like he's with me, and he's good company. But, I haven't yet figured out how to introduce him to my friends – Max and Violet. It's like he's a secret companion that I keep in my room. My MP3 player is on shuffle and another Matthew and the Atlas song comes on. It's mostly acoustic guitar-based and I can see why Danny loves it. It's not so far away from his own style.

Yesterday, I checked my phone for messages, the first time I'd checked in a few days. It's weird; on the outside my phone was part of me, like an extension to my hand. In here, with the brick-phone I have, I barely think about it. I had messages from Mum and Dad. No one else has my number, although I should really message Danny. Mum and Dad say they're coming to visit soon, when they get clearance from Dr Gilani.

A nurse's alarm sounds in the main reception area down the corridor. I pull my earbud out. I've heard this alarm only twice since being in Hillside, and both times it was serious – someone hurt, or about to be hurt. I wonder if it is Jasmine again. Last time she'd taken a plastic knife from the kitchen, broken it in half and was threatening to cut her own wrists in front of one of the nurses. I'm not sure she would have done it, or even if the piece of plastic was sharp enough, but Nurse Simon raised the alarm in any case, bringing all the available nurses into the dining hall. One of the nurses directed the rest of us out of there while someone talked her down.

Jasmine is one of the longer-term patients in Hillside. She keeps flipping out because they're going to transfer her to an adult unit now that she's turned eighteen. She's not happy about it. She told Violet that moving to an adult unit might as well be a death sentence. People don't come out of the adult units.

Aside from her outbursts, she seems pretty switched on to me. Whenever I've spoken to her she has an enviable clarity of thought. She told me that she'd never transfer to an adult unit, that she'd discharge herself as soon as she could. She's convinced that Hillside overprescribes the drugs to get her to appear more out of it than she really is. Then there are rumours about some of the treatments in those adult places. Max talked about electric shock treatment, but I'm pretty sure she read that in a magazine and that they stopped that way back in the sixties. But who knows what pills they push on the patients to keep them agreeable.

I don't know the truth of it, but if there was someone in this place who I'd say had it all together, then it would be Jasmine. I wouldn't bet on Hillside in a battle between the system and Jasmine.

Izzy's door swings open and she joins nurse Camilla running down the corridor. They don't see me. I stand to follow them. By the time I get to the corner, there are three other girls with me, watching to see what's going on. Jasmine is in a stand-off with three staff. Simon is out front. He must be the one who raised the alarm and is now the lead negotiator. He's flanked by Izzy and Camilla. Jasmine puffs out her chest and stands firm, looking ready for a fight. She has no weapon as far as I can see, but Simon keeps his distance in any case, his palms raised.

With each step forward by Simon, Jasmine steps back. She's talking to Simon but I'm too far away to hear. The whole thing reminds me of one of those American shows where the hapless cops try to corner the nimble offender who evades their attempts to get the cuffs on.

The three girls watching with me drift away. I lean up against the wall as Jasmine finally seems to give up and allow Simon to guide her to sit on a chair in the corridor. He puts a hand on Jasmine's arm and she pushes it away. Izzy crouches to speak to her for a moment and then she and Simon head off together, leaving Camilla to talk to Jasmine. I guess Izzy hasn't remembered our appointment.

Camilla helps Jasmine to stand and keeps a hold on her as she leads her away. Jasmine twists and gives the nurse a heavy shove in the chest with her free hand. Camilla stumbles. The tight grip she has on Jasmine's arm is the only thing that keeps her from falling over. Her face flushes with colour.

Then Camilla slaps Jasmine's cheek.

I gasp. Camilla's head flips in my direction and I raise my hand to my open mouth. She gathers herself and releases Jasmine's arm, flipping from aggressor to comforter. I slip back around the corner of the corridor and head to my room.

Chapter 20
Day 12 in Hillside

I didn't speak to Jasmine again after that. I feel bad for it too. I wanted to, but there was something about her that made me uneasy. I felt sorry for her, but not enough to overcome my own stupid hang-ups and reach out to her. Something in her eyes made me question myself, challenge my own motivations, my own sense of what was important, what was real and what seemed to be part of a big charade. She'd never do anything to hurt me, I know that, but she scared me nonetheless.

It was twenty-four hours later when Jasmine was transferred out of Hillside to an adult unit, up the country somewhere. She didn't say goodbye to anyone, or she wasn't allowed to. I don't know.

A couple of days later, Camilla calls me in to her office and I sit in the seat opposite her like it's me who's being transferred out. That's what it feels like. She's asked me in for an update meeting, to see how I am feeling.

She says how well I'm doing and asks if there is anything I need. I try to say that all I need is to get on with the psychology when she interrupts me. 'The pressure is so much sometimes,' she says, 'and we don't get paid any more than any other nurse, even though we have to be specially trained to deal with all sorts in here.' She pauses then, and she even looks a bit tearful. I can't believe this is happening. 'We get trained in restraint techniques, but in the heat of the moment... it's scary, and there's not always time, you know?'

I stare at her. I think she's asking me if it's OK that she slapped Jasmine. I keep quiet, and she puffs out her chest. 'Jasmine is OK. I've checked again today and she's settling in to her new unit.'

'That's OK, then,' I say, trying not to sound sarcastic, knowing that the last person I need to be going up against in Hillside is Camilla. She gives me a look that reminds me of Mia's controlling, calculating expression of half-threat, half-innocence.

Chapter 21
Day 14 in Hillside

Max looks directly at new-boy Archie, the only boy patient in Hillside, and asks what his story is. The rest of us stare at Max without saying anything, then back at Archie.

He's tall with straggly, curly hair flopped on top of his head. His smart, pressed navy trousers look as if they have sparkly flecks in them, a weird mix with his tatty, old, white high-top Converse. And his white shirt still has the shop creases in the sleeves. The combination is so far away from working that it might just be super cool.

'I'm still working on it,' Archie says, his voice soft. He looks away from Max and shrinks in his seat. For a split second he reminds me of Danny. Not the outwardly confident Danny who doesn't give a shit

about what anyone thinks, but the other side of him –
the side that allows his vulnerabilities to be on display.

Max straightens up on the sofa, her back to the
window in the boys' lounge. 'Well, welcome to the H-
blocks, Archie. I'm Max, and these are my friends.' She
sweeps her arm theatrically at me and Violet. 'But be
careful because they are both a bit mental.' She pauses
and Archie looks at the three of us in turn.

Max continues, 'We're all in here to try to figure
out shit, so whatever you decide your story is, you're in
good company.' Max rests back and we look at Archie
for what feels like ages. He leans back in his seat,
smiles and visibly loosens up. Violet looks over at me
and rolls her eyes at Max.

A group of girls comes to the door of the boys'
lounge, poking their heads in for a moment to see the
new arrival, then go on their way.

'H-blocks?' Archie asks.

'That's what they call Hillside House,' says Max.

'Who does?' Violet asks.

'The nurses.'

Violet frowns. 'Why? Because it begins with H?'

'I don't know, I've overheard them call it that a few
times.'

'It's a prison,' I say and they all turn to look at me.
'The H-blocks was a prison in Ireland.'

'That's about right,' says Max. 'That's fucking

lovely, that is, the nurses referring to this place as a prison. What hope do we have?'

Violet rolls her eyes at Max again, then turns to Archie. 'I'm Violet. Nice to meet you, Archie,' she says, reaching behind her for a guitar that I'd not noticed before.

'Whose is that?' I say.

'It's the house guitar. It lives here,' Violet says. The sight of it immediately warms me in a way I can't explain. I have to stop myself from reaching out for it to play something.

Violet looks at Archie and gives him one of her rare smiles. He smiles back and she starts to pick haphazardly at the strings. The sound of the guitar is thin and slightly out of tune, but it settles my mind more than any talking session I've had since being in Hillside.

'Where are you from, Archie?' Max asks.

He tells us he's from Minstead, a small village not far from where I live. I look at him again, thinking he must be at a school in Linford, same as me, but not my school. Probably one of the posh schools out in the villages. I think for a moment what it might be like to be in school with people like Max, Violet and Archie. I can't imagine it. Just a thought of school and I feel the pressure like I'm actually there. The overwhelming scrutiny. The fear of not doing what's expected – what

Mia and the others require of me. My mouth dries up and I sink back in my chair.

'How long have you guys been in here?' Archie says.

Max relates her Hillside story so far. She's been in for more than three months. She jokes about being *mental*, but she doesn't mention her PTSD. Her manner is blasé, but inside she's as tangled as I am – a different tangled, but messy all the same.

'I've been in and out of the dark side for as long as I can remember, more Vader than Skywalker if I'm honest,' she says without humour. Her head twitches a little. It's something I've noticed before; it's almost undetectable but definitely something. It creeps in and cuts her off, like a stress tick. She looks down at her feet. 'That's enough about me. Charley, your turn.'

'Are we really supposed to talk about our issues like this?' I say.

'Look, we are all ill in here, all on some kind of medication, and all in therapy. This is a psychiatric ward. It can't be that bad to talk about it,' she snaps, and her stress tick is nowhere to be seen.

I keep quiet, deciding not to fight this battle with Max.

I miss home, my dad, the viewpoint bench on Butser Hill, looking out over the horizon. Dad was always just there, not pressing too hard with the questions, in case I broke. I look at Archie's shoes. The soles are clearly coming off.

'I'm not asking for details.' Max's tone is more conciliatory, looking at me.

'Mine's a mixture of things,' I say, 'everything and nothing.'

'What does *that* mean?' Max is annoyed again.

'I just mean it's not one big thing, it's a few things piled up. And the eating thing is part of it, with a bit of OCD and anxiety in there too.' I stop there.

Talk of anxiety takes me back to the panic attack I had in bed last night, and I tighten my grip on the armrest of my chair.

It wasn't unusual to wake with a jolt in the early hours, my head spinning and random images streaming through my mind, too fast to register or make sense of. Last night, my window saved me. I stared at it, and the sky gradually brightened as I watched. I opened it wide and knelt so I could breathe in the clean air as if in an act of worship. I stayed there until long after daylight arrived, long after my foot went numb, squashed under my arse.

Violet is still picking at the guitar strings, a discordant accompaniment to my thoughts. 'Bipolar,' she blurts. The rest of us look at her and then at each other. We let out a laugh as it seems she isn't going to say anything more. I feel suddenly bad for making light of her illness. I try to recall what I can of my knowledge of bipolar but fail miserably.

'It's under control,' Violet says. 'I'm medicated. The tricky thing is getting the meds right, which no one can ever seem to do. As soon as I think they have it, they change it.' She continues to play the guitar, her hair flopping back over her face.

'PTSD,' Archie says, quietly. 'But I'm not sure what that means for me at the moment. I'm working on it.' He looks relieved to have shared, and then a little confused about what to say next.

No one says anything.

MAX BANGS impatiently on the keyboard of the computer in the OT room. 'This fucking thing is so slow, it's impossible to do anything on here.'

I have my own problems with a sticky letter on my keyboard. 'You don't realise how often you need the letter "a". Hey, Max, who's that bloke you mentioned, ages ago?' I say.

Max gives up trying to import images for the finishing touches to her English assignment and twists round to face me. 'What bloke?'

'Elsie something.'

Max is wide-eyed. 'She's a girl, not a bloke. I forgot

about that. Elsie Fisher.' She takes a shifty look around and draws her seat closer. 'Listen,' she says, getting comfortable. 'Elsie Fisher was a patient here when she was fifteen or sixteen.' Max speaks in a low whisper so the nurses can't hear. 'The rumour is that one winter, in the middle of the night, she escaped.'

'Escaped?' I say. 'It's not a prison, not difficult to get out of here. You mean she ran away?' I tuck my hair behind my ears so I can hear her better.

'They never found her. She never turned up anywhere; just disappeared.'

'Dead?'

'There's no evidence that she died,' Max whispers. 'She just disappeared.'

'How long ago?'

'Years ago. Like, ten years ago. Anyway, listen, here's the interesting bit.' Max hushes me again. 'Apparently, as the rumour goes, she camped out some-where nearby.' She pauses. 'And has done ever since, living off the land.'

'Oh, come on.'

'Seriously: she's been spotted several times in the area over the years. I'm not making this up, I heard it from a nurse,' she says.

I'm not sure if Max is winding me up or if she's been wound up by the nurse. 'Which nurse?'

'Conor. He's not here anymore.'

'Convenient.'

'I'm serious,' Max says, no signs of amusement in her face.

I turn back to my computer to see if I can find anything about Elsie Fisher.

'What are you doing?'

'Research. When did you say it was?'

'The nurse said it was about ten years ago.'

'OK. Elsie Fisher...'

Nurse Lisa comes over and lets us know we need to move on to the art section of the room for the next activity. I bring my leaflet back onto the screen. 'Can I just finish this before I go, Lisa?'

'Sure, you can catch up with Max when you're done,' she says. I give Max a wink and she gets up. I smile to myself. Lisa is a great nurse. I have three duty nurses in Hillside: Simon, who's kind of useless, awkward and maybe a bit simple; Lisa, who's brilliant; and Camilla, who I think might literally be a witch.

I bring the internet back up and continue the search for Elsie.

MAX'S MUM IS SKINNY. And pale. She's around Max's height but she has long, straggly, dark hair. She's wearing an old black leather jacket that hangs loose around her shoulders. Her eyes glisten under the light as she holds out her arms to greet Max.

Max has been moping in front of the TV all afternoon, saying that her mum wasn't coming, again. Then Simon came in and said that she was here, at the same time as my mum and dad arrived. We came to reception together but I dropped back a bit so I could see what Max's mum was like.

They embrace, but Max's arms hang in the air like she can't bring herself to hug her mum back. I turn my attention to my own parents.

They both look at me as I approach, sizing me up as if searching for signs of recovery in the two short weeks I've been here. Mum is wearing a long, rainbow-striped jumper and jeans. She's straightened her hair. Dad's in an old black T-shirt and the usual faded blue jeans.

'Sorry we're so late,' Dad says.

I embrace them both at once, one arm around the neck of each. The greeting is awkward. All of us are conscious of the glare of the nurses and don't quite know what we are supposed to do next. We exchange public small talk for a minute, then start towards the door, Dad having decided we should sit and talk in the car for the little time we have left.

'How is it?' Mum says.

'Awesome,' I say.

'Charley, you know what Mum means. How are you getting on? You sounded bad on the phone the other night.'

'I'm sorry, Dad. I don't know, it's weird. I don't know how I'm getting on.'

'Have you met anyone nice?' Mum says. They turn their expectant faces to me in the back of the car, desperate for some snippet of positive information, something to confirm that I'm OK, that I'm recovering.

'Yes,' I say, 'I've met some nice people.' Their expressions loosen. Mum allows herself a smile.

'Are you eating OK?' Dad asks.

'I don't exactly have any choice.' We are quiet again and the atmosphere is tense.

'Not much has happened,' I say. 'I keep expecting to get into psychology sessions to help me figure stuff out, but it hasn't happened yet.'

'It will, love,' Mum says.

'Don't wait for the psychology,' Dad adds. 'Listen to the nurses and the other staff that are there to help you.'

'I will. I am. I just need to get the plan straight in my mind. I'll see Izzy soon.' I pause, looking at my reflection in the car window without much recognition.

'We forgot to bring your guitar, love. I'm sorry,' Mum says.

'It's OK, there's one here I might be able to use.

And the new boy, Archie, he plays too. He has his own guitar with him.' I pause. 'How's Lucas?'

'He misses you,' Dad says.

'Yeah, right. I bet he hasn't noticed I've gone. He'll only realise I'm not there when he wants me to set up his *Minecraft* server or something.' We laugh, and I picture Lucas's face. He *will* miss me, I know that. I miss him. I miss his stupid questions, and the way he talks.

I even miss his annoying dubstep.

Chapter 22
Day 16 in Hillside

I scuff right foot first into the boys' lounge.

Max and Archie are sitting on the sofa. No sign of Violet. The floor-to-ceiling blinds are hooked open on a window handle so the August evening sunlight sneaks in, giving the room a warm glow.

I want to tell Max about what I've read on Elsie Fisher. But Simon is here, sitting, reading a magazine, so I slump down in a space between Max and Archie to wait.

'Avoiding nurse duty, Simon?' I say. He glances at me before turning back to his magazine.

I turn to Archie. 'One of the gang now, Archie?' I say, giving him a friendly nudge. He grins at me, tilting his head forward and peering through his perfect ringlets over the top of his glasses, then returns his attention to the TV without saying anything.

'He's graduated. He's one of us now,' Max says.

'How was your mum yesterday, Max?' Archie asks.

Nurse Simon looks at his watch, gets up and leaves the room.

'Fine,' says Max.

'She looks nice,' I say.

Max stares at me. 'Fucked in the head, you mean? Or nice, as in alcoholic, had a drink recently so is relatively calm, and good job she made it here in her car?'

'I just mean—'

'Or do you mean nice as in she looks like she's been way too busy to have a shower recently so when I go to hug her I can barely stand in her air space?'

Archie looks as if he is about to say something but Max starts up again.

'You don't have a clue,' she says. 'Look at your perfect parents in their cool-kid clothes and their hundred-quid haircuts.'

'Fuck off, Max,' I say, unable to stop myself. I feel an irrational anger, not towards Max but towards my parents for being so normal, so sorted. So suffocating. I get no space to think. One of them is always there: monitoring, advising, planning my every move. 'They're not as perfect as they look, and it's not my fault they are who they are, I didn't choose any of it.'

'Hey,' Archie says. 'Neither of you two have sole claim to fucked-up parents. That's what parents do. They fuck you up. We're all in the same psychiatric unit.'

We are quiet then. Thinking. Too many thoughts at once: Mum, Dad, school, Mia, Danny, Max, Hillside...

'Sorry,' Max says to no one in particular. Archie slings his arm behind me and puts a hand on Max's shoulder.

Conversation is sparse. It's easier to let the TV distract us than it is to talk. I look up, periodically, hoping for Violet to walk into the room.

Max breaks the quiet. 'They've been talking about fostering as an option for me,' she says.

'Who has? Why? What about your mum?' asks Archie.

'She can't cope. You saw her yesterday.' She looks at me. 'It's been coming a long time and they can't keep me in here just because Mum can't cope.'

'That sucks, Max,' I say.

'Does it? I don't know. I mean, I'll still see Mum, I just won't be staying with her. They're looking at a local placement so I still get contact. Feels a bit of a relief, to be honest.' Max looks down at the floor. 'Anyway, we're looking at options. But, like I say, it will be local, so when all you nut-bags are out of here you won't be getting rid of me.'

We are silent again, drifting back under the power of the TV.

'I found Elsie,' I say, remembering my excitement to tell the others, 'when I was researching yesterday.'

'Is this the Elsie Fisher story you were telling me about, Max?' says Archie.

'It's true,' I say.

'What do you mean?' Archie asks.

'OK, listen,' I say, 'I was looking for information on Elsie Fisher in relation to Hillside House from about ten years ago, but I couldn't find anything. So, I was starting to think that Max was probably just talking shit.'

'I'm not—'

'Hang on, Max. Then, I found something about an Elizabeth Fisher, sometimes called *Elspeth*.' I pause for breath. 'It's a short step from Elspeth to Elsie. Anyway, Elizabeth Fisher – or Elsie – was a patient here, just over ten years ago, like Max said. There are some newspaper articles. The story made the national press when she went missing. Some of the reporting is a bit confused, with the different papers saying different things. Anyway, then everything in the news seemed to fizzle out when the country lost interest, and they never found her. In the end they said she was missing, presumed dead.'

'Wow,' Archie says.

'That's not all,' I continue, 'it's become one of those stories on the conspiracy-theory web, and there are some pictures of her. One from less than a year ago.' I unfold a black and white printout of a web page with a picture of Elsie. It shows a bedraggled figure with long, frizzy dark hair covering her face. She's wearing loose-fitting clothes with a big hoodie top and a rucksack on her back. She's clambering over a fence looking back over her shoulder towards the camera.

'Shit,' Archie says, looking closely at the picture.

Max grabs the printout. 'Told you. You both thought I was making it up.'

'I did think you were talking crap,' I say, leaning over to look at the picture. 'She looks familiar now that I look again... the frizzy hair... ' I glance at Archie and then back at the picture. Archie lunges at me and the three of us laugh.

'You think she's out there?' Max asks.

'Yes,' I say, at the same time as Archie says, 'No.'

Archie screws up his face. 'Come on, Charley, you don't believe this?'

'It's there in black and white,' I say. 'It looks like she just opted out of the system, society or whatever. Took her chances on the outside, not giving a shit.'

We are quiet for a moment and I muse on the idea of this girl out in the wild, living rough for all this time. My mind drifts back to the flash of light I saw at the base of the tree on the hill when I first got to Hillside. I'd not thought much of it at the time. I allow my imagination to roam, enjoying the idea of it all.

Simon pokes his head around the door. 'Five minutes, girls,' he says, then ducks back out. Archie looks up with a frown as Simon's head disappears.

'*Girls?*' Archie says. 'For fuck's sake.'

Max and I laugh.

'Where's Violet?' I ask. Archie shrugs.

'She's on a downer,' Max says. 'She's in solitary, with the witch-nurse, Camilla.'

'Solitary?' Archie asks.

'It's not *solitary*, Max,' I say, turning to Archie. 'She means Violet is in the special care flat, where she can get more one to one. She's been there before, more than once.'

'Same thing,' Max says. 'Suicide watch.'

Archie raises his eyebrows. Max's language is crude, but she's right. If Violet is in the special care flat, then they think she's at high risk of being a danger to herself. She'll be on full-time supervision for a bit.

'She was very down yesterday when I saw her in here,' I say. I was on my own, trying to tune the house guitar until I broke one of the strings. Violet sat with me on the floor for a bit and we talked. She said she was going to get me to play that "Supermarket Flowers" song by Ed Shearan that she liked. I told her the guitar was screwed and asked if she was OK.

'She said that her pills were making her feel crap. They changed the dose again. She said they struggle with what they can give her because of her age.'

'You'd think someone would've made a wonder pill by now,' Archie says.

'Seems to be trial and error mostly,' I say. 'I asked her what it was like.'

'What *what* was like?' Max asks.

'Her dark place, as she calls it.'

Max straightens in her seat. Violet hasn't spoken much before about her dark times. 'What did she say?'

'She said it's a bit like a dream, or a nightmare. It's like she's stuck in treacle or something, bound and gagged. She wants to respond and talk to people, to say what's going on, you know, but she can't – no energy to open her mouth, like she's numb.'

'Sounds terrifying,' Archie says.

'She seemed more sad than scared,' I say, and we are quiet then.

I feel anxious, my skin prickling.

Then I feel bad for feeling anxious when Violet is a million times worse right now.

Then I feel more anxious.

WE DON'T SEE Violet for three days. Then we glimpse her in the dining hall with her nurse. She looks drained, her head down and hair lank over her face. But we still can't talk to her. On the fifth day, she's in the dining hall again and she seems brighter. She makes eye contact with me across the room.

Later, in the girls' lounge, Archie is using super glue to stick the rubber sole of his Converse back on without taking it off.

'Are you not going on home leave?' he asks me, concentrating on his shoe.

'Not allowed out,' I say, watching him work.

'Too mental?' Max asks.

'No one knows how mental I am because I haven't seen Izzy since the initial introduction,' I say. 'Is that super glue, Archie? Surprised they let you have that in here.'

'Smuggled in by one of the girls. You'd be surprised what's available on the H-blocks black market.' He smiles up at me and then turns his attention back to his shoe.

'Don't glue your toes together,' I say.

'His feet are already webbed.' Max grins.

'Up yours, midget.' Archie turns back to me. 'Why

haven't they allocated you the other psychologist? She's really good.'

'I guess she's busy.'

'Well,' Max says, 'my mum hasn't got her shit together – no surprise there – so I'm staying here.'

'Me too,' says Archie. 'They're still *evaluating my needs*, but that's fine with me to be honest. I can't face Dad right now.'

'Is your mum not around?' I ask.

'No,' he says in a tone that invites no more questions.

Violet breezes in. 'Hey, guys.' She holds out her hand for a high-five with Max before sitting on the floor cross-legged in front of us.

'You look better,' I say and she beams, peeling her hair away from her face.

'Awesome,' Max says. 'Fab Four back together.'

'I think it's Famous Five,' Archie says, still concentrating on his shoes.

'The Fab Four were The Beatles,' I say, immediately thinking of Mum.

'Who are the Famous Five?' Violet asks.

'A bunch of posh kids from the forties.'

'Alright,' Max says, 'settle down. We can be whatever we want.'

'Can we be like the X-Men?' says Archie.

'The X-Women,' Violet says.

'Can I be Wolverine?' I say.

Max frowns at me. 'Why?'

'Because he's fit.' I grin.

Archie says, 'I should be Wolverine. You can be Super Girl.'

'She's crap,' I say.

'I like her,' says Violet. 'I'll be her. You stick with Wolverine, Charley, Archie can choose someone else.'

'Archie's Kick Ass,' Max says. 'I can just see you in a Lycra all-in-one.'

'Keep dreaming,' says Archie. 'Whatever. We're a team.' He stands and pulls Max to her feet. 'Group hug, come on.' He puts an arm around Max's shoulder and flaps his spare hand. 'Welcome back, Violet,' he says, pulling her in on one side and me on the other.

Two girls come in and head straight back out at the sight of us. We wobble in a huddle, trying and failing not to laugh.

Chapter 23
Day 21 in Hillside

I t's hot in the girls' lounge; with the tall windows it's like a greenhouse. We head to the boys' lounge for the afternoon, shaded on the north side of the building. Our school sessions ended early because of the heat. They said we could spend the afternoon as we liked. In groups, they said. Nurses circulate, supervising our interactions. Thankfully, Nurse Simon's idea of supervision is to sit in the nurses' station with a magazine.

I sit with my legs curled under me in the armchair with my hair pulled back in a ponytail as I try to keep cool, reading through a bunch of printouts on Elsie Fisher I got from the computer room. The tips of my fingers are black with ink from the printer.

The information on her is thin and contradictory. What must it have taken for her to plan, prepare and eventually get out? Not just out of Hillside but out of everything; life. She must have planned it. You can't just walk off into the countryside and survive on nothing. What about her family? I wonder if they know if she's OK. I could never do that, could never leave my family.

Max is slumped on the sofa in a sleeveless top, reading a magazine with Violet dozing in the foetal position, her head on Max's lap.

Archie's on the floor, his back up against my chair. I ask him, 'You heard from your dad?'

'Kind of. He's on some big case or something, so his secretary tells me.'

'Is he one of those court prosecutors, all dressed up?'

Archie smirks. '*He's* the one in the curly wig, and I'm the one in the psychiatric ward. At least he's earning a load of money so it's nothing but the best for me: top school, quality therapists.' A bitterness comes through in his voice.

'How come you ended up in here then, if you have such good therapists on the outside?' Max says.

'Dad's appointed therapist refused to see me in the end.,' Archie smirks. 'The man was an idiot. Probably the best that money can buy and he didn't have a fucking clue how to deal with the stuff in my head. The shit that goes on up here.' Archie taps the side of his head. 'It's complicated. None of us conforms to the user manual. He wasn't a great listener.' He pauses. 'In the end, I told him to kiss my arse. Nicely, you know.'

'How do you do that nicely?' I smile.

'Well, I actually gave him a rundown of why he was so shit at his job, but he didn't take it so well. I didn't really mean it, you know; I was just pissed off with it all. He told me I was a spoilt brat, which I think wasn't an example of good customer care. So hence the "kiss my arse" thing, which led me to here.'

'What, forcefully? Straitjackets and men in white coats?'

'No.' Archie laughs. 'I'm a willing patient, pleased to get out of that fucking house with the staff, the twat of a therapist, the home-schooling bullshit and Dad...' He trails off.

'It's an odd existence,' he says, fiddling with his copper bracelet. 'Dad is never there anyway, and my mum's things are still all over the place. The people Dad paid to sort it out after she died didn't really know what was Mum's stuff and what wasn't, so they left a load of things.' He pauses. 'I'm glad they did leave stuff, gave me a chance to collect some things, to keep, you know.'

'How long ago did she die?'

'Six months. No, must be seven.' He fiddles with his bracelet again, scratching it like he's trying to remove the remains of an old price sticker. We are quiet then.

'Hey, have you seen the view over the fields from the top floor?' I ask no one in particular. Max looks up from her magazine, turning it to show me her artistic flare, where she's been adding facial hair to the airbrushed models.

'I'm on the ground floor,' Archie says. 'So is Violet.'

Max throws her magazine onto the side table. 'You can't see anything from my room because of the award-winning design that put the lift block right outside my window.'

'You want to come and see?' I say, looking expectantly at their quizzical expressions.

'We're not supposed to go into each other's rooms,' Archie says.

I roll my eyes at him. 'The nurses have just left so they won't be checking on us for at least an hour, and how do they know we haven't just gone to our own rooms?'

Archie stands. 'OK, fine.'

Violet jumps up to join me and Archie, and Max drags herself off the sofa. 'What's so good about it then, Charley?' she says.

We sneak up the stairs to my room and I have to shush Violet and Archie's giggling as we bundle through my door, the four of us filling the little room.

'Yeah, nice view,' Max says, motioning towards the clothes strewn across my floor. I kick the laundry to the edges so they can get into the room, and we bunch together at the window. No one speaks.

The darkening sky is a clear, pastel grey-blue with just a few static clouds. The sun is heading towards the brow of the hill. The solitary tree on the top of the hill stretches its thick branches confidently above the woods on the surrounding slopes, like a conductor presiding over her orchestra. I open the window and the cool air gives some relief. Violet pulls her cardigan around her chest.

'Wow,' says Max, sarcastic, sitting down on the bed and picking up my phone.

'It's nice,' Violet says, pointing at the tree. 'Makes me want to go *there*.'

'Looks like a good climber,' Archie says. 'Reckon I could get almost to the top of that one. I should have brought my binoculars.'

'Binoculars?' Max says.

'Yeah, I've got some in my room.'

'You are kidding?' Max says.

Archie shrugs. 'How far do you think it is to the tree?'

'One mile down into the valley, then one mile up the other side,' says Violet.

'Hang on,' says Max. 'Are we just going to let the

fact that Archie has binoculars pass by without comment?'

We laugh. Archie shrugs again and says, 'Always useful.' He turns back to the window. 'You reckon we could—'

'Don't even think about it,' Max says. 'They won't even let us out of the building without a psychological assessment and a nursing escort. You think we'd get to that tree before they have the police dogs out?'

'Maybe not,' I say, still looking out over the valley. We are quiet for a moment, the three of us staring over the landscape as the sun's glow retreats further. 'Hey, do you see that?' I say. 'At the foot of the tree – there's something moving.'

'No,' says Violet.

'There,' says Archie. 'There's *something* there. You reckon...Can't be Elsie?' he says, straining his eyes.

'It's probably a fucking cow or something,' says Max, standing and squinting into the distance with us. 'I can't see anything. There's nothing there but a big frickin' tree.'

'There!' Archie says as something moves at the foot of the tree. It's too far away to see what it is. Too small for a cow, but maybe a sheep.

'Squirrel,' says Archie.

'Shut up!' says Max. 'Way too big. It's either a sheep or an Elsie.'

'I've been reading about her again,' I say, drawing a look from Archie, and one from Max. 'I downloaded some more stuff from that conspiracy-theory website. It's interesting once you get past the bollocks about aliens. She was due to go into care once she got out of here. She had bipolar.'

'Like me,' says Violet, under her breath.

'And other stuff,' I say. 'She had some emotional difficulties, identity issues. She was confused. She got a lot better over the time she was in here.' I pause. 'And when she went missing, they said she was close to being discharged, anyway. But maybe that's why she did a runner.' I look at Violet. 'She didn't want to go back to where she was before.'

'I can relate to that,' Archie says.

'Me too,' Violet says, as darkness closes in around the hill.

'The interesting thing is that one of the websites says that she's part of a movement,' I say.

'Bowel?' Max says. Archie groans.

'A direct action group. A weird bunch of hobo extremists, according to the more conservative websites. Living outside of society.'

'Doing what?' Max says. 'Fighting for rural equality? Equal rights for trees?'

'Equality and freedom in general, from what I can gather,' I say.

Max frowns. 'How does she do that from a bivouac?'

'They keep under the radar,' I say. 'It's like an offline community thing. I guess. The ultimate rejection of society.'

I scan the space at the foot of the tree one more time but see nothing unusual. There's a noise from outside the door, someone approaching down the corridor. Then a knock. We freeze, looking at each other like mouth-breathing zombies. I place a finger to my lips.

'Charley, are you in there?' It's nurse Camilla.

'Coming,' I say and move around my room to create some noise. Max has her hand over her mouth, stifling a laugh, which makes Archie snort as he rams his own hand over his mouth.

'Everything OK, Charley?' Camilla calls, her voice clipped.

'I'll come downstairs in a minute. Do you want something?' I say.

'Just checking in. Have you seen Max or Violet?'

'Try the boys' lounge?'

'I'll check. I'd like to see you downstairs in a minute, please.'

'Witch,' Max whispers.

The moment we hear her steps fade, we explode

into action. I open my door a crack and peer down the corridor.

'She's gone down the far staircase. If you take this staircase you can get to the girls' lounge,' I say to the three bunched-up escapees behind me at the door.

Violet looks at me, confused. 'You said boys' lounge.'

'Exactly, so you've got about one minute to get to the girls' lounge before Camilla realises you're not in the boys' lounge.' I raise my eyebrows, waiting for the penny to drop.

They spill out of my room and towards the near stairs. I stand at my door and smile after them, bumbling their way down the stairs to outwit the witch. I step back into my room and close the door, leaning with my back against it.

I roll and light a cigarette and kneel at my window, resting my arms on the windowsill. I tilt my head and cushion my ear, peering at the view, the tree.

No sign of any movement.

AT LUNCHTIME, the dining room has a feel of melancholy – more than usual. It's quiet. No one seems to be talking, and it's as if something's happened. No sign of Max. Violet is sitting with Archie and two other girls. Nurse Lisa is already sat at my table and she nods for me to sit.

In front of me is a plate of food that looks bigger than yesterday. 'This is more than before?' I say.

'Same. You're still on maintenance.'

'Looks like more.' The mince is stodgy. I push it around my plate, between the potatoes and broccoli. I force a small mouthful, my hand shaking a little as I raise the fork to my lips. It feels harder than yesterday. This is supposed to get easier.

Lisa watches.

I take a drink from one of the two plastic cups and wince at the under-diluted lemon squash. I follow it with a gulp of water from the other cup.

'Let's get on with it then, Charley,' Lisa says, not unkind, folding her arms over her fluffy cardigan.

I take another mouthful. The girl with the blonde hair who struggles more than I do – I still don't know her name – seems to be refusing her food. A nurse is gently encouraging her. I can't hear what she's saying. I watch for a moment as I move the food around inside my mouth, trying to build up to swallow.

I can feel Lisa's eyes on me.

The lump of mince slides down my throat and I gag as my throat constricts. I take some water. 'I can't,' I say. 'Not today.'

'It's not optional,' Lisa says, matter of fact.

I try to catch Violet's eye for a little bit of solidarity. I need something to break the tension. She's deep in conversation with Archie. After a moment, Archie looks up and sees me. He seems to register my discomfort and gives me a broad smile. I smile back and it helps. The heaviness of the air in the dining room seems to ease off a little.

I turn back to my lunch.

My parents arrive late. Mum is a good three paces ahead of Dad as they walk across the car park. I pause Danny's music on the MP3 player and shove my earbuds into my pocket. A nurse lets Mum and Dad in and I stand to give Mum a hug. She's not wearing any make-up, looks tired and struggles to raise a smile. I smile at Dad over Mum's shoulder and he joins to make a three-way hug. He apologises for being late again, mumbling something about a problem on the A31.

We persuade the nurse to let us use the little time we have to walk in the grounds. I lead the way to the back of the main block. I want to see if there is somewhere to get a view of the valley that's visible from my room. We stop at a wooden seat at the back of the residential block. As soon as we sit down, Mum asks if everything is OK: am I making some progress, is there light at the end of the tunnel, and all that.

'I guess,' I say, then pause. 'It's confusing, still. Izzy has been off for ages so I've not had psychology and I'm still not really sure what I'm supposed to be doing.'

'Izzy?' Dad says.

'My psychologist.' I crane my neck to see over the hedge line that separates us from the valley and the hillside. The hedge is as thick as a solid wall.

'Are you eating OK?' Dad asks.

'I suppose. I'm eating. It's not so easy, though. I still feel guilty when I eat.'

'Why? You shouldn't...' Dad starts to say but trails off.

'No shit, Dad. I know what I'm *supposed* to feel, but it's not that simple, or I wouldn't be here.'

'Are you managing to eat in the time allowed?' Mum asks.

'Mostly, but it's weird in the dining room because some people are struggling big time, more than me, and I get confused. If I eat normally, then what does that mean? Does that mean I'm well and don't need to be here?'

'Charley, try to work on the issues that *you* need to focus on, not what others are doing,' Dad says.

I tighten my fists, digging my nails into my palms. I can't seem to get anything right. This place is my last resort. What is there if this doesn't work? If they send me home, then it's like they're saying I'm OK, and I'm just making a fuss, the pain isn't real. Then I'm fucked. 'Like Jasmine,' I say under my breath.

'Who?' Mum says.

'Oh, nothing. Someone who was in here. Jasmine. They sent her away, to an adult unit.'

'That's different,' says Dad.

'Kind of,' I say. The system was failing her. What chance did she have? A few days after she left, after Camilla fed me the line that she had settled in to the adult unit, we learned the truth – that she'd left the unit voluntarily, then tried to take her own life.

I can't straighten my thoughts and I'm relieved for Mum distracting me, pulling me away from the tangle with mundane stories of BB, of work and her day-to-day.

Twenty feet in front of us, the dense hedge stretches to either side, a mass of green. It must go around the full perimeter, like we're in a prison camp.

'Do you want me to talk to them?' Dad says.

'Who?'

'The staff, to see if there's any more help we can get you?'

'No, it's fine, Dad. Izzy should be back soon. I've written some things down in my notebook that I can talk to her about.'

There's a small gap in the hedge, about three feet wide, with what looks like a pathway through, over a stile. A sign for a public footpath sits above it.

'Have you met some nice people?' Mum asks.

'Yes,' I say.

'Are we allowed to know?' Mum says.

'Sorry, I was thinking. There are four of us that kind of hang out.'

'That's brilliant, Charley,' Mum says. I think about my friends. They don't feel real. None of this feels real.

'It's good, you need people here you can talk to,' Mum says, but I'm distracted. I want to take a peek over the stile. Mum shuffles up closer to me and puts her arm around my shoulder, snuggling in. 'Hopefully you'll get some home leave soon.'

'Hope so, Mum. How's BB?' I pause, then quickly add, 'And Lucas.' I smile at Dad as he rolls his eyes at me.

'Lucas is OK. He misses you; keeps asking when you're coming home,' Mum says. 'BB's a pain in the butt like she always is when you're not around.'

'You're bottom of the pecking order, Mum,' I say.

'We'd better get you back inside, Charley,' Dad says, looking at his watch. He stands up and rubs the base of his back. Mum hugs me closer.

'I'll ring you tomorrow, after I've seen Dr Gilani.'

'What are you seeing her for?' Dad asks.

'My review. It's routine. Hopefully we can figure out a plan.'

The air in the reception area is stale and warm with the sweet smell of the apple air freshener that periodically squirts out of the automatic dispensers in the toilets.

Warm air holds more germs, I think to myself. Or does it hold more moisture? I can't remember. Perhaps it's that moist air can hold more germs, and warm air can hold more moisture. Whatever: stale, moist, warm, germy air leaking from the toilets makes me want to be outside again.

The nurse swipes Mum and Dad out of the building and I stand in reception as they walk across the car park. Mum climbs into the driver's seat and Dad stands at the passenger side, rubbing his eyes for a moment before gently lowering himself in. The car pulls away leaving a black hole that threatens to suck me in – the air is thin and I can't quite catch my breath.

Chapter 24
Day 23 in Hillside

Last night I woke to the sound of activity in the corridor, people talking in hushed, urgent tones. I heard the faint sound of an alarm in the nurse's station. Something must have happened, like someone was sick, maybe.

I couldn't sleep. My mind raced at the possibility of a sick-bug going around. I couldn't shake the thought that I probably already had it. A door slammed then, as if someone had let it swing with the full force of its self-closing spring.

I calmed down eventually. I imagined Dad there, lying on his back next to me, narrating his fictional MI6 adventures of the week, taking me away for a while.

Now I'm waiting to be called for Dr Gilani's ward round. It's like I've been confined to my room for bad behaviour.

She doesn't actually go *around* as 'ward round' suggests she might. I have to go to her. I had one of her intimidating reviews once before, early in my stay. I was collected by a nurse and we walked over to the admin building, where there are mainly just offices and a few therapy rooms. Then I was shown into a big room, like a boardroom, with an oval table. I thought of *The Apprentice*. Dr Gilani was at one end, with people on either side. With me and the nurse who brought me from the ward, there were seven or eight of us in the room last time.

My bedroom door is open but nurse Casey knocks anyway, then peers her long face and shaggy hair around my door. She reminds me of a spaniel.

This time the walk to the admin building feels shorter and I'm not so nervous. The boardroom is hot and the air heavy with moisture, despite the blinds being closed to keep the sun out. The scent in the room is a sickly mix of body odour and perfume.

Dr Gilani is in the same seat as last time. She doesn't bother looking up from her papers. The eating disorder lady is on her right, looking at me with a smile as I find a seat. Izzy isn't here, but Lisa and Simon are, sat together. Lisa gives me an unconvincing smile.

Dr Gilani finally looks up. 'How are you doing, Charley?' I shift in my seat, trying to interpret the heavy atmosphere in the room. 'Charley, the team have some concerns we want to talk to you about. And then we can make a plan of action to resolve and move forward.' She looks down at her notes. My heart sinks and my head spins as I try to think what I've done.

'As you know, Charley, the hospital has particular rules and requirements of its young people that need to be followed if we are to be a success and help you get better,' she says. 'I am a little disappointed in you, I must say, Charley.'

My mouth drops open but I have no words. She continues, 'You started well, but you've slipped. You have been eating too slowly, watching other people eat and slowing to their pace.' She pauses and I try to steady my breathing.

'This is a problem for us,' she says. 'We are concerned our work here is becoming counter-productive and you are developing an eating problem that was not there, or not as bad, when you first came.' The others are silent, waiting for a reaction. I look down. My skin is prickling with anxiety. My eyes are welling.

She doesn't get it. I can't describe the feelings of worthlessness that come with sitting in the dining room with all the girls that are suffering. I can't just shovel my food in like I'm on a holiday camp. If I did that, they'd all think I was fine and then that would be it, the support would be withdrawn and I'd be back where I was before. I'm sick. I'm sure I'm sick. I *know* I am sick.

But it's an invisible illness, and I can't find the words to explain it.

Dr Gilani's eyes are on me. 'We are proposing a period of extended home leave for you to reflect on these matters, and on whether you feel Hillside is the right option for you. You need to consider the hospital rules: the agreement we have between us on the non-negotiable requirements, OK?'

Eating disorder woman says something about developing healthy habits, but I can no longer focus on what she or Dr Gilani are saying. Tears silently roll down my cheeks and I'm desperate to get out of the room.

I check the space between me and the door to confirm that I can get there without anyone having to move out of my way. Casey, the nurse who brought me in, is opposite me, tapping on her phone, seemingly oblivious to the discussions in the room. She stops what she's doing and bites around her thumbnail until she can pull it off with her teeth, spits it onto the floor and returns to her phone.

Dr Gilani says that Mum and Dad will collect me tomorrow, and asks if I have any questions. I shake my head and stand up, turning away from them and shuffling along the table towards the door.

Casey gets up and comes to the door. Dr Gilani speaks once more as I fumble with the handle.

'Charley, we all want what's best for you. We just need to work out between us how we can get you there.'

She's a blur then, just visible through my tears. I don't know what to say. What am I supposed to say? They are the experts. They are the ones mapping out my pathway – I'm just trying to move along it.

I nod and step out of the door. Casey delivers a sideways glance of concern to the rest of them and follows me out. She'll have me on suicide watch on the way back. In fact, she spends most of the walk back coming up with different ways to ask the same questions: if I'm OK and if I want to talk.

I can't even think, how can I talk? I'm so ashamed. I need to lie down.

'No,' I say. 'I'm fine.'

Part Four
Limbo 2

Chapter 25
Day 1 back home

The morning after I get home, Lucas bounds into my room in his tatty old yellow pyjama bottoms and the top with the faded Stormtrooper on the front. He screams as he jumps onto my bed, almost losing his glasses. He sits cross-legged and beams at me. His bed hair is brutal: short, blonde and skewed to one side.

'Hey, Lucas. Missed you.' My thoughts immediately depress me: *a young person exposed to so many other people in school – how do I not breathe in his air?* My heart sinks at the strength of the feeling, the fear of germ transfer, the pull to edge away from him.

Yesterday, when I left Hillside, it was like a dishonourable discharge. The nurses seemed to be avoiding my eye, and even Max and the gang were acting weird. I'd let everyone down.

'What's it like there?' Lucas asks.

'It's OK.' I try to think of a description that Lucas can relate to. 'It's like a cross between a hospital and a youth hostel.' I pull my duvet up over my nose.

Lucas scrunches up his face. 'How many people?'

'About fifteen of us. All girls except one boy.'

'One boy? Why?'

'Most kids there have an eating disorder of some sort, and I guess it's mostly girls that have those kinds of problems.'

'Why?'

'Pressure on girls to look right, to have the perfect body, to be thin. All the pictures and stuff on TV show beautiful thin bodies.'

'Boys too, though. Boys in my year talk about their six packs.' Lucas taps his tummy.

'You're kidding me. That's ridiculous.'

'I know. Not me; I don't mean me.'

'Don't let anyone judge you by what you look like.'

Lucas nods. 'Are you better?'

'Not yet. But I will be.'

Lucas seems to relax a bit then, and we start catching up properly. We talk for nearly half an hour, and I even forget about trying not to breathe his air. He tells me about school, his friends and his drumming. I tell him about the others in Hillside. I try to describe Max, Archie and Violet.

'Is Archie any good on the guitar?' Lucas asks.

I ponder the question. He *is* good. Perhaps not technically, but he has a connection with the music he plays. 'He's great,' I say, the image of Archie in my head drawing a smile as I realise I miss him already, and I miss the girls.

LATER, Lucas and I go for a walk up Butser Hill with BB. We rest on the viewpoint bench at the top. It's the best time of day, when the sun is just sneaking down over the trees. Today, there's a spectacular red-orange glow in the sky. Pink light reflects off the clouds.

BB's nose is in the dirt following a scent along the line of bushes at the ridge. Lucas is unusually quiet. I study his profile as he gazes out at the sunset. I'm surprised at how grown-up he looks. He's started using wax in his hair to shape it to one side, and he's got taller in the time I've been away.

Secondary school is just around the corner for Lucas. I can't imagine my little brother going up to that big, faceless melting pot of shit that will take away his innocence and his optimism. Maybe he'll be OK. Maybe he'll be brave enough to bypass the social politics. I make a mental note to let him know, at the right time, that if it crosses his mind to send a picture of his penis to some girl, then that is a bad idea, and that no girl wants to see a picture of his dick.

I smile. He glances down at my arm. My sleeve has rolled back, showing some of the scars. He looks disappointed, worried. 'Did you try to kill yourself?'

'No, Lucas, I'd never do that. Don't think that.'

'Looks like you did.'

'That's not it, Lucas.' I search for an explanation, something that will make sense. I never wanted to have this discussion with him. I feel ashamed. Each scar is a permanent record of a selfish moment, something that I'll have to keep talking about, rationalising and explaining to people that I get close to.

'I was ill. More ill than I am now. Or at least as ill, but not getting any help like I am now.' I pause. 'I didn't try to kill myself, though, believe me. It's more of a coping thing.'

BB trots over to us, tail wagging so hard it makes her back legs unstable. The glow in the sky has reduced to a rich crimson.

Lucas looks at me again. 'It makes you feel better?'

'No. I mean yes, sort of. Temporarily. But it isn't real; it's short-lived relief and then it just makes me feel like I need to do it again. It gets addictive.'

The sun slips further behind the trees, and I pull my knees up to my chest to keep warm.

'Addictive? Like Mum is with smoking?'

'Yeah, like that.'

'Have you stopped now?'

'I'm trying to put it behind me. It's still confusing.'

Lucas frowns. 'If it's about addiction, then I reckon you need self-harm patches, like Mum's nicotine patches.' He shoots me a reserved smile.

'Self-harm replacement therapy. A pain patch?'

'I can help you with a pain patch.' Lucas grins at me and holds up a clenched fist. We laugh.

I want to hug my little brother. I need it. And he needs it too, but he won't instigate it. It's been so long like this that it's not natural for him. And I can't silence the voice in my head. Lucas is the most likely source of sick-bugs.

'I don't want you to worry, Lucas, OK?' He nods, looking out at the view again, now a meagre strip of red holding up a dark mass of sky. 'I'm working on it.'

Lucas looks again at my arm, turning his head for a clear view. He runs his finger over the scars as if he's trying to read me, to read my arm as if my pain is written there in braille. 'They're bumpy. Do they hurt?'

'Not really.'

'Battle scars. Mum said that it's a battle you have, that you have to slay the dragon and you are bound to get some battle scars.'

I smile. 'That's right. It's a fight.' I run my own fingers over the inside of my arm.

'Why do you always cover them up? You hide them.'

'I guess I'm scared of what people might think of me. People might not understand.'

'You can't help it if you're ill.' He pauses. 'If I'd slain a dragon and got some battle scars, I'd be showing *everyone* at school.'

'You are so right, little wise Yoda boy. I'm not proud of them, but I've no reason to be ashamed of them either.'

'Exactly.'

I LIE STARING into the darkness when Dad comes into my room on his way to bed. 'Are you asleep?'

'No. Come in.'

'How are you doing?' he whispers, taking a seat on the edge of my bed.

'Weird day.'

'I'll say. Must be a bit odd being back home?'

'Feels like I've been suspended for bad behaviour.'

'Don't think of it like that,' he says as he shuffles up next to me and we both stare up at the ceiling. One of the photoluminescent stars I stuck up there when I was a kid glows brighter than usual.

'My head is a mess,' I say. An understatement. Each time I try to figure out what's happened, and what I should be doing, the tangles just tighten and leave me more confused. I get what Dr Gilani was saying, and the potential for Hillside to exacerbate my issues, but I had hoped for a bit more guidance, something to help me through. 'The last thing I expected was a telling off.'

Dad lets out a sigh and is quiet for a minute.

'I think it's just a bit of a nudge,' he says.

'What do you mean?'

'A reminder for you to keep on track. There's so much going on in Hillside, so much pain. The point is that you need to block all that out, focus on your own journey.'

'I...'

'Try not to worry. Use this time to take a step back from it all. See if you can figure out a bit of a plan for when you go back in. What you need from them to get yourself on track.'

'I will.'

'We can talk about it, me and your mum.'

We are quiet then. Dad's breathing slows, and it feels like he's dropped off before he says, 'Those bears are an enigma, you know?'

I laugh, pleased that he's changed the subject to something lighter. 'Evil, more like.'

'Hmmm. I always thought so. But something happened over there in the week that has given me pause to reflect.'

'Are those bears more crafty that you thought?'

'I met one, a bit different to the others... He said something that sticks in my head.'

'What did he say?'

'I'm just trying to remember his name... *Ice P*, that's it.'

I laugh again. 'Ice P...?'

'He said that all is not what it seems...'

'Did he deliver the message in a kind of rap?'

Dad sits up. 'Yes! How did you...'

I nudge into him and we both laugh.

Chapter 26
Day 2 back home

Mia and Ada head towards me, deep in conversation. They look just as I remember, both in black leggings and vest tops, both with long brown straightened hair.

I didn't speak to either of them while I was in Hillside, but word gets around. Before I came home, I asked Mum to speak to Ada's mum about it, just so the stories would remain under control and have at least some elements of truth.

Ada sees me nursing a mug of green tea under the green and white canopy of the café and speeds up to greet me. I stand for a hug, holding her for a few seconds.

Her smell takes me back to when we were kids. She still uses the same shampoo. I tighten my grip and she hugs me back. An image of the three of us at seven or eight years old flickers in my mind as if tentatively emerging from a suppressed corner of my memories. Thoughts of us back then are painful, not because those times were difficult, the opposite in fact. It was all so simple back then. When did it all get so complicated – so tangled?

Mia catches up and opens her arms. 'You look good, Charley,' says Mia. 'You don't look that thin.' She steps back to observe me. My jaw must visibly drop at Mia's comment because Ada quickly changes the subject and drags Mia into the café to get drinks.

I slump back down. The flicker of hope I had when I arrived at the cafe – the tiny possibility that things might be different – had evaporated. I feel like I'm back on the same roundabout that flung me off a few weeks back. My anxiety levels rise to a six.

They get back with drinks and I look at Ada. 'So, what's new?'

Mia sits next to me. 'Katherine and Matt have spilt up,' she says.

I roll my eyes. 'I thought those two were made for each other. That boy is a dick.'

'It's Katherine that was the nightmare,' Mia says. 'He's better without her.'

'I doubt that.'

Mia bristles, her tone sharpening. 'You haven't *been* here, Charley, have you?'

Ada intervenes again to change the subject. She talks about Mr Watkins, the RS teacher who left under an alcoholic cloud.

'He was one of the good guys,' I say. I always liked Mr Watkins. He chaired the debates in class about interesting stuff. He was a staunch feminist, and he didn't take any shit from the boys when they started on their sexist rants.

'He was creepy,' Mia says.

I decide not to press the issue. 'Any news on the Arena competition?'

Ada and Mia exchange a glance. 'We weren't sure if you were coming back,' Mia says. 'We're putting something together.'

'Cool,' I say.

'They're giving out free tickets to our year group again this year,' Mia says. 'So that means everyone's going to be there like last year. It's going to be awesome.'

'Who's in the band?' I say, hoping beyond reason that I'm still in. Ada looks at her feet.

'I'm on vocals and bass,' Mia says. 'Ada is on drums, and Matt will be on lead guitar.'

Ada looks at me. 'Matt hasn't said he'll do it yet, and if you're back, Charley, then maybe you can do it?'

'But he will,' Mia says. 'And he's really good, been playing for years. And he's got an awesome guitar.

We're going to step the tempo up a bit with Matt on his electric guitar.'

'That's great.' I turn to Ada. 'I'll make sure I get a ticket.'

Mia is animated now. 'We need a demo. Two songs. Danny is going to help us record them.' The mention of Danny hits me in the chest. I've not spoken to him yet.

'Have you asked him?' Ada says.

'Not yet, but he'll help me.' She winks at Ada.

She's got to be winding me up? She knows that me and Danny are close – or at least we were.

'We think there are two spots, one from each school,' Ada says. 'Two winners that get to play support, with a headliner that's usually someone quite big...'

I zone out and look past Ada to the high street. My mind drifts to Hillside House. Sitting here with Mia and Ada, it's like I've not been away – nothing's changed.

It's like I never left.

When the top of the hill comes into view, I can see Danny is sitting on the viewpoint bench, gazing out over the west ridge. He's side-on as I approach and his shaggy brown hair hangs down over his eyes. The sight of him seems to bring a freshness to the air that blows away a little of the darkness. He looks different; his hair is longer and his skin seems darker.

'Hey, stranger,' he says as I sit next to him. 'I was surprised to get a message from you. Thought you'd left the planet.'

'Sorry. It's been a bit intense, I should have—'

'No explanation needed. It's good to see you.'

'Thanks for the music,' I say, holding up the little MP3 player. 'Bit of a lifesaver in there.'

'Thought that might be the case. Have I converted you to the Atlas yet?'

'I'm coming around.'

He smiles then rifles in his pocket, pulling out another MP3 player, a red one. 'Try this,' he says. 'I'll swap you.' He holds out a hand. 'It's got new stuff, and it's got everything that's on the blue one. It's an upgrade, if you like.'

We swap MP3 players. 'Thanks,' I say. 'Really. I appreciate it. Nice to have some music to take me away from it all. It's weird being home, wading through the same old shit-heaps.' Danny snorts a laugh. 'And talking of which, I saw Mia and Ada earlier.'

'How'd that go?'

'You know Mia.'

'Maybe we should end her? Take her out.' Danny smiles at me. 'I know a man who knows a man—'

I silence him with an elbow in the ribs. 'I'm not sure that the solution to not having many friends is to knock off one of them.' I pause. 'But thanks anyway; nice offer and all that. I can't say anyone's ever offered to kill for me.'

I look at Danny. I've not seen him for so long and I take a moment to remember his kind face. He has a good profile: nice contours and big eyes with long dark eyelashes that most girls would be proud of.

'Mia says you're helping with their recording for their demo?'

'News to me.'

I should have known Mia was talking shit. 'Are you doing anything yourself? For the Arena competition?'

'No, why? Are you offering to be in my band?'

'I'd love to, but the thing is, I'm in this loony bin, and anyway I think we'd need more than a two-piece. I don't think we'd cut it with one musician and a sidekick passing out on stage.'

'So I'm just a sidekick?' Danny says, laughing. 'Maybe you're right.'

'You can join Mia and Ada,' I say. 'They've got Matt with them now.'

'Not sure I can be in the same room as Matt for long enough to get through a whole song.'

'I know what you mean,' I say, glancing at Danny to gauge any reaction. I'm pretty sure he knows nothing about what happened. No one does.

'Let's jam some stuff when you come out.'

'You mean, *if* I come out.'

Danny gives me one of his half-smiles. 'They'll have to let you out eventually, when you're no longer a danger to society.'

'I might be a danger to Mia.'

'We can jam some stuff, if we've got time before the deadline. Then, maybe we can find ourselves a rhythm section, and put something down on tape.'

I feel a flutter of excitement. 'I don't know,' I say. My excitement is tinged with fear and embarrassment about my inability to handle being on stage. And, the stage in the Arena is a world away from the Year 11 common room. Why would I put myself through it?

'Come on, Charley. We can see how it goes. No pressure.'

'You think I can dial in to the performance on Zoom?' I grin. Danny laughs.

I think about my friends in Hillside. Maybe Archie would help. He could even be our third member. The thought of getting back into playing is too much to pass up, and the possibility that Archie could be with us is tantalising. 'I'll practise with Archie,' I say.

'Archie?'

'Friend of mine on the inside.'

'We can do the song we recorded for my assignment?' Danny suggests. 'That went down pretty well, and you already know it.'

'I have one I'd like to have a go at too. Archie might do the bass guitar, so then we just need drums. And you and Archie can sing?'

Danny rolls his eyes at my obvious ducking away from the front-person position. 'Whatever you say. Can you tempt Ada away from the shit-heaps to come and drum for us?'

'Great name for their band.' I laugh. 'Don't think it would be good for me to poach Ada, though.'

We are silent then. Birds flutter between branches in groups, playing and chasing. In the distance, the sprawling oak is the centrepiece, the focal point for everyone that rests at the top of Butser Hill.

'I love that tree, the way it's stretching and reaching,' I say.

'Like you?'

'Maybe.'

'Reaching for what?'

'Like all of us, I guess. Everyone's searching for something, some reason or other for why we're on this complicated fucking planet.'

We are quiet again for a few minutes, breathing in the silence together, with no awkwardness.

Danny sighs. 'You can simplify it.'

'What?' I say, waiting for one of Danny's philosophical musings about how I should separate myself away from the unhealthy influences.

'Simplify the complicated stuff.'

'You're not going to talk about opting out again?' I smile.

'Can be liberating. Break it down. What are the biggest shit-heaps? Start with *one* of them.'

'Mia,' I say, 'and all the other clones.'

'Why?'

'Why what?'

'What's Mia got to do with anything of any meaning in your life? She's nothing; a tiny blip on your timeline. As insignificant as the human race on the timeline of the planet.'

'Did you just liken Mia to the whole of humanity?'

Danny smiles. 'Kinda.'

'Mia's the boss. She has the power. Without her, there's nothing but friend-wilderness. Tumbleweed. And solitude.'

'Sounds peaceful.'

I look at him. 'Come on, Danny, we've been here before. With Mia, I get along, I get by.'

'You get by. Is that what you've been doing this last year or whatever: getting by?'

'I guess.'

'And how's that been going for you?'

My thoughts are muddled. I can't imagine not having Mia on side. The idea scares me as much as ever. 'We used to be so tight.'

'Do you think that if they all knew the *real* Charley, they'd disown you? Or do you in?' Danny smirks.

'You never know with Mia.'

'Well, I think I've seen the odd glimpse of the *real* Charley and I'd say you stand a reasonable chance of making it.'

I look at him. 'Maybe I don't know who the real Charley is.'

'Then that's your challenge, my little friend.' He nudges into me and stays close as we look out over the ridge. I think about germs for a moment, migrating from Danny and onto me, but there's something in Danny that helps me to push the thoughts away.

He's on my side, I think. Not the side of me that normally shows up, but *my* side. Maybe it's time I was too.

Part Five
Hillside 2

Chapter 27
Hillside - Day 24

'Hello, girls,' I say, poking my head around the door of the boys' lounge. Max and Archie give a cheer and Violet jumps up for a hug.

'How was it?' Archie asks.

'Yeah, fine,' I say, standing with Violet. 'Made me think a bit, get my head in the right place. I kind of have a plan brewing, some stuff to think on. I feel weirdly optimistic.'

Archie smiles. 'How long you back in for?'

'Discharge meeting in a couple of weeks, depending how I go. I can't stay much longer than that or they'll do a Jasmine on me.'

'A what?' says Archie.

'Kick me out, or put me on the list for an adult unit.'

'My fostering is going through,' Max says.

'That's great,' I say, but Max's expression is not so clear. She looks scared, but hopeful.

'I've met them. Will be a fresh start.' She forces a smile.

'Me and Violet are staying in forever,' Archie says, giving Violet a little nudge but getting no reaction.

'You'll get there,' I say.

I try to catch Violet's eye but she keeps her head low and I can see her mood is dipping again. I feel for her. She's suffered too much pain for someone her age, and there doesn't seem to be a clear route out for her. It feels like I at least have some control over my destiny, what I need to get myself in a better place with my mental health. The short trip home, as painful as it was to be ejected from Hillside, has given me a renewed sense of direction. I know what I need to do, and I know what I need from Hillside.

I put a hand on Violet's shoulder as I sit next to her. She leans into me, resting her head on my arm. The four of us are quiet then for a while.

'Hey, Archie,' I say. 'I saw my friend Danny yesterday. He has a crazy idea that we can concoct some kind of demo tape for the Arena band competition.'

Archie looks dubious. I fill him in on my discussion with Danny and the details of the Arena competition.

'Sounds impossible,' he says, but a sparkle in his eye tells me he's interested.

'It probably is. Let's see.' I reach behind the chair for the house guitar. 'Why don't you go and grab your guitar?'

~

We jam a few tunes in the lounge for a while, then, later, we congregate in my room. Playing together with Archie felt good. He can really play, and we had an immediate connection in the timing and rhythm. The competition feels like a serious possibility.

Looking at the countryside beyond the window, Violet says, 'We've got to see that tree before you all get out of here.'

'Before *we* all get out of here, Violet. You too,' I say.

Archie sits on my bed. 'No chance,' he says, leafing through one of my books. 'We'd never make it.'

Max slides off my bed and stands with Violet at the window. 'Maybe,' she says. I try to figure what she's thinking. 'We could go at night.'

'How would we get there?' Archie says. 'We don't know if there's a road or a path there; it's miles away. And what about Elsie?'

'What about her?' I ask.

'What if she's over there?'

'Then we can have a chat,' Max says, smiling. 'She's not a serial killer, Archie. She's like us.'

Archie stiffens. 'As well as being a direct-action nature-terrorist.'

'I think, if she exists,' I say, 'us being there would be enough for her to stay away.'

Violet nods.

I lean close to the glass to peer down at the hedge line. 'I saw a footpath, when I was down there with my mum and dad the other day.' I point down to the ground outside my window.

Max leans to look. 'Show me.'

'There.'

'Yes,' says Max. 'It goes through the woods, so it probably leads out the other side over... there.' She points to the opposite hill. The trees thin out in the fold of the valley and thicken again on the other side, as if something has ploughed a clearing along the riverside. The oak stands on the opposite hill, like its sister at Butser Hill.

Archie shifts his weight from foot to foot. 'We'd never get away with it. How would we get out?'

'Through my window,' Violet says. We all turn to her. Her eyes have a little of their sparkle back. I smile. The Violet I know is coming through. 'I'm on the ground floor,' she adds.

'The windows are restricted,' Archie says. 'They

won't open enough for us to climb out.' Violet smiles and pulls out her lock-picking kit from the pocket of her hoodie.

'Violet! You are the dog's,' says Max, and Archie and I laugh.

'The *dogs*?' Violet frowns.

'Never mind,' says Max. 'You reckon you can deal with the restrictor lock with that stuff?'

Violet grins. 'It's just a lock.'

THAT NIGHT, three knocks on my door startle me, even though I know it's Archie.

I tiptoe to let him in. 'Why'd you knock, you moron?' I jump back onto my bed and unlock my phone again.

'In case you were naked or something,' he whispers.

'Shh!'

Archie rolls his eyes at me as he sits on the bed. Earlier, when we practised the two songs together in the lounge, Archie quickly picked up the chords and wrote all the lyrics down. We refined the guitar parts and played around with bass lines, then agreed to meet in my room after lights-out, by which time I guessed I'd have heard from Danny and we could figure out what to do.

'OK, we've got a plan,' I say. I try to keep my enthusiasm levels high, despite not being wholly convinced by Danny's plan. And, in any case, not sure I'd ever be able to follow it through if the miracle happened and we managed to get to the auditions.

'Is it legal?' asks Archie.

'Sort of. Listen.' I wave him to be quiet. 'The recording has to be in by next week. So, we need to record it as soon as we can. Preferably this week.'

Archie raises his eyebrows. 'I'm waiting for the killer explanation of how the fuck you think we're going to record a demo when half the band are banged up in here and we don't have a drummer.'

'We're not going to get a drummer in the next few days, so we just focus on getting the two songs recorded with the three of us, as best we can, then if we get through to the Arena...' I pause. There is no chance of that. 'Then we can recruit a drummer.'

'Sounds OK,' Archie says slowly, 'and...?'

'And what?'

'And how do we do the recording?'.

'Oh yes, this is the good bit. Danny is going to drop his M630 at—'

'His M6 what? Speak English.'

'M630, six-track, digital recording thing. He's

going to drop it at my parents' house, *in* the guitar case with his bass guitar, so my dad can drop it here.'

'OK,' Archie says, 'so we can record our bits onto the M630 thing, the bass, your guitar and vocals, then what? How do we get it back to Danny in time for him to put his bits on and send it off for the competition?'

'We have to record it while my dad is still here, then I can give it back to him with our stuff recorded and he can take it home again. Then Danny will pick it up.'

Archie does not look convinced. 'More flaws than the Empire State, but let's just focus on the big ones. Assuming your dad is cool with driving all the way over here to drop off the guitar, what happens when he gets here and the nurses want to look through the case and find the electronic gear? They'll want to check it out, electrical-test it or whatever.' Archie folds his arms and tilts his head.

'Danny says the case has a pocket at the bottom. I'll make sure the nurses don't see it. They won't be that bothered. They'll see the guitar and that will be it.'

'What reason do you plan to give for getting your dad to wait while we do the recording? Will you tell him what we're doing?'

'I'm not supposed to have visitors this week as I've just got back here, so I need to persuade the nurses that he's just dropping something off and taking something else back. Then we can quickly record it while he waits.'

'What happens when the nurses realise you're taking ages to get whatever it is that he's taking back?'

'They won't find us till it's too late and we're done anyway. We can do it in the boys' lounge and the others can keep guard, delay the nurses. Have faith, Archie.'

He's silent for a moment. If I know Archie, he's searching for holes in the plan.

He smiles at last. 'Worth a go.'

Chapter 28
Hillside - Day 26

'What did you say?' Camilla shifts in her seat and leans back, glancing at Simon. The way they're sitting opposite me, I'm not sure if it's like they're interviewing *me*, or the other way around. Camilla's perfume is sweet and overpowering. I glance over my shoulder to see if the window is within reach. It's of the type that doesn't open.

I turn back to them. 'I've refocused,' I repeat.

'Good,' Simon says as Camilla looks increasingly uncomfortable.

'There are things I need from you, though.' I open my notebook on the table between us. Camilla flinches.

In the days since my readmission, I've been ordering my thoughts and devising my own plan for recovery, detailing it all in my notebook. Whenever I lose focus, I try to recall a picture of Danny's face, his encouragement. It keeps me going. If I am going to get through this shit, I need to take control, and Hillside needs to help me.

'What is it you think you need, Charley?' Camilla asks through tight lips.

'I need some guidance.' I point at my notes. 'In the four weeks I've been here I've had one psychology session. That's it. They're supposed to be weekly.' I look at Simon. He deflects my gaze onto Camilla. She's unconvinced by my allegation of lack of psychology, so I tell her to check my records. 'I can't do this on my own,' I say.

'It's complicated,' Camilla says, her tone soft. 'Your needs are carefully evaluated by the team with input from everyone who has contact time with you here – the nurses, OT, schooling sessions, and not least the management of nutrition and exercise.' She leans forward in her seat, getting into her flow. 'There are things that you don't see, things that are happening behind the scenes to ensure your smooth pathway to recovery.'

'Well it might be nice if you share some of that with me, so I can understand how to progress. I can't do that if no one fills me in.' I slump back in my chair. I catch the smug look from Camilla and re-double my resolve. 'I want to talk to Dr Gilani,' I say. 'I don't believe that it's right that I don't have the psychology sessions.'

Camilla shakes her head and is about to speak when Simon finally contributes. 'It's true,' he says, looking at Camilla, then back to me. 'You should be seeing Izzy at least once a fortnight and preferably once a week.' Camilla shoots him a look and he trails off.

'We know Izzy has been oversubscribed,' Camilla says.

Simon butts in again. 'Camilla. Please. Charley is right. Whatever the pressures on the system here, and I know it's tougher than it's ever been, we cannot get away from the fact that Charley's pathway requires a level of psychology that she's not getting.'

I feel like crying. Simon has never stood up to Camilla before. She looks away and lets out a sigh of defeat. It's like she's failed to protect the precious resources of Hillside from the greedy inmates. I can't help but smile. I look to Simon but he avoids eye contact. He shrinks back into his chair.

'You want me to take your plan? I can look at it with Izzy,' says Camilla. 'She's in tomorrow.'

I pull the two pages with my plan out of my notebook and hand them to Camilla, then close it. 'Good.'

I leave them sat in the airless box room and head

out into the corridor, squeezing my earbuds back in as I go. It's Danny's latest playlist. Something by Muse comes on, and there's a little spring in my step as I head back to the lounge.

Chapter 29
Hillside - Day 27

Archie is agitated. He plays a bit of air bass as we wait for my dad to arrive with the recording gear. I watch as he recalls the notes and occasionally panics when he forgets a bit.

'Calm it, Archie,' Max says. 'It'll be fine. You'll be fine. Stick to the plan. Meditate or something, but shut the fuck up.'

Archie peers through the window towards the car park. 'I can't see how we're going to set up and record two songs in the time you expect your dad to wait in the reception area.'

'Archie, just sing it through with me; it'll take your mind off things.'

'Blue Ford!' Max shouts, making Archie jump and Violet scream.

'Calm,' I say. 'Let's get ready. Archie, can you

arrange things in here? I'll go meet my dad. Girls, take your posts.'

Violet positions herself directly outside the lounge door. Max settles way down the corridor in the seating area near reception, where she makes like she's reading a magazine. Everything is in place. I stroll into the reception area as nurse Simon is swiping Dad through the door.

'Hi, Dad.'

'Is this what you wanted?' he holds the guitar case. I thank him and ask if he'll wait while I get some bits for him to take back, and then I turn away.

Simon frowns. 'Hang on, what's in there?'

Dad and I share a look of 'What the fuck does it look like is in the guitar-shaped case?'. Simon stutters that he knows it's a guitar and, while still looking annoyed, he waves me away.

'I'll just be a minute; you two chat for a bit.' I turn to head back, discovering my speed-walking skills. I pass Max and she winks. Then to the boys' lounge. Violet looks relieved to see me and guides me through the door.

'Archie, calm down,' says Charley. 'You won't be able to play if you're like this. What's the worst that can happen?'

He settles down enough to focus on arranging the equipment that we pull from the guitar case, including two microphones for the vocals and two guitar leads.

Archie plugs in the final lead. 'This is ridiculous.'

We're ready to go, red light blinking on the M630. I run a test, record a few seconds through the microphones and strum some chords. I play it back. The guitar comes through but the microphones aren't picking anything up. Archie checks the leads, fumbling at the connections. I reach for the M630 and flick the switches on the microphone channels. Red lights come on.

Archie stutters something incoherent. I run another test. It's good. I look Archie in the eye as he positions his bass guitar.

We both take a deep breath. 'Ready,' we say in unison.

We play Danny's song first, then mine, straight through with a short gap in the middle. One take. No time for a second go.

'It's good,' I say. A noise outside the room. Violet stalling a nurse. We throw the gear back into the case and squeeze in the guitar. As Archie closes the zip, the door opens and Camilla barges in, red-faced and flustered.

'Charley!' she says. 'You're supposed to be getting something for your dad! He's waiting. I've been looking all over for you.' She stands with hands on hips. Archie and I take a step backwards from Camilla's anger. Violet is just behind Camilla in the doorway, a massive smile on her face.

I motion to Archie. 'He had the guitar that I need to give to Dad. I've just found him. Archie, you are one difficult boy to chase down.' I smirk at him and look back to Camilla. I catch sight of Violet shoving her hand up to her mouth to stifle a laugh.

Camilla hasn't finished with us yet. 'So, what's with all the sentries stationed up the corridor.' She nods at Violet and does a double take at her sniggering.

'They were helping me find Archie,' I say. She looks around the room as if expecting to see something else untoward: contraband perhaps, or a stowaway with their feet poking out from under the curtains.

She waves me out of the room. She's clearly frustrated but can't pin anything on us. I grab the guitar case from Archie with a wink and head back up the corridor. I give Max a high-five as I pass her, obvious enough for Camilla to notice.

'Sorry, Dad. I'll explain, one day.' I give him a smile and he looks intrigued. 'Can you take this one back? Danny will pick it up later.'

Dad looks at the case and frowns. It's clearly the same guitar. 'I won't ask,' he says out of earshot of Camilla and Simon. I give him a hug and turn to head back.

Chapter 30
Hillside - Day 29

Three days after my session with Simon and Camilla, I finally get an appointment with Izzy. Simon is the one to let me know, and he seems almost as pleased as me. 'It's just a short, ten-minute session, but it will kick you off,' he says.

'Thanks, Simon. I appreciate what you said with Camilla the other day.'

'Good for you, Charley. Taking the initiative.'

'Thanks.'

I knock on Izzy's door and she immediately calls for me to come in. 'Sit down, Charley. I'll be with you in a moment.'

Her office is full of books, papers and files. It's more like a library than a hospital treatment room. I sit in the chair opposite her as she files papers and slots them back onto the shelf behind her. 'Right,' she says.

'We have a full session planned for next week, so this is a simple check-in, OK?'

'Sure.'

'Simon reminded me that you've not had the psychology you should have had, is that right?' I nod. 'And you didn't see anyone else while I was away?'

'No.'

'Well, I'm sorry about that.' She leafs through what must be my file. 'You did the right thing raising it with the nurses.'

'Did Camilla and Simon give you my plan?' I ask, placing my notebook on the table.

'Yes, I've been going through it. It's good. It's well thought through and it really helps us structure the next steps, these final stages.' She looks me straight in the eye and I'm reminded how beautiful she is: a pale complexion, dark hair and fringe.

'I can see you're motivated. We can work with that.' Her tone is soft, encouraging. She flicks through some of her own notes and we go over what she calls a *mind-mapping* process to draw out some issues, and barriers to recovery. We talk about friends, family, thoughts and feelings. And self-image. Body image. We also talk about emetophobia and OCD, and the work I've already started on shortening my rituals. She sets me goals for the coming days, before we meet again next week.

'Let's keep it simple,' she says. 'I think you already have a good grasp on what you need to do, but I don't want you to go too quickly. It can be counterproductive if you try to do too much too soon.'

'In what way?'

She looks at her watch. 'We can talk more about this next week, but for now, keep with the plan, OK?'

I nod, but I can't help think the session is barely long enough to be useful. I sigh, and Izzy seems to read my thoughts. 'So we focus on our own eating regime? Yes? And we let others worry about their own processes?' I nod again. 'And the OCD rituals, we deal with those bit by bit. For now I just want you to limit as much as you can, but then *notice* the feelings. Acknowledge the feeling it gives you and sit with it for a time. Breathe. Then move on. OK? Make sense?'

'Yes.'

Chapter 31
Hillside - Day 30

I wash and rinse my hands at the basin in my room, just once, like Izzy said. 'Notice the anxiety. Breathe through it. Don't give in to the OCD.'

I avoid looking at myself in the mirror. I won't wash my hands again. Not here. Not this time.

Well, I could wash them just once more. That would be less than the usual three times. And much less than three lots of three.

Not this time.

Anxiety pushes pins and needles from my chest to my neck.

My cheeks are numb.

I stand motionless for another minute. The anxiety level stabilises at about eight and a half, high enough to make me sweat.

I maintain my breathing: *in for three... hold... out for five.*

The anxiety subsides a little. I'm surprised how quickly I'm back down at a level four, then three. I puff out my cheeks and wipe my forehead with my forearm. Panic averted. Anxiety levels down to manageable levels. I think of Izzy and feel like heading straight for her room to tell her what I just did.

I open my bedroom door with my foot and head out, shaking my hands dry as I go.

In the dining room, I sit opposite Lisa. She gives me one of her smiles – like a virtual hug.

At the next table, a girl is sat with her head down and to the side, trying not to look at her food. She's alone but for her supervising nurse.

'New girl?' I ask Lisa.

She nods and says that I should keep focused on my own table. The girl is maybe thirteen years old, with her hair pulled back in a high ponytail. She's crying. I try to catch her eye to transmit some compassion, but she's too distracted.

I look at my food, and for the first time in as long as I can remember, it looks good. It is more than a simple challenge, a task to get through. It is something I know that I need, and I want it. I want what it offers me – a way to the start of something healthy, and meaningful. Almost as soon as I feel it, the sense of optimism is tinged with a little darkness, as if I am being reminded not to get smug. Don't think that it will be easy.

I look up at the girl. She continues to refuse her food. Tears run down her cheeks as she looks to the side, towards the window, as if searching for something to save her from the impossibilities before her. I have hope for her, though. She's in a good place. I want to tell her that there's a way through, and with time she'll find it. I hope she finds the key to unlock how her own particular puzzle is configured.

WHEN I WALK INTO THE BOYS' lounge, Max, Archie and Violet are bunched up on the sofa. Archie looks up. 'You look tragic,' he says.

'Charming.' I rub my eyes, feeling the fatigue from the near panic attack at my hand basin. It felt different to the usual post-panic bitterness and tiredness. The full on panic attack was avoided, so the deep low was also absent – less of a lingering sense of depression. But, I guess, I still look like I've been through the mill.

'What?' Max says, her voice raised. She stares at Violet. 'Say that again.'

Archie and I turn to Violet.

'I picked the window lock,' she says.

'So it's open?' Max asks, her grin broadening. 'It swings open enough to get through?'

Violet nods. 'It was easy. Easier than the store cupboard in the kitchen.'

I sit on the armchair, then look at Max and we laugh. 'Violet, why did you pick the lock on the kitchen store cupboard?' I say.

'I was hungry.' More laughter.

'So we have a route out?' Max says.

Violet nods.

Archie shifts in his seat. 'What if one of the nurses sees that you've busted the lock?' he asks.

'They won't,' says Violet. 'I've closed the window and you can't tell it's de-restricted unless you really look hard. And even then, they'll just think it's broken.'

'We're not seriously going?' says Archie. 'What will we even do when we get there? Why take the risk? What's the point of trekking all the way over there?'

Max smiles. 'Because we can,' she says.

'We can hunt for signs of Elsie,' I say. 'We might even see her.'

'Seriously?' Archie says. 'There is no Elsie Fisher.'

'We all saw the movement at the tree,' I say. But I'm not sure if my conviction that Elsie Fisher is more than a conspiracy story is anything but wishful thinking. I love the idea of someone from Hillside breaking away and choosing freedom from the institution, and freedom from the shackles of her mental illness. It raises questions in my mind about the seeds of mental illness. Like Danny would say – opt out; give yourself a break from the pressure of it all. That's what Elsie Fisher has done, and as far as I'm concerned, she exists in every way.

'We'll need torches,' Violet says.

'Are we up for this, then?' says Max.

I look at Archie and he looks at Violet.

'I'm in,' says Violet.

We all look at Archie. 'OK, OK, I'm in, but don't say I wasn't the voice of reason. Don't say I didn't tell you it was a bad idea after we get savaged by wild animals, or stuck in a hole or something.'

Violet laughs and leans into Archie. He smiles and slings an arm around her shoulder.

Max springs into action. 'We each need to take a little rucksack or something, with supplies.'

I frown at Max. 'What supplies?'

'I don't know, food and stuff.'

'Let's just take ourselves. We don't need to take *stuff*,' I say. Max looks a little disappointed and I feel momentarily bad for dampening her enthusiasm. I give her a nudge. 'Take a bag. But keep it light.' She grins.

'When?' says Violet.

I smile. 'Friday night? Friday is a good day.'

Max stands up as if to give a speech. She looks

wired: her curly, beetroot-red hair sticks up in random places and her eyes are wild.

Archie stretches back, curving his long torso into the sofa and straightening his gangly legs. His feet get in Max's way and she gently kicks out at his familiar old fucked-up Converse as she crosses the room. She closes the blinds and pokes her head out the door, no doubt checking for eavesdroppers.

Archie and I glance at each other in amusement. 'What is she like?' Archie says, loud enough for Max to hear. She ignores him. Violet slips off the sofa and onto the floor, wrapping her arms around her knees, pulling them up to her chin as she looks up at Max.

'So,' Max says. 'Everyone is in?' The three of us slowly nod our heads, remaining silent for a minute. Max adds: 'And we go Friday?'

'What time?' Violet asks.

'None of us is on any kind of night supervision, so as soon as it's lights-out we can RV in Violet's room,' Max says.

'RV?' Archie says. 'Speak English, Max.'

'Rendezvous.'

'Eleven o'clock is a good time,' I say. 'That will give the nurses time to settle back in their room.' I think about how we'll get to Violet's room, past the nurses' station. It will be easy enough for Archie as he's on the ground floor, but it's more of a challenge for me and Max. 'It will take us about an hour to get to the hill.'

'So, we'll be there by about midnight?' Violet says. 'We can light a little fire at the top, to keep warm.'

'See if we can entice the mythical Elsie to join us,' Archie says with a hint of sarcasm. 'How are we going to light a fire, though?'

'I'll get some matches from the kitchen store, then we can collect some wood at the top,' Violet says, as if it's obvious.

'Hunter-gatherer,' I say, winking at Violet.

'What?' says Archie. 'You're going to pick the lock on the kitchen store cupboard? Again? Before Friday?'

'I know that lock, so I can be quick. Actually, I can go now. I don't have to do it at night. There'll be no one in there now.'

'You sure, Violet?' I say.

'Yes. Come if you want?'

I stand with Violet. 'I'll be your getaway driver.' I lean over for her to get on my back and I piggyback her down the corridor to the kitchen.

Violet is right. There's no one to be seen. I drop her off my back and position myself as a lookout. She pushes two metal pins into the lock on the store cupboard. Click. She twists the second pin. Another click. In less than thirty seconds, the door is open and Violet is inside. There's no sign of any staff, so I glide over to the store to take a look. It's stacked floor to ceiling with food stuff: cereals, dry pasta, tins of soup and tomatoes, beans. Violet is on a stepladder, reaching for a big yellow box of matches from an open multipack.

'Violet, is that wine up there, next to the matches?'

She checks out the bottles. 'Why have they got wine in here, anyway?'

'Maybe left over from a nurses' Christmas dinner or something,' I say, wondering whether they would miss a couple of bottles. 'Grab two. Chuck me the matches first.'

I stuff the matches into the front pocket of my hoodie and reach back for the wine. Violet closes the door while I stash the bottles up the front of my hoodie. We stow the wine and matches in Violet's room and head back to the lounge.

On the walk back, Violet is quiet, and I ask what's up.

'Nothing,' she says.

'Is it about sneaking out of here?'

'No. It's nothing,' she says, as we arrive back at the boys' lounge.

'Hey, girls,' I say.

'Did you get them?' Max asks.

'Yep,' I say. 'Violet is a master criminal.'

Violet grins. 'We got wine too.'

'Wine?' Archie blurts. 'How'd you get wine?'

'From the store,' I say.

Max beams at me. 'Excellent,' she says. 'Where is it?'

'In Violet's room,' I say. 'Are we all ready?'

'Absolutely,' Max says.

Archie nods. 'Yep.'

'Violet?'

She smiles. 'Always ready.'

Chapter 32
Hillside - Day 33

Lisa studies me, her head tilted. 'OK, Charley?'

'Fine.' I tuck into my pasta. 'Are you going to miss me?' I ask.

'Are you going somewhere?'

'Can't stay here forever.'

'That's what I like to hear.'

I give Lisa my shifty look. 'I'm planning my escape.'

'Best to leave by the front door, when you're ready.'

'I guess.'

'Well, I'm not saying I want to see you back, but I will miss that beautiful voice of yours. I love hearing you guys playing and singing in the lounge.'

'Ah, and so says the lady with the voice of an

angel.' Lisa sometimes sings with us. She especially loves the oldies.

I finish my pasta in good time. My stomach is bloated. A familiar nagging guilt sinks in as the food settles. I question my progress, then push the thoughts away.

Lisa is impressed. 'Good.'

I finish my drink and take my empties to the kitchen hatch. Max looks over at me as I leave, then follows, with Violet not far behind. Max cracks a joke but I don't hear it, don't want to hear it. She must sense my discomfort because she drops the humour and silently links my arm with hers. Violet takes my other arm and together we push through the double doors.

Izzy PULLS a bunch of papers from the filing cabinet behind her desk. She seems happy, as always, as if nothing is wrong with the world. Even though she knows, more than most, that all is not right.

We talk about my progress with controlling the OCD rituals, and the levels of anxiety. 'Remember what I said about taking it slowly? One step at a time?' she says.

'What's the problem with moving quickly? Surely the quicker we go, the sooner I can crack it?'

'We need to be careful,' she says. 'It can get a bit like whack-a-mole.'

'Like what?' I say.

'You know, where the mole pops up and you have to hit it with a hammer and it pops up somewhere else?'

I frown at her.

'If we squeeze too much,' she says, 'too quickly, in one place, problems can pop up somewhere else in a way we aren't expecting, maybe in a form that's worse, or not so easy to manage. One step at a time. Does that make sense?'

I nod.

She says, 'Just focus on the *next-right-thing*, Charley. When you are feeling overwhelmed, remember that you can't control everything and you don't *have* to untangle all the thoughts and confusion, you can just focus on one thing, just do the *next-right-thing*. That might be taking a bath or writing a message or whatever. One step at a time.'

She pauses and I have to concentrate to arrange the information that she's just planted in my head. In the disorder, Matt pop-ups ping into my mind and I knock them down again as best I can. An image of his face haunts me – his smell, and the sound of his breathy voice in my ear. It's exhausting. Izzy reads my discomfort. 'What is it?' she asks.

'I've been struggling with flashbacks to something that happened a while ago.'

'Do you want to tell me about it?'

'No.'

'Take your time.'

'Maybe.'

'No rush.'

'A thing with a boy at school. Not *in* school, it didn't happen *in* school, it was at his house, but with a boy *from* school...'

Izzy interrupts me. 'Slow down, Charley.' Her voice is soft and her pace measured. I look up at the ceiling, take a deep breath in, hold, and then the words come.

All of them.

My vision blurs as I stare out of the window in Izzy's room. She says something but I don't hear her.

'Charley?'

I come around. 'What?'

'I was asking if you've told anyone else? Your parents? Or the police?'

'Just you,' I say, feeling sick at the thought of anyone else knowing.

'You know what he did is wrong? A crime?' She is slow and deliberate with her words. 'You were brave, escaping like that.'

'I was lucky. I got a good swing at him with my

elbow.'

'From the description you gave me, Charley, we are talking about attempted rape.'

The word jars. It shoots across at me like a bullet from a gun. I lean forward and lower my head into my hands. 'He's sick in the head. When I saw him after, at school, he had no sense that what he did was wrong...'

'You went to school after that?'

I nod. I'm feeling wobbly. It would take just a light breeze to knock me off my chair.

'You know we're going to have to tell someone about this?'

I jerk my head up and look Izzy in the eye. 'I have. I've told *you*.'

'Someone else, I mean. We have to talk to the Hillside social worker, and we may need to speak to the police.'

I shake my head. 'Don't we have some kind of therapist-patient confidentiality?'

'I'm also bound by a duty of care.'

'Shit. Great. There's no point in telling the police: it's only his word against mine and he'll deny it.'

She makes some notes and I turn my head again to look out of her window. A starling lands heavily on a flimsy branch of a tree outside. The branch is too weak for her and it bends almost out of sight before she launches off again.

Chapter 33
Hillside - Day 35

They put us in the lounge of the visitors' flat for the police interview. It has the feel of a place that's in disguise, like some of the therapy rooms. I move to put down my glass of water but I can't reach the coffee table so Dad takes it from me.

After Izzy had spoken to the social worker, things kind of snowballed.

Mum and Dad came in and we talked. Mum was distraught. She blamed herself at first, for not seeing my pain and my vulnerability – for not looking after me. I tried to explain that there was nothing she could have done. No one can plan for behaviour like that.

I wondered if Dad might get all masculine and threaten to go and *sort him out* – but I should have given him more credit. He was calm. He was saddened, and, no matter what I said, like Mum, he drew some of the blame onto himself.

The social worker told us they were obliged to contact the police. Then, within twenty-four hours, here we are in the plastic lounge.

It feels full to bursting with all of us in here. Mum and I are on one of the green sofas; the two women police officers are on the other one. They look uncomfortably close to each other, both folding their arms in front of their chests and pulling their shoulders in. Izzy and my dad are sat at a little dining table to the side. The whole thing feels fucking weird.

The plain-clothed police officers ready themselves, like they can't begin until we get to the agreed start time. I feel a familiar sense of apprehension, about to open up the wound once again to squeeze out more of the infection for everyone to see and judge. Mum puts a hand on mine and brings me around.

'It's OK,' one of the police officers says. She has broad shoulders and short curly hair. Despite her deep, chain-smoker's voice, her words put me at ease. As I talk, they both nod, agree and reassure, always reinforcing each other's words and sentiments.

When I finish talking, I cry until I can hardly breathe.

The police officer steps over to me and pulls me in to her shoulder. 'You've done really well, Charley.'

I ask what will happen to Matt, now, and the shorter police officer takes over the talking. She says that they will take it a step at a time, that a prosecution is possible but unlikely. She says she expects him to receive a formal caution. 'It will be added to his record, so that if there are any other incidents, particularly of a similar nature, he would be subject to the full force of the law.'

'He gets a second chance,' I say, almost to myself, but the police officer reacts as if it were a question.

Her voice remains calm. 'Further action is possible if the prosecution service decides to pursue, and you agree it's what you want. But I'm just telling you what I think will most likely happen under the circum-stances.'

'What circumstances?' I say.

'Where evidence is limited. But let's not get ahead of ourselves. The first step will be to talk to him, and you should be aware that he will know that you've spoken to the police. If he makes any contact, you should let us know straight away.'

'He won't contact me here,' I say, thinking that he doesn't even know I'm in Hillside.

'We know what he's capable of, so you will need to be aware,' the short one says – and I get the feeling she means more than his attack on me.

'Do you mean he's done stuff before?' I ask, and the

short one nods while the tall one says that they can't divulge any information on that.

AFTER THE INTERVIEW, Mum and Dad are allowed to take me off site for a bit so we drive to the nearest café. Dad buys three teas and says how proud he is of me for opening up, and how hard it must have been to relive it all.

Mum is fuming. 'What is it with teenage boys that they think they can take what they want?'

'That's what it's like—' I start to say.

'We've gone backwards,' Mum interrupts. 'We're supposed to have moved on. There's barely even a pretence of respect and equality.'

'They think it's funny to touch up a girl at the end of the night at a party,' I say. 'That's their banter.'

'Why do girls these days accept it?' Mum raises her voice and draws a look from the couple at the next table.

'Some of them at school just think it's funny too. Anyone who complains is a fucking weirdo tight-ass or, God forbid, a *feminist*,' I say. I've never understood why feminism seems to be so derided in school, as much amongst the girls as the boys.

Mum agrees with me. 'Why?' she says. 'I don't get

it. Why is feminism such a dirty word? Everyone should be fighting for equality, and if they are, they are a feminist, simple. Your dad's a feminist.' She looks at Dad. He nods.

'Look, Mum, the girls want the boys' attention and the boys want sex, so guess what? It's not rocket science.'

'It's demeaning; it's fifty years back.'

'Come on, Mum,' I say, 'that's not fair; you can't blame the girls.'

'Not you, Charley, I know that you wouldn't accept it. I just can't understand why your generation accepts this imbalance, this power that the boys have.'

'Why do you think I'm any different?' I say under my breath as Mum goes on.

'It just staggers me, all the shit that's come out in the media over the last few years, and it just keeps coming. Men in positions of power and influence, taking advantage of women and girls.'

'Mum...'

She won't stop. 'And all of it legitimised by celebrities, the leaders of the church, the US president, for fuck's sake. What hope do we have if the US president is able to normalise sexual assault?'

'Mum...'

'It's so sad that it's the same with the next generation, the generation that's supposed to be progressive, the future...' she says. 'What? What did you say, Charley?'

'Nothing.'

'Charley?' Dad says.

'Well, it happened to me.'

'What did?' Mum says.

'I walked into it, with Matt.'

Mum's face reddens. 'No,' she says. 'This isn't your fault, Charley, it's...' She grasps for words. 'That boy took advantage when you were vulnerable. That's not right, it's not OK – he is the *only* one that should be ashamed.'

Chapter 34
Hillside - Day 38

I press the light button on my digital watch. Four minutes to go. I watch as it glows for a second then blinks out, leaving an imprint of my watch face on my retina.

A sound outside in the corridor: a creaky floor, someone standing there, ear against my door. I hold my breath and strain to listen but it's nothing. Just my imagination.

My watch bleeps on the hour and I pull off my cover and swing my legs out of bed. Already clothed, I just need to squeeze on my trainers and slip my torch into my back pocket. The corridor is dark, lit only by the light from the stairwells at each end. Adrenaline is flowing now: anxiety, but a good kind of anxiety.

The sound of a creaking door stops my train of thought. Max's face peers from her room. She grins at me with a double thumbs-up. Out in the open I see she's wearing a black balaclava rolled up to just above her eyebrows and a camouflage, army-style jacket. She looks as if she's going hunting.

'What's in there?' I whisper, nodding at the small black bag on her back.

'Nothing,' she whispers, and I frown. 'It's for the wine.'

At the bottom of the stairs, we peek around the corner of the wall towards the nurses' station. At about twenty feet away, their door is open. Nurse Simon is sitting at his desk, tapping at a keyboard.

'Crap,' I whisper.

'What is it?'

'Simon.'

'Let me see.' We switch places so Max can get a look. 'We only have to get to the corner, maybe ten feet,' she says.

With no more discussion, she steps out into the open and freezes, legs astride, like a gun-slinger, staring in Simon's direction. She walks backwards towards the opposite wall, keeping her eye on him, then ducks out of sight.

My turn. I follow Max's technique, stalking in a slow-motion rewind towards her with my eyes on Simon. He's hunched over his keyboard so that his head is out of my line of vision, obscured by the wall. I hope that he's dropped off to sleep at his PC.

After I've taken two more steps, he leans back in his chair so that his upper body and head are in full view. I'm sure to be in his peripheral vision. I stop dead.

He stands and stretches his arms above his head, arching his back and yawning, still facing his screen. I pray he won't feel my eyes on him.

Then he moves. He turns away from me and heads to the other end of his office. I launch myself and Max grabs me as I fly around the corner. We both stifle laughs with our hands as we head towards Violet's room.

Max knocks gently on the door: two knocks, one knock, three knocks. She listens.

'Did you make up a coded knock with Violet?' I whisper through a smile.

'No, but I used the universal secret-door-knock sequence,' Max says. I give her a what-the-fuck look, then open the door. It's dark. Archie and Violet are sat on the bed, staring at us. Max jumps when she clocks the two of them.

'What?' I whisper at Archie and Violet. They break their rigid stares and Max smothers another laugh behind her hand.

'Nothing,' Violet says. 'You were ages.'

'Took us a while to get past the nurses' station,' Max says.

Archie looks at the window. 'We doing this, then?'

Violet retrieves the wine and matches, and Max continues to hustle. 'Ten seconds, people. Look sharp.' She loads the wine and matches into her rucksack. 'Let's move out: we want a nice, clean dispersal.'

Violet pushes open her window. It swings freely without its restrictor lock and she looks at me with pride. I hold the window open. She drapes her leg over the threshold and slides down onto the grass. She steps backwards and a security light bathes the entire rear side of the building in blinding white light. Violet jumps, stepping back towards the building and squeezing herself up against the wall.

'Stand still,' I whisper. I hold my breath until the light goes out.

'What's going on?' Max says from behind me.

I lean out of the window and whisper to Violet, 'We're going to have to see if we can edge along this wall and then leg it across the grass when we get opposite that opening over there.' I point to the public footpath sign.

Max hands me her rucksack while she pulls her balaclava down over her face. The only openings are the two eyeholes and a sinister, circular mouth hole, her pink lips exposed. She clambers out of the window like a hapless SAS operative. I pass her the rucksack, unable to make eye contact in case I can't control my laughter.

We line up with our backs against the wall.

'I'll go,' says Max, twisting on her head torch and positioning herself for a clean run. She makes it to the stile in just three steps. The security light doesn't trigger so the rest of us go together. Max holds out a steadying hand to Archie as he stumbles on the stile. Violet follows him into the blackness. I can see the darting beams of their torches as they take their first steps into the woods.

I pause on the stile to look back at the plain red-brick façade of the hospital building. It looks industrial, a warehouse closed up for the night. No sign of movement, and no indication that anyone is on to us yet.

OUR TORCHES LIGHT the woodland floor as we trudge down into the valley. The ground is soft under a sprinkling of leaves, needles and twigs that give the surface a satisfying crunch. I look up and strain to catch a glimpse of light from the moon or stars but there's nothing. Just the vast, black umbrella of trees.

We relax more as we get further from the hospital, and our whispers grow to a normal level of conversation. Archie asks if I've heard anything from Danny on the music.

'He got the recording, and he's put his own stuff down. He said it sounded good by the time he sent it off.'

'We have a chance then?'

'No drums though,' I say. 'Long shot I reckon.'

Archie speeds up to catch up with Max. 'You reckon Elsie is around here somewhere?' I hear him ask, ducking under the low-hanging branches and flashing his torch into the thick undergrowth. He and Max are now side by side, leading the way, him in his green retro army coat down to his knees and Max with her thumbs tucked in to the straps of her rucksack, balaclava rolled up above her eyebrows.

'I thought you were a non-believer?' says Max. 'If she was here, she'd have been killed by the badgers by now.'

Archie doesn't respond, but Max presses: 'They're devious.'

'Devious? Shut up, Max, badgers aren't *devious*,' says Archie.

'You'll see,' Max says, looking into the trees, 'they're night hunters.'

'They don't hunt humans.'

'Not before we started to encroach on their habitat. They've evolved.'

'Shut up, Max.'

'They can live on human flesh.' Max lets out a mock scream while shining her torch into her own face. Archie jumps and hits his head on a low branch and Max dissolves into laughter.

'Fuck's sake, Max,' Archie takes off his black beanie to rub his head as we all walk on. He recovers and gives Max a heavy sideways nudge so that she stumbles off the path for a moment.

After twenty minutes, the trees ahead of us open up and the light of the moon penetrates for the first time since we left the hospital grounds. We step out from the trees and stop to take in the view. We are a few hundred metres away from the base of the valley, looking across a sparse grassland. A river snakes across our field of view. The surface of the water scatters the moonlight onto its banks.

If Elsie exists, I can understand why she might want to live off the land in this beautiful place. A wooden, arched footbridge stands between us and the hill on the other side. I shiver in the breeze and step forward in silence with the others into the mono-chrome landscape.

We head for what looks like a clear path, dodging the rabbit holes and cowpats. I feel more exposed and vulnerable out of the trees and scan the edges of the valley for any buildings that might have a line of sight to us.

I step onto the footbridge and the sound of my shoes on wood echoes in the space below. Violet leans over the handrail, examining the surface of the water, while Max stomps on to the far bank and scans the path ahead. Archie and I look downstream. A fresh breeze tickles the back of my neck. I shiver and pull up my hood.

The river drifts away from us along the floor of the valley with moonlight glinting on its wind-ruffled surface. There's no movement within my expansive field of view. No animals, no people. Even the river looks static but for its sparkle. It's peaceful, and I relax further with every breath of the clean, unspoiled air.

Violet is distracted, looking up the side of the valley towards where the oak stands. Archie nods downstream. 'Makes me want to go fishing. You know, wading in through that wide, shallow section and standing there flicking a rod around.'

'Sounds technical, Archie,' I say.

'I don't know the jargon, but I've done a bit of fly fishing with my dad. It's relaxing. You feel connected, to the river and the environment.' Archie reaches into his inside pocket and pulls out a set of binoculars, lifting them to his eyes and scanning the river downstream. Violet and I can't help laughing.

'What?' Archie says. 'Can't leave home without the binoculars.'

'In the dark?' says Violet.

'Plenty of light from the moon.'

Violet edges closer to me. 'Look at those two.' Archie is stooping and Max looks as if she's trying to convince him of something, some unlikely bit of trivia. 'They look good together.'

'Together?'

'Yeah. Don't you think?'

Max turns back to us. 'We ready then, team?'

Violet and I look at each other and smile as Max and Archie lead the way again.

The path splits the wooded area in two so that the sky is visible between the trees on either side. The moon helps to light our way, and at the top of the hill the steep gradient eases off and the sprawling tree comes into view. It looks as if it's been quietly waiting for us. Up close, its size is breathtaking. Its massive trunk sprouts three thick branches that droop to touch the floor, too big to hold their own weight.

Archie picks up a fallen leaf. 'Oak,' he says and spreads it out in his hand, tracing its edge with a finger.

'We'll take your word for it, Archie,' Max says, walking around the base of the tree and kicking at the ground. Archie continues to examine his leaf, then turns his gaze upward into the branches, a look of awe on his face. I look over the valley. The outline of the hospital buildings is visible, back-lit by the moon.

'She's definitely been here; look,' Max says.

'Who?' says Archie.

'Elsie, you idiot. Look, there have been campfires here before – lots of them by the looks of it.'

'Could be anyone.'

'Yes, Archie, because there are a lot of people living off the land out here.'

'What do you think she lives on?' I ask.

I glance over at Violet. She's leaning up against the tree, her body is turned away from us. She looks as if she's found something, or she's trying to hide something. As I lean to see what she's doing, she covertly pops two yellow pills into her mouth and swallows them down as natural as anything, without any water. She catches my eye and looks away. I decide not to say anything in front of the others. I'll leave it till later.

Max builds a fire as Archie watches in awe. 'Can I light it?' he asks.

'I'll do it,' Max snaps and reaches into her rucksack for the matches. She lights the inner core, which flares and quickly grows, then she smiles and rests back on a log.

Violet puts a hand on Max's shoulder and sits next to her. She holds up her hands to the growing fire, illuminating her palms. Max takes a tobacco pouch from her rucksack, placing it in her lap. She pulls out a cigarette paper and passes the Rizla packet to Archie.

'Since when did you two smoke?' I ask.

Max looks at me briefly and winks. 'Me and Archie have one now and then,' she says, carefully placing a filter and expertly rolling between her thumbs and forefingers. I find my own tobacco and start to roll one for myself. Archie and Max gawp at me for a moment, then laugh.

We sit in silence, tiredness drawing us in to the flames. Max sheds her coat, her face flushed. In the still air, the hot smoke rises in a tight plume, then breaks free and melts into the night.

Max passes the wine around. When the bottle gets to me I take a long swig, feeling the warmth trickle through my chest. I slump, relaxed, and I breathe out fully for what feels like the first time in days.

'That's good,' says Archie, looking at the bottle in his hand.

'OK, gang.' Max flicks away her cigarette. 'A game.'

'What game?' asks Archie.

'Truth or dare,' she says. Archie and I both groan but Max insists. 'You start, Charley.'

'It's your game, Max. You start.'

'Truth,' Violet says, tucking her hair behind her ears, keeping her eyes on the fire.

'What do we do now?' I say.

Archie laughs at me. 'Someone needs to ask Violet a question,' he says. 'Anything you like, and Violet has to tell the truth.' Archie squashes his cigarette butt under his shoe and kicks it towards the fire.

Max leans forward. 'Tell us which of the nurses you'd go for? Who's your crush? You're not allowed to say no one.'

'I'd have to go for nurse Laura,' Violet says. I smile as the realisation comes.

'What?' Max splutters in disbelief. 'You're a...?'

'Max!' Archie and I say in unison.

Max looks affronted. 'I didn't know, that's all.'

'Yes.' Violet smiles. 'It's good to say that out loud, actually.'

'How long have you known? I mean, when did you...' Max fumbles her words.

Archie laughs. 'Max, she's gay, she's not got a terminal illness.'

'I've always known I wasn't really into boys, since I was young, maybe seven or eight, but I've never talked about it. I've not had boyfriends *or* girlfriends.'

'Is it still a secret? I mean, do your parents know, Violet?' I ask.

'No one does. I'm not even sure I knew for sure until recently.'

'So how do you feel now? Is it clear in your head?'

Max says. 'Or do you think you might swing both ways?'

'Max!' Archie says, rolling his eyes, to a look of innocence from Max.

'It's OK,' Violet says. 'I've not spoken out loud about it like this before, but now it feels right. Like I've finally allowed myself to think about it. To be honest with myself.'

'Good for you, Violet,' I say.

'Thanks.' She smiles.

Archie frowns. 'Which one's Laura, anyway?'

'Youngish, with the crazy blonde bangs,' Max says.

'She's kind,' says Violet. 'I mean *really* kind, not just nurse-kind. We've talked a lot. She's clever. She makes me think about stuff. She's passionate about women's rights, equality and respect.'

'She's a feminist?' Max says. 'Like bra-burning and all that?'

'Max,' I say. 'For fuck's sake.'

'I'm a feminist,' says Archie, looking at Max, then me. 'We all are. If you're not, then fuck me, you're a sexist, by definition.' Archie stands and goes around the other side of the tree for a piss.

'Truth or dare, Archie?' Max shouts after him.

'Dare!' he calls back from the darkness.

Violet looks over at Max. 'What now?'

'We need to come up with a dare that he can't turn down.'

'So long as the rest of us think it's reasonable,' I say.

'Easy,' Violet says. 'Climb this tree.'

Archie steps back into view with a grin on his face, looking into the branches above our heads.

'With nothing on,' Max adds, winking at Violet.

Archie looks horrified. 'No way.'

'Maybe you're right. You with nothing on would be more of a challenge for us than you – from this vantage point, anyway.' We laugh. 'You just go climbing, Archie, and bring us back a leaf.' As she speaks, Max hands Archie her head torch. We watch in silence as he clambers up into the branches.

'Such a boy scout,' Max says, rolling her eyes.

'Your go, Max,' I say.

'Truth. There's no chance I'm climbing anything.'

Violet and I look at each other, silently conspiring. I decide to try for a truth on Max's PTSD. Max considers, pulling her tobacco pouch out of her coat and staring into the embers of the fire. 'I've not been able to say much to anyone about it, not even the psychologists.' She pauses, rolling her cigarette. 'Too many triggers.'

'We can think of a different—'

'Give me a minute.' She licks her cigarette paper. 'I can talk about the general, not the details, OK?'

'Max, let's not—'

'It might help,' Max says, lighting her roll-up. 'Do you remember the school shooting in Castlecam, about five years ago?'

'Kind of,' I say, a vague recollection.

Max pokes at the embers with a stick. 'That was my first year in secondary school. It was a Monday, just after the October half-term. I only remember bits, feelings, mostly. Then some odd details. Apparently, my brain is protecting me.'

'Shit, Max,' I say.

She takes another drag on her roll-up. 'I know. Three people died. God knows how many traumatised. The smell after he'd fired the gun is the thing that still sticks in my nose. A smoky, chemical kind of smell. If I smell something like that now, it spins me out. Two of the kids who died were in my class. Two boys. Not my friends, particularly. I'll never forget the funerals. Their families.'

Archie calls down that he's at the top of the tree, and he's coming back down. Max glances up then continues. 'I have some tinnitus in my left ear as a reminder, something to go with the images that flash through my head. Sometimes the ringing in my ear is a trigger.'

'Trigger for what? Flashbacks?' asks Violet.

'I don't know if I'd call them flashbacks. More like

anxiety episodes. I don't go all in a trance or anything like that. I get these waves of anxiety, nausea and feelings similar to the ones I had on the day.' She pauses. 'When I first got here, to the H-blocks, it was hard. That corridor in the main building did it for me at first. I needed therapy to get over having to walk down the corridor to the therapy room.' Max gives a wry smile. 'I couldn't see a way through it for a long time. It's only recently I've had any sense that there's light at the end of the tunnel; something to aim for.' She looks up and takes a deep breath, letting it out slowly through pursed lips. 'Anyway, that's kind of it. I was only young.'

'Max, that's terrible,' Violet says.

Archie lands back on the ground with a thump. 'What is?'

'Another time, Archie,' says Max.

'Brought you this, Max.' He hands her a big green oak leaf, bigger than his hand. 'That's from the highest point of this tree reachable by any human, which means it's probably from the highest point around here for miles, maybe even the highest point in the county.'

'I am truly overwhelmed, Archie. This is a special moment and a proud day,' Max says, inciting Archie to play-wrestle her into submission.

The wine goes around some more, keeping us warm.

'I'll go again,' says Violet. 'Dare.'

'You've already been, you don't have to,' I say.

'It's OK, I fancy a dare.'

'I dare you to finish that wine,' Max says, pointing to a half-full bottle.

'Max, no!' I say.

'Dare me to go and check out that shed thing over there,' Violet says, pointing to a small, brick-built outbuilding that I hadn't noticed before. It's tucked away in a clump of trees, next to a feeding trough and what looks like a watering point for animals.

'OK,' says Max. 'With no torch, and bring back something from inside; something interesting.'

'Let her take a torch,' I say, 'otherwise she won't be able to see anything.'

Violet twists the end of her torch to bring it to life and points it towards the brick building. It has a wooden stable-type door and no windows. She wades through the long grass, some fifty yards or so. Max makes stupid ghost noises. I guess she's trying to raise the tension, but it just makes Archie laugh.

'What do you reckon is in there?' asks Archie, straining to see into the darkness.

'Hey,' says Max, standing, 'that could be where Elsie is hiding out. Maybe we should go take a look.'

'Let's see what she finds,' Archie says, a hand on Max's arm.

Violet pulls at the door. It eventually opens and she disappears out of sight.

Time passes. I stand and start towards the shed but then she emerges, pushing open the bottom half of the stable door with something over her head.

'What the fuck?' Max says. 'Is that a sack on her head?'

We crack up laughing. It looks as though Violet has pulled a big hessian sack over her head, down to her shins, and is staggering back towards us like a disorientated zombie.

'What the...' Archie's words trail off.

'Violet, you are nuts,' I say when she's within earshot. I stand and help her over the final ten feet, so she doesn't fall into the fire. She sits on her log seat, her head turning from side to side comically inside her sack. Max and Archie laugh.

Violet eventually pulls the sack off, breathing heavily. 'Hot in there.'

'OK, Violet, good work. On the laugh-o-meter you're in the lead,' Max says.

Violet looks over to me. 'Go on then, Charley.'

'Truth,' I say, with a feeling of mild dread.

They think for a minute. Max says she has one for me. 'Tell us why you were talking to the police the other day. What did they want?'

The others look at her and then to me. 'Police?' Archie says.

'Yes,' says Max, 'they stand out a mile off. You went into the visitors' flat with them.'

'Max,' Archie says, 'Charley doesn't have to—'

'It's OK,' I say. 'I was going to talk to you guys about it, anyway. Letting these things go is part of my journey.'

'You sound like a therapist,' Max says. I ignore her.

'Max is right. In psychology I told Izzy about something that happened to me and it set some wheels in motion that ended up with the police.'

The others remain quiet, their faces turned towards me. A vivid picture of Matt's face comes into my mind again, as if he has taken over a portion of it and comes out whenever he wants. 'There's this boy at school, Matt,' I say. Bottled-up anger and shame bubble away together. I describe the incident again, like I did to the police, my mind sticking for a moment on his violent twisting of my arm, pushing my face into the table. The others all looking at me, speechless. I explain how I escaped, giving him a crunching blow to the nose. I look over at Archie. He has his fists clenched. As I speak, I revisit my decisions in my head and can't help seeing how naïve I'd been. 'I feel like such a twat now, looking back,' I say.

'Don't blame yourself, Charley,' says Archie.

'There were signs, you know? Signs that are obvious looking back. He's a narcissist, he can't see past his own gratification, can't possibly do wrong, in anything. I should have seen it.'

'This bloke,' Max pipes up, 'he basically tried to rape you. Are the police picking him up?'

I shrug.

'He can't get away with that,' says Archie.

Chapter 35
Hillside - Day 39

In the dining room, Max and Violet are sat at their usual table. Max is slumped in her chair, food already eaten, sipping tea from a mug. Violet looks sparky, talking to the nurse. She catches my eye and gives me a smile and a wave of her piece of toast. No sign of Archie yet.

We were subdued on the walk back last night, physically and emotionally tired. When we rested at the footbridge, the sky brightened, and we were cold. I had a strong sense of something having shifted. My path out of Hillside seemed clearer.

By the time we moved off again, silent but connected, daylight had arrived, and the sun was already burning off the early mist. Me and Violet lagged behind the other two and I asked her about the yellow pills.

'They help keep me calm.'

'They let you take them, without dispensing them?' I said, knowing that there's no way Hillside would let patients self-administer drugs.

'I have a way to get the pills from the med centre. I only take a few a week, just to keep topped up. If I didn't, then I'd spend most of my time in the secure unit, fighting with the mania.'

'How do you get them?'

'Don't tell anyone,' she said.

I thought for a moment.

'Promise,' she added.

'OK, I promise. As long as I think you're OK, I won't tell anyone.'

It was Violet's turn to think for a moment. 'OK,' she said. 'The med centre is easier than the kitchen store cupboard. I can get in and out in less than ninety seconds.' She looked proud. I couldn't return her smile, and I wasn't sure I'd be able to keep it to myself.

Lisa is at my table, a quizzical look on her face, as if she suspects something has gone on. 'How are you doing, Lisa?' I say, as I scoop honey from an individual carton and pour it over my porridge.

She scrutinises me, arms folded over her chest. 'Better than you, I reckon, Charley.' She peers over at Max, then back at me.

'Didn't sleep so well,' I say, the truth.

'I can see. Looks like Max is struggling too. Anyone would think you two have been up to something, your rooms being next to each other.'

I avoid eye contact. 'Just one of those nights. Noisy birds outside.'

Archie shuffles in as I start on my toast. The sight of him reminds me that I need to tell him I got a message from Danny this morning about the Arena competition. We didn't make it to the live auditions.

When I read it, my heart sank, the news affecting me more than I thought it would. I had a feeling we wouldn't get through, and it shouldn't have been a shock. But I must have been resting a lot on it. The chances of getting into music college on the back of the lack of work I've got through this year are minuscule. The Arena competition was the back door that's now slammed firmly shut.

Archie's hair is flat on one side where he slept on it, and he's wearing the same clothes he had on last night, his jeans muddy at the bottoms. Thankfully, Lisa has her back to the door and doesn't see him walk in. I can't help a smirk. He gives me a vacant sideways glance before he sits down with Max and Violet.

'You've made great strides since you came back in,' Lisa says. 'At our planning meeting this morning we agreed that you can come off supervision, which reflects your progress with the eating.'

'Off supervision?'

'It just means you no longer need a nurse to sit with you for the supervision period after a meal. You still need to take the rest period, but not necessarily strictly supervised.'

'That's good,' I say. Progress is good. I want, and need, to get better. But with progress comes the withdrawal of support, which scares me.

THERE'S a smell of bonfire in the boys' lounge. Max is slumped against Violet on the sofa, looking ready to go back to bed. Violet looks ready for anything. I sit next to Max just as Archie walks in. He stops inside the door and looks at us through bloodshot eyes. We all laugh at the sight of him. Two other girls stop by the door at the sound of our laughter but Max gives them a stare that sends them on their way.

'Walking dead,' says Max, nodding at Archie. Archie looks around the room, head lowered and mouth slightly open.

'I like the look, Archie,' I say. 'Don't listen to Max. People pay a lot to get their hair like that.' Finally, a twinge of a smile appears at the corner of Archie's mouth. 'Danny messaged me,' I say. Archie looks up and I tell him that we didn't make the cut.

'Fuck-shit,' he says, slumping down on the armchair. He looks at the three of us. 'Everyone feeling chipper, I see. Am I the only one that was out last night? I'm sure I saw you lot there?'

'You can't take the pace, Archie,' Max says as her own eyes droop to half-closed.

Archie reaches for the guitar behind the sofa and then seems to think better of it and sinks deeper into his chair. 'At least it was good to get to the top of that tree,' he says. 'There was a great view through a gap in the branches up near the top. You can see for miles along the valley.'

'No sign of Elsie?' I say, looking at Archie with a half-smile.

'She might have been staying in that shed thing,' says Violet.

We all look at her.

'What?' Max says. 'You said it was just farmer stuff in there.'

'I just mean that she *could* have been there, you know. It was a good place to hide out, sheltered, so it's possible.'

'I knew it!' Max erupts. 'She must be staying there. She must have been there all this time. We should go back again.'

'It didn't look like anything, Max,' says Violet.

'If she's up there,' I say, 'then she's been living like that for years. I say we leave her be.'

Violet nods. 'I'm with Charley.'

Chapter 36
Hillside - Day 44

Max's discharge day arrives.

It's been nearly a week since our trip up to the hill. Despite Max pushing for us to go again, we never quite got around to it. And now it's too late.

Violet has been in a dark place. She's slipping further every day and I can't break through her protective shell. Archie, too, is uncharacteristically down. He will miss Max more than anyone else will. He's been getting more subdued by the day as her discharge date slowly but surely edges closer.

I wash my hands in my room and look at myself in the mirror, my fingers dripping dry in the basin. The hand towel is clean. I know this because I never use it. I don't remember the last time I used a hand towel. I've never seen the point in washing your hands and then re-contaminating them on a towel. But this one I know is clean, and I know that every normal person in the world would not think twice about using a hand towel.

I reach for it.

I dry my hands quickly and return the towel to its hook. Anxiety creeps up to a seven.

A darkness teases me. Self-doubt nips at my ankles. All my failures seem to gather at the door, waiting for me to stand aside and let them take over. The music is dead, the competition lost. I can feel the contamination on my hands.

I take a deep breath and release to the count of five in my head. Eyeing the hand soap, I resist repeating the wash. Just one wash is too much too soon for me. A single wash and then the use of a hand towel is pushing things too far. My hand hovers over the hot tap. I ache to release the hot, scolding, germ-killing water. I withdraw my hand and look myself in the eye in the mirror.

I breathe.

I think of Izzy.

Sit with it. Notice it. Acknowledge it, and then allow it to pass.

My face radiates heat as the hot flush reaches a peak. Sweat forms on my forehead and my hands are clammy. I close my eyes and try to control the spinning. Anxiety peaks and I can feel it turn. From and eight down to a seven. I'm coming through it.

My eyes open again, I blink away the blurry background, and my face comes into focus once more. I'm down to a six and the anxiety continues to drop.

Five.

I can't help a smile as the anxiety slips down to a four and feels as if it's continuing to reduce. My face is cool as the perspiration evaporates and I return to a normal stress level. I look at my hands. They are dry. The urge to wash them again is there for sure, but it's far from overwhelming.

I turn and make for the door, barely thinking about it as I reach for the handle with my hand for the first time since being in Hillside, rather than opening it with my foot.

Outside the door of the boys' lounge, Max's bags are stacked. The four of us sit together in the lounge, waiting for her new foster parents to arrive. The atmosphere is heavy – it feels so final. We don't know when we'll next be together, if ever.

Max's big maroon Dr Martens boots stick out of the bottom of her long, flowing brown skirt. I've never seen her wear a skirt before. She sits in the armchair and crosses her legs, a distant stare in her eyes. Violet and I are on the sofa, still in our pyjamas. Violet is barely there – monosyllabic. She's battling against a slip into darkness and this time it's like none of us can hang on to her.

I look at Archie sat on the floor, fidgeting, unsettled. His features seem drawn, like he's not slept in a week. He isn't ready to be in Hillside without Max.

It was a bit like this after Jasmine left, even though we never really hung out with Jasmine. It's the change that throws us off kilter, the realisation that nothing is fixed, and anything can happen. Just when you think things are settling into a rhythm, it changes, and you have to once more find your way in an unfamiliar environment. Without Max the days will be grey.

'What's your plan today, Max?' Archie asks without making eye contact.

Max shrugs. 'Nothing.'

'You're gonna miss us, you know?'

'Might come back and see you tonight. Maybe I'll break in.'

Archie laughs. 'That'll be a first. Someone breaking *in* to somewhere like this.'

'Like an opposite-Elsie,' I say.

'My foster parents have a dog,' Max says. 'I'm going to ask if we can take it for a walk up that hill that you were talking about, Charley. Butt-Head Hill or something?'

'But-*ser* Hill, Max.' I smile. 'It's beautiful up there.'

'I'll have a look,' Max says. 'When you get out we can go for a walk up there together, with the dogs?'

'You bet,' I say. 'Archie and Violet too.' I nudge Violet's arm but she doesn't respond.

Simon breezes purposefully into the lounge, saying that it's time. We are all still for a moment before Max pushes herself up from her seat.

Without thinking for more than a split second about germ transfer, I stand and fling my arms playfully around her neck, rocking from side to side. Over her shoulder, beyond the tall windows, the sunlight disappears behind a cloud. I force enthusiasm into my tone and say, 'It's been great. You're special, you know that?'

'Special needs,' Max says.

'Aren't we all?' I step back to let Archie say goodbye.

'Bye, Max,' he says, stepping up to hug her.

'I'll be seeing you, Archie,' she says.

'I hope so.'

'Make sure of it.'

They pull apart and smile at each other. Max turns, bends down to Violet and whispers something. They make eye contact and Violet's arms creep around Max's neck. Archie and I exchange a worried look.

'Later then, losers,' Max says as she turns and heads out of the room without looking back. She grabs her bags and strides off towards the entrance lobby, a burp echoing down the corridor as she walks away.

Chapter 37
Hillside - Day 46

Two days later I'm allowed to sit at the same table as Archie in the dining room for the first time. I grin as I pull up a chair next to him, but he's distracted.

'I got a message from Ada,' I say. 'She got through to the auditions with Mia.' My tone is upbeat as I try my best not to sound jealous. I've been analysing my feelings about the whole thing and I've decided I am happy for them. I'm sad that me, Danny and Archie didn't make it, of course, but I hold no malice for Ada and Mia getting through. That's what I keep telling myself, and if I do that enough, it might become true.

Archie raises an eyebrow. He's been miserable since Violet went back into the special care unit. She hasn't yet emerged from the darkness that came down when Max left Hillside.

'She'll get through,' I say. 'Like before. She's strong.'

As I say this, nurse Lisa comes into the room with Violet, heading towards us. I'm flooded with relief, thinking she must be pulling through. As she gets to the table, I quickly realise she isn't back on form. Her head is down, hair covering her face.

'Hey, Violet,' I say, trying to catch her eye as she sits at our table. Lisa plants herself next to Simon. He gives her the briefest of looks before going back to his magazine tucked inside a psychology journal.

I wonder if I should tell Lisa about Violet's trips to the med centre, whether that would make any difference to what she's going through now. Maybe she's had too many pills, or maybe she needs more, I don't know.

Violet shifts in her seat and lifts her head, her hair falling back from her face. I beam at her and she forces a half-smile and puts her hand gently on top of mine on the table. Archie places his hand on top of Violet's to complete the sandwich, and we sit in silence.

I WAKE WITH A START, wired and spinning into a fully developed panic attack. It's three in the morning. I sit bolt upright and gasp for air, already up at a level seven. I get a hold on it, forcing the spin to a stop with sheer determination.

The panic attack subsides, but there's no hope of going back to sleep. I climb out of bed and splash water on my face at my basin, dabbing it dry and checking my reflection in the mirror. I don't look like the girl that I have in my mind's eye. I look older in the mirror, more solid, like a real person.

I step over to my window. The light from the moon is bright, illuminating the tops of the trees that carpet the hill down into the valley. I can't see the river from my window but I imagine it: the reflections on the surface of the water, the sparse landscape. I only have a few more days in Hillside and the prospect of leaving brings mixed feelings. I'm scared more than anything else.

As I strain to see the tree on the opposite hill, the outside security light comes on below my window. I squeeze my face up against the glass to see what triggered it. Nothing. The light goes out and I look back up into the distance.

I try to see if there is anything at the tree, if Elsie is out there. It's too far away and its base is in darkness. I look at the ground outside my window. The security light hasn't triggered again, but I can't shake a feeling that something isn't right. Something – some*one*, more like – must have triggered it. There is no way that

Archie or Violet would go out without saying something to me.

The urge to go to Violet's room is too strong. I quickly dress, grab my phone and edge my door open.

I glance at Max's door on my way past, half expecting her to appear in her army get-up. At the bottom of the stairwell, I peek around the corner towards the nurses' office. The door is open but there's no sign of anyone, so I scurry across the corridor and towards Violet's door.

Without knocking, I squeeze the handle down and push open the door, enough to get a line of sight to her bed. I use the torch on my phone, fully expecting to see Violet tucked up in bed so I can go back to my room and stop being crazy.

She isn't there. The room is empty. I look to the window: it's been propped open with a book. My heart pounds. Why would she go out on her own? I have to go after her. I grab the orange book from the window and throw myself clumsily over the threshold before turning and replacing the book. I run straight to the wooden stile. The security light triggers but I ignore it and launch myself over the stile and into the woods.

I settle into a steady jog. When the trees thin and light begins to penetrate, I turn off my torch and pick up speed, racing to the edge of the woods where I stop to catch my breath, looking down into the valley. No sign of Violet. Maybe she never left the hospital grounds?

I try to see if she's on the bridge but I'm too far away. I stuff my phone back in my jeans and break into a run, frightened for Violet and still sensing something is wrong, that she needs me.

Then I see it.

Something in the water at the bridge. Something big enough to be a person. Violet.

I pick up speed, sprinting down the hill without taking my eyes off the shape in the water. I trip on something, a tuft of grass or a rabbit hole, and fly into the ground, turning my head just in time to avoid my face hitting the mud. My shoulder takes the full force and I roll twice before coming to rest with my face in the dirt and a hand in a cowpat. My shoulder feels bad; dislocated, maybe? I sit up and force myself to my feet. Walking at first, then back into a run, close now to the bridge.

It is Violet in the water. I can see her, a hundred yards away. I sprint. Fifty yards. Twenty. She's face up in the shallows. Not moving. I hit the edge of the river, hard, splashing the freezing water up over myself and onto Violet. I half fall, half jump and kneel next to her in the shallow water. Pain shoots through my knee as I catch it on a stone.

I force myself to be calm, to remember the first-aid

training from school. I can't do any good if I'm not calm. I look at her. No obvious signs of injury. Is she breathing?

'Violet, can you hear me?' I lean down and listen for breathing. The water burns my skin it's so cold. 'Violet, can you hear me?' No response. Nothing. I put my ear to her mouth and nose. I hold my breath.

She is breathing. It's shallow, but she's breathing. I prise her shoulders gently out of the water and try to lift her to my chest, to relieve her from the cold. She's so heavy; I'll never get her to the bank of the river. I gather myself and count to three, then pull her close to my chest and step backwards towards the bank using all my strength. I get her out and on to the grass. I pull off my hoodie and cover as much of her as I can then take out my phone. It's wet and my heart stops for a moment when I press the buttons and nothing happens. At last its screen glows orange and I dial 999.

Exhausted, I lie down next to Violet and pull her close to try to warm her. I give directions to the emergency operator.

'Ambulance is coming,' I say, the phone slipping from my hand and onto the bank of the river. I can hear the faint voice of the operator on the other end but I have nothing left in me.

'They know where we are,' I whisper, more to myself than to Violet.

Chapter 38
Hillside - Day 48

The therapy room has been transformed into a makeshift police interview room. Less than forty-eight hours after I found Violet in the river, I'm sat on one of the low chairs positioned around the coffee table. Nurse Simon is next to me and two people I don't know, police I guess, not in uniform, sit opposite me.

The woman speaks first. 'Hello, Charley. My name is Sarah, and this is my colleague, PC Steven Banks. I think you know Simon?' I nod. 'Now, I am sure there are lots of rumours about what—'

'Is she going to be OK?' I interrupt.

Sarah pauses and glances at her colleague before answering. 'I'm afraid we don't know yet. Violet's very poorly. We think she hit her head pretty hard when she went into the water. Last night she slipped into a coma.' She pauses again. 'If it's OK with you, we would like to ask a few questions, so we can get a better idea of what happened.'

She leans forward in her seat, clasping her hands together. She doesn't look like a police officer. She's probably in her late thirties, tall, slim, with shoulder-length brown hair and good skin. She's casually dressed. Her long denim skirt looks stiff and uncomfortable, and she's sitting awkwardly in the low chair with no room for her long legs.

'Sure,' I say.

PC Banks writes something on his pad. He's wearing a suit and tie. The bottom of his shirt has come untucked at the front, revealing a bit of hairy blubber.

My memory of the incident is hazy. The ambulance took me to the hospital with Violet, and when I got back to Hillside to see Archie, he was frantic. The nurses wouldn't tell him anything so his imagination had been going crazy.

'She's alive,' I said to him.

'Where is she?'

'Hospital.'

'How bad?'

'I don't know,' I said.

Archie said that he'd heard that the med centre door was unlocked and there were pills missing. He asked me how I knew to go after her. I've still no idea. Other than the security light, it was just a sense.

Plain-clothes Sarah asks me questions about Violet's state of mind and whether she'd given any signs of doing something like this. She doesn't get it. It's difficult to put into words how Violet has been this week and how she normally is when she's in her dark place. But we all expected her to come through it, like always.

I try to imagine my friend walking to the medical centre in the night, on her own in the darkness. Did she mean to overdose? What was going through her mind when she was focusing on the lock, turning the pins until it clicked and released? Did she think of us? I wish I could have been with her, to talk to her.

I picture her face from when she was in her good place – her mischievous, playful eyes. Then I picture her lying in the water. Was she on her way to the tree?

Chapter 39
Hillside - Day 50

I need to run. I haven't felt it this strong since before Hillside, and I can't shake it. My skin prickles with nervous energy. I can't untangle my motivations – the mix of feelings and needs to burn calories, and just to feel the fresh, cold air on my face. Right now, I don't care.

As soon as it's lights out, I creep to my door and out into the darkness of the corridor. With little care for any noise I make, I slope down the stairs and across the way towards Violet's room. No sign of any nurses.

My heart sinks as I consider that they've probably fixed Violet's window and I won't be able to get out. Looking both ways, I turn the handle of Violet's door.

Locked.

I push harder, twisting the spherical handle. It won't budge. 'Shit,' I whisper, then kick the bottom of the door, the noise ringing out through the corridor. I hold my breath, expecting Simon to come striding towards me to find out what all the noise is about.

Nothing.

I lean harder into the door, but it doesn't budge.

I take a step back and hold my breath, listening for nurses. Nothing. With my back against the wall of the corridor opposite Violet's door, I launch myself at the side with the handle and hit it with as much force as I can muster, which turns out to be more force than probably I needed. The door gives way easily and slams back against the wall in Violet's room. It seems to me to be the loudest slam of a door I've ever heard, and I quickly turn to close it behind me, inspecting the splintered frame and hoping that it's not so obvious from the outside.

As soon as it seems no one is coming, I turn to the window. The lock is just as Violet left it. The window swings open easily and I clamber out, my back to the wall so as not to trigger the security light. I look towards the opening in the hedge and am reminded of the last time I was here, just a few nights ago, when Violet was freezing to death in the water. I head the other way, edging along the perimeter fence until I arrive out front, then push my way through the hedge until I emerge on the side of the road.

No cars. No streetlights. No sound but the distant rumble of the motorway.

I pull up my hood and I run.

The feeling as my feet pound the tarmac takes me straight back to my running with Danny. I pick up speed a little to increase the pain and distract me from my tangled thoughts. In less than five minutes my lungs are heaving and muscles burning. As I emerge from under the cover of trees and I bear left, dipping to a steep decline towards the valley, the light of the moon illuminates the road. My running shoes slap the tarmac as I lean back and take longer strides on the down-slope.

A car approaches in the opposite direction and I pull my hood tight around my face, looking down as it passes. It slows as if deciding whether to stop, then speeds up and its rear lights disappear around the corner. I take a sharp left into a narrower road and as the landscape flattens into the valley my legs wobble and I trip.

I reach out to stop my body hitting the road and the full force transmits up through my hands. I cry out, rolling across the road and scraping my knees and hands.

I moan and sit up, inspecting my knees.

Not serious, I think, and I pick the gravel from the palms of my hands. I sit for a moment, looking up at the starless sky. The moon has retreated behind the clouds and once more the countryside is all but pitch-black.

At the end of the narrow road, I recognise the sound of the river that runs through the valley and I head towards it. Through a small field and over a stile and I'm on the riverbank. I look right and contemplate how far I am from home, then left, and consider that I am probably less than twenty minutes from base. The river would take me to the footbridge in the field below Hillside. Hesitating a moment longer, I take a left and pick up speed as the light of the moon brightens the pathway.

I sprint the final hundred metres to the footbridge, clomping onto the wooden deck and leaning over the handrail, panting.

There's a deep chill in the air, and the river looks cold and uninviting. The water turns angrily as it squeezes past the bridge piers and hurries downstream. The spot where I found Violet is just a few feet away and I picture her body in the water.

A flicker of light catches my eye and I look towards the great oak on the hill. An orange glow flashes across the surrounding trees and then slips away as if teasing me. I strain my eyes to see but there's nothing. I stand there on the bridge for what feels like hours, but is probably no more than ten minutes. Then, I scan the trees on the edge of the hill to find the opening that leads towards Hillside House. My eyes fixed on the location, I start to run, my mind pushing me on, but my body resisting.

What is this? Is this about calories? Have I learned nothing, made no progress?

I slow to a steady jog as I enter the trees, the endorphins pumping freely. I tackle my own questions. This run is not about my weight. It's not about burning calories. This is all about clearing my head – untangling my complex thoughts. I don't feel that aching need to push myself to maximise calorie burn.

Above my head, the moon is bright enough to penetrate the canopy of leaves, guiding me back to my room. I take a deep breath of the cool night air and it filters through my lungs like it's cleansing my body.

THAT NIGHT I dream of polar bears.

At one stage I wake and I'm not entirely sure whether they might exist for real, then I look over at my window and remember where I am – the side of a hill, not the polar ice cap.

I drift back into sleep, and the dream catches me once more.

Something's happened. The atmosphere is
tense, as if the war has reached its climax, and
the final battle is coming. The bears have been
driven back to the edges of the ice landscape
with nowhere to turn but the open seas.

Dad isn't here, and I worry for him.
I am alone on the ice. Nothing but white
planes in all directions, and a row of bears in
the distance.

Instinctively, I walk towards the bears lined up
on the edge of the ice, water lapping at their
feet. Three of them turn to look at me, their fur
bristling in the cold white wind. They look to
the sea, and then back at me. It's as if they are
deliberating which is the greater of threats.

I count them.
Six, no, seven. One with blood stains across its
back and I'm not sure if the blood belongs to
the bear or to something else. Someone else.
One of Dad's team? Or even Dad?

The leader of the polar terrorists, the biggest of
the bears, teeth showing, scuffs its foot on the

ice. It takes a step back from the edge of the
water and glares at me. The others turn too.

The seven bears start to walk towards me,
slowly at first. Then they pick up speed,
accelerating to a canter.
I continue to walk towards them, maintaining
my pace to make out like I don't care. Like I'm
not scared.

I falter a little.
I slow then stop.

There's nowhere for me to run if these bears
continue on their path. Nothing but a wide
expanse of exposed ice. I lock eyes with the
leader as it nears. Maybe a few hundred feet
away. Then, as if hearing a starting pistol, or
smelling my fear, all seven bears break into
a run.

Chapter 40
Hillside - Day 55

I wake early on my last day in the H-blocks, unable to get back to sleep.

Max is in my head.

On Saturday, she came to visit me and Archie and she looked so different. Her hair was shorter, and she had new clothes. We saw her pull up in a big old car out front, then stroll across the car park like she was totally cool with everything.

Archie didn't recognise her at first. 'Who's that? It's not...' he said, his mouth open.

The sight of Max looking so relaxed and comfortable did something to me on the inside – brought a little fire to my belly. She was an inspiration, a reason to make something of the opportunity I'd been handed by Hillside. She made me want to go home.

The sight of Max affected Archie too. He had a way to go before discharge, but she brought a twinkle to his eyes I'd not seen before.

She had her foster parents' dog with her so Hillside wouldn't allow her in the building, but Archie and I were allowed to sit outside with her for a bit. We talked about Violet mostly, and about Max's foster parents. They sounded perfect for Max – relaxed and open, structured and attentive. Max seemed happy, like she was determined to make a go of it.

After Max left, we caught snippets of information about Violet but nothing official. Lisa said there were sleeping pills missing from the medical centre, but they don't know how many she took. She also said they don't know whether she would recover. 'She would have died in the water,' she said to me. 'You have a remark-able, intuitive connection to Violet.'

Looking at the peeling wallpaper above my bed one last time, I try to summon the 'remarkable, intuitive connection' I'm supposed to have to Violet but feel nothing. I don't feel her. I rip the paper off in long strips in my mind.

After weeks, months of therapy and self-reflection, I'm being ejected back into the world. Am I any different to how I was on the day I arrived? I'm not *fixed*. I don't think I'll ever be fixed.

Later, Izzy is bubbly, humming to herself as I walk in for our final session. She nods at a chair for me to sit down, then softens her tone and asks if I want to talk through what happened with Violet. I shake my head.

She leans forward a little to look me in the eye. 'Let's keep your mind occupied and focused on your recovery plan.'

She gathers a bundle of papers: a pack of information to take away with me. There are 'soother packs' for difficult times, activity sheets, distractions and reminders that I can use when I'm thinking about self-harming. Then there are phone numbers if nothing else is working.

We talk about my eating, and what she calls the minor blip I've had over the last couple of days, with all that's happened. I describe my progress with my OCD rituals, how I have limited some of them, pushing through the anxiety curve.

'Each time you complete the anxiety cycle,' Izzy explains again, 'without completing the OCD ritual, the peak of the anxiety is reduced. Your brain eventually learns that the ritual doesn't help. So you need to press on with that. Just take it a day at a time.'

She says I don't need to be perfect all the time, as long as my overall trajectory is on an upward, improving trend. I tell her that I'm not convinced I'm on an upward trajectory. It feels like I use so much energy just to stop from slipping, there's little left for any upward anything.

She digs into my file. 'Do you remember when I first saw you? We talked about your friends and family, and school, and the problems with some of those interactions?' I nod, although our first session is hazy in my mind. 'And talking about your friends and your eating, you said...' Izzy looks down at her notes. 'You talked about fitting in... needing to get thinner and have the right shape body... controlling food intake. You also talked about keeping up with the social media apps, and all that, so you can engage with the girls at school. Do you remember?' I nod again. 'And how have those things changed, if at all?'

I think about it, trying to figure if anything has shifted. I do feel like those things aren't so big. 'I still *feel* them. I need to fit in,' I say. Izzy sits back in her chair. 'But, I know I need to eat. I can't restrict intake like I was.'

'And when we talked about self-harm, you said you needed it, that it was a defence system.'

I have to think for a minute. 'Sounds strange hearing it like that. The self-harm is complicated. I wouldn't call it a defence system.'

'Have you done it since you've been in here?'

'No.' I look at the skin on the back of my hand and see the marks I'd made with my nails a week or so before, in a moment of confusion. I look up at Izzy. 'It's like an addiction. But it's more than that. I think it's about outwardly showing my inside pain.'

Izzy nods. 'You haven't self-harmed for some time. Why is that?'

'It's not allowed in here. And I haven't needed to because the support has been there, all the time.' I think again about the deep end of the pool that I'm being thrown into as soon as I'm out of here. Izzy seems to read my mind and reminds me that there are things I can do when I get out, materials in my pack to help me avoid the dark places.

'You talked about the need to fit in.' She looks again at her notes and relays to me what I'd said to her before, about keeping people sweet and looking right. She asks me if my feelings on those things have changed in Hillside. I think for a moment and feel a burning determination in my gut.

'Like I said, I do need to fit in. I'm not going to be a recluse, a loner.' I pause. 'But, I need to be myself. I need to be *true* to myself, and not just conform to other people's expectations.'

Izzy smiles and leans forward. 'You've made progress. You have the tools and the understanding.

You need to focus now, and use what you know.' She pauses. 'You've done well, Charley. You have an amazing capacity for self-reflection. You just need encouragement, and a little nudge here and there.'

'The dolphin,' I say to myself, remembering the metaphor for mental health support being a dolphin, swimming alongside, nudging and encouraging. As opposed to the kangaroo, its young smothered and protected in the mother's pouch.

AFTER LUNCH, Archie and I shuffle along the corridor and into the boys' lounge. There are five others in there watching the TV, so Archie links his arm in mine and turns me around to head straight back out. 'Time to let the boys' lounge go.'

We duck into my room and walk over to the window, peering out over the fields, through the drizzle and gloom. I can only just make out the oak tree in the distance.

'Do you reckon she did it?' Archie says. 'Tried to kill herself, I mean?' The raindrops on my window distort the landscape. I think I can make out some movement at the tree but can't be sure.

'No, I don't think so.' I sit on my bed with my back leaning against the wall. I tell Archie about how Violet had propped open her window with a book. *What book was it?* An orange cover.

'That doesn't mean she was planning to come back. Probably just autopilot.' Archie lies back on my bed, puts his hands behind his head and closes his eyes. He kicks at me with his feet, playfully. 'Get your butt out the way, I need to stretch.'

I lie on my side next to him, for comfort, and for some closeness, my head under his arm. A fleeting thought of germs slips away with barely a flex of mental muscle. Here with Archie reminds me of lying with Dad. He pulls me in to his chest. I feel him relax, breathing deeply. I close my eyes.

DAD TURNS the key in the ignition. The car sparks into life with a tune from my old playlist drifting through the speakers, taking me back. The flashback is short-lived. I return Dad's smile as he turns up the volume.

He pulls the car out of the car park and I look around to see Archie standing forlorn at the window in the lounge. I wave, but we are gone before I can tell if he's seen me.

The evening roads are deserted. We twist and turn along the narrow, single carriageway at speed before pulling out onto the main road, accelerating away. I rest my head back and look out of the side window of the car as we glide along the smooth, tree-lined road with the sunshine forcing its way through the clouds and scattering light across the windscreen. I breathe out some of the tension of the H-blocks, and breathe in a level of apprehension about what's to come next.

Part Six
Outside

Chapter 41
Home - Day 1

The smell of the house isn't as comforting as it should be. The memories are complicated.

Lucas rushes towards me, and I drop my bags so I can shield myself from his impact.

'Hey, Lucas,' I say, as he wraps his arms around my waist. My heart races at the thought of germ transfer and I puzzle at my own reaction. With Archie, last night, it was easy. Yet with Lucas the risk feels so much greater. I can't bring myself to hug him back so I stand there like a fucking idiot with my arms out, as if he's infected with something. I've been home for just one minute and I've already let the fear of contamination win out, as it always has.

'Missed you, Charley. Are you home for good now?' he says in his beautifully innocent, squeaky voice, then releases me as I wriggle awkwardly away from him.

'You bet,' I say, forcing a smile and reaching for my case. BB scampers into the room towards me, over-shooting and skidding past on the wooden floor before jumping up to greet me.

'Your fans have found you then, Charley?' Mum says from across the room in the doorway, smiling when I look up at her. She's wearing a knee-length dress over jeans, her hair pulled back. She has puffy bags under her eyes.

I manage just over twenty minutes of Mum, Dad and Lucas fussing around me before I escape to my room. My bedroom is spotless and fresh with new bed linen. Mum has been busy redecorating, covering up the old space, but the little reminders are still there, glaring at me from all four corners of the room. I switch on my phone then kick off my trainers and lie on the bed, turning onto my side to message Ada. The two big springs that poke up at me through the mattress are still there, pushing through Mum's superficial cover-up.

I think of Mia, already starting to worry about how I'll survive the school day, how I'll cope without Max, Archie and Violet. I send her a short, friendly message, to smooth the way.

I message Ada and she's happy that I'm back. She asks if I'll join their band for the audition and I feel a mix of excitement and fear at the prospect of playing on stage at the Arena. I say I'll think about it, not sure that Archie and Danny will see it as a great idea for me to play without them.

I head for the shower and turn the water on. I feel a rush of thoughts and images of my old routines as the steam billows up and out of the plastic cubicle. I lean in and turn the temperature up to maximum. My thoughts drift to Izzy. What would she say to me right now? I contemplate scalding myself. I think about Mum and the look of concern on her face that has become such a permanent fixture.

I turn off the water and walk back to my room. Shower can wait.

From the big leather armchair under my window, I take in the view of the clear night sky. Dotted with stars and a bright but distant half-moon, it offers some hope; something more than all of this.

Dad pops his head around my door on his way to bed. He asks if I'm OK and I say that I am. He comes in and sits on my bed for a minute, looking out of my window with me. He tells me it will be OK, that we'll get there, then he stands and kisses me on the forehead and turns to leave.

Mum comes in a few minutes later and sits down on my bed, in the same spot Dad has just left. Her face is grey and lined. She looks ill, and I wonder how much of it's down to me.

'Get some sleep,' she says, stroking my hair. 'It's been a long day.'

I nod and say goodnight.

It's been a long day. It's been a long year. But I am home, and I will be stronger.

Chapter 42
Home - Day 3

Over breakfast, Mum and I are both on edge. I sense her watching me, calculating how much I'm eating, looking for signs of any restriction of calorie intake. The tension is uncomfortable so I leave early and take the longer route to school.

It's overcast. Butser Hill is deserted and foreboding in the gloom. The bench at the top is too wet to sit on, so I keep moving. I try in vain not to think about what it will be like in school. I'm not ready for it. I have no idea what Mia is going to be like. She's not answered my text. It's her unpredictability that scares me the most.

Then there is Matt: I know the police have spoken to him but not charged him with anything, but I don't know how he has reacted. Is he sorry? Will he be angry, want retribution?

On my way down the west slope a group of three boys skirts the foot of the hill, on their way to school. They are too far away to recognise but I figure they must be about my age.

They look at me and nudge each other before one of them shouts 'Hey, psycho!' so loud I'm sure it would have been heard across town. They laugh and push each other around, looking as if they are preparing themselves for a follow-up. I stop still, feeling threatened, unsure of what they might do. There are no other people in sight and I'm aware of being alone in a secluded area. I watch them jostling each other as they walk away.

One of the boys drops back and turns to give a piercing wolf whistle with his fingers in his mouth before rejoining his friends. What is going through their minds as they scream abuse at the mental patient, then wolf whistle? Maybe I'm easy prey? Maybe they'll do the mental case a favour. The crazy, fucked-up girl is begging for it; she'll be grateful for the attention.

A dog walker passes in front of me. The black Labrador stops in his tracks at my feet as if I've interrupted his line of scent. He looks me in the eye, panting with his tongue flopped to the side. He looks as if he's smiling. I smile back. 'Thanks,' I say, and the dog trots away, glancing back at me once – still smiling.

I look up, glad to see that the boys have gone.

Tension racks up as I continue to walk. I try to remember Izzy's action list for returning to school, but it's lost in the muddle in my head.

When I walk through the school front gate, my mind straightens a little, like a turbulent stream forced through a grille. In the corridor, the place feels weird: alien and yet horribly familiar.

A HUSH COMES over the Maths room when I arrive for first period, quickly followed by low murmurings as people clock me. Most of them wouldn't know, or care, about why I've been out of school for so long, but there will have been rumours.

I walk in the direction of Mia and Ada at the back of the room but I'm intercepted by a girl I hardly know, Tammy. 'Hey, Charley, where have you been? Someone said you had a baby. Is that true?'

'No, Tammy.' I smile weakly as I dodge around her, praying that this isn't the story of my absence.

Mia's group goes silent when I reach them. My heart sinks and the knot in my stomach tightens as I look across their faces and ready myself for rejection. I see Ada and she smiles at me, opening her arms for a hug. Two of the girls exchange a look of amusement at my being there, a joke about the hospital perhaps.

'Good to see you, Charley,' Mia says, to my surprise. Before I can respond, Mr Sparks scuffles in, carrying too much in his arms, shouting at the class to sit down while he drops bits of paper on his way to his desk. Mia offers up a chair and I sit next to her.

Chapter 43
Home - Day 5

I've been back at school for three days now, and every day has been tough. Mia is unpredictable. One minute she's my best friend, and the next she barely acknowledges me – just blanks me. And she's still got it in for Danny.

I've tried to steer clear of Danny in school just to keep things on a level with Mia and the girls, but it's getting difficult. I miss him.

She's stepped things up today, making jokes about him in the canteen. I try to keep out of it, but the rest of the girls are all laughing just as Danny appears at the end of our table. He stands next to me, his head down to avoid looking at the others, his eyes on me. He already looks so disappointed and I feel really awkward with him here in front of Mia and the others. Then Mia puts the boot in. 'What is it, Moon Face?'

Ada frowns. 'Mia, come on...'

'What?' Mia feigns innocence. 'It's a beautiful round face, that's all.'

Danny looks at me for support and I shrivel in my seat. 'Danny, let's chat later, eh?' I say, thinking I just need to avoid a confrontation. I can't afford to slip again like before. Danny walks out, saying nothing.

I call after him, but Mia cuts me off, yelling, 'Moon Face, don't go!', to the delight of the girls.

Danny's pain still lingers in the air when Matt struts into the canteen. I've not seen him because he hasn't been in school much, but I know Mia is in the process of hooking up with him, so I knew it was only a matter of time before I'd have to face him. I wanted to tell Mia about him, what he did. But the words never come.

He approaches with his usual swagger. And the oily, sculpted hair perched on his head in a curl. My heart races. The sight of him takes me straight back to his kitchen: the fear, the disturbed look in his eye and the pain in my shoulder. My mind spins. How could it possibly be fair that he gets to swan around as if nothing's happened?

He says hi to Mia and kisses her on the lips, then turns to me. 'They let you out, then, Charley?' He laughs and drapes his arm around Mia's shoulder. I am dizzy with anger and fear, not sure whether I should punch him in the face or walk away but unable to do either. I feel sorry for Mia. I say nothing but look straight into Matt's eyes. I can read nothing, no hint of acknowledgement of what we both know happened: his attack, the police, his caution.

I wonder about Katherine, and how Mia has managed to prise Matt from her clutches without getting a kicking.

Mia speaks again, breaking the silence. 'So, it's next Saturday, the Arena audition.'

Matt nods at her then turns back to me. 'You fancy joining, Charley, a bit of backing vocals?' He has a smug look on his face. Before I can say anything, Ada is pleading with me to join, with guitar as well as backing vocals. She looks at me expectantly.

I avoid looking at Matt, and a glimmer of excitement rises in me. The chance to play in a band, at the Arena. My heart tells me to go for it, but my head reminds me that there's no way I can occupy the same space as Matt, not for anything. 'I don't think so,' I say.

'Charley, please, we need you,' says Ada.

I look her in the eye and find I am nodding slowly. I tell myself that I am strong enough, that Matt won't dictate what I do.

I feel excited, then. And we agree to rehearse after school. If I have the music, I can block out Matt, and maybe I can move on.

Chapter 44
Home - Day 7

The mood in the car is solemn as Mum pulls into the hospital grounds. I do *want* to see Violet, but for reasons I can't get hold of, I'm scared. The last time I saw her face was on the bank of the river at Hillside.

Mum drops me at the front of the main building, promising to pick me up later. I head to the entrance and step through the automatic doors.

I'm pleased to see the hand sanitiser and pump it three times. It gives a comforting stinging sensation and a rapid cooling as it evaporates, and I imagine the germs evaporating with it. I resist the urge to pump some more and head through to the reception area.

The warm, germ-laden air slows me down and a dryness catches in my throat. I try to stop myself breathing too heavily for fear of the hospital germs getting deep inside my lungs.

I can't remember if I touched the door as I came into the reception. The door will probably be the most contaminated surface in the whole hospital, and the hospital is probably the most contaminated building in the town.

I take a breath and settle myself before pressing the call button for the lift.

When I get to Violet's ward, a woman with short dyed silver hair and glasses approaches me in the foyer where she'd been getting some water from the cooler.

'You must be Charley,' she says with a warm smile, her hand on my arm.

'Are you Violet's mum?'

She nods. 'Good of you to come. Violet's not very good company, though, I'm afraid. There's no news to speak of; we're just praying for her to come back to us now. Thanks to you, she has a chance, however small.' She sits on a chair up against the wall next to the water cooler and motions for me to join her.

I sit and look down at my feet for a moment. 'What do you mean by *small* chance?'

'The prognosis is not good. I don't want to give you false hope.' She pauses. 'She's suffered for long enough. It's all down to the medication, unfortunately; we could never seem to get the right balance. Her biological mother also suffers. She has it mostly under control now with the right pills, but she's had it hard too.' She looks down the corridor as if waiting for someone to arrive. 'We got the worst of the mania under control when she went into Hillside.'

'Mania?'

'That's what brought it to a head, what led to Hillside. A few months back, she slipped into some unusual behaviours, out of character.' She pauses. 'She would get quite hyperactive, speaking so fast and incoherently. She deteriorated quickly and was hallucinating by the time we got her some help.'

'Sounds terrifying.'

'It was, for all of us. It was horrible. Poor Violet. They had her sedated and on anti-psychotic medication that seemed to work. But the low moods were something we never got under control.'

'She'll get there,' I say.

Violet's mum turns to me and smiles unconvincingly. 'She's had some pretty tough times in her little life, but this is the worst. The doctors don't think she's coming through it this time.'

The pain in her expression scares me. Her eyes glaze over and fill with tears. 'You need to know that,' she says, placing her hand on mine. I see that she's serious. I'm shocked at the thought that Violet might not make it through, might not wake up.

'She'll come through,' I say firmly.

She smiles. 'How are *you* doing, anyway? Have you been discharged now?'

'Yes. I'm getting there.'

'That's as much as you can hope for, I think. You just need to keep battling. You're so young. You have so many wonderful experiences ahead of you, so much life to live yet.' She seems to drift into her own thoughts again. 'She told us so much about you, Charley, and Max and Archie. She's fond of you all.'

We are quiet again before she asks if I want to see Violet. She says that she's about to be taken for some tests, but I might be able to see her before she goes, or I could wait until she's back.

'I need to see her.'

Violet's mum nods gently and leads me to the ward, leaving me alone with her daughter.

She's lying on her back with her eyes closed and arms by her side. She breathes deeply and steadily, each breath with the help of a mechanical device and tube connected to the mask on her face. Her hair is immaculate, recently brushed. There is a smattering of cards on her bedside table. I approach the chair next to the bed where a magazine is propped open at a cross-word puzzle. I carefully move it to the side and sit down, leaning in towards Violet.

Her face is pale, reflecting the white LED light

from above her bed. I put my hand on hers. It's soft and cold with a tacky feel of moisturiser.

'Hi, Violet. It's Charley,' I whisper, taking a look around, feeling oddly self-conscious. 'I just wanted to see if you were OK... I mean, I wanted to see you.' I raise my voice above the sound of her breathing support. 'I miss you; we all do.' The bed next to Violet's has a curtain pulled around. It's quiet and I wonder if there's anyone in there.

'I wanted to ask you about some stuff, so I hope you're planning to wake up soon?' She looks helpless, so young and vulnerable. I can't *feel* her. It's as if she's already gone and there's just a shell. I cry then. For Violet. And for her parents. I cry for others too, like those at Hillside that are fighting for some kind of a life, wading through the sticky, sinking bog of mental illness, either desperate to keep their heads above the surface to breathe, or worn out trying. Relenting. Slowly disappearing.

I look up to see a nurse walking towards us with Violet's mum. I wipe the tears from my face and stand up. Violet's mum pulls me into a hug.

'Can I wait?' I say.

'Of course. She'll only be a few minutes – why don't you get some tea from the café downstairs and then come back up?'

I make my way back to the lift and my chest feels so empty it's like I left a part of me back on the ward.

THE COFFEE GIVES ME A BOOST. I'm both high and exhausted at the same time. On the way back up in the lift, the momentary weightless feeling after each acceleration makes me dizzy.

On the ward, I look towards Violet's bed, the last one on the left-hand side. My peripheral vision is hazy, as if I'm staring down a long tunnel with just Violet at the end. My feet are stuck to the floor and I stand at the entrance to the ward feeling as though there's no hope left in me. As my eyes regain some control, Violet comes into focus. There is someone at the foot of her bed sat motionless on a chair. The same chair I was sitting on before. I guess that it's Violet's mum.

I start walking, and within a few metres it's clear that it's not Violet's mum. They look towards me and stand. It's a girl, perhaps twenty-something. I stop about thirty feet away from her. She looks straight at me. She's about five foot six with long, curly, unkempt hair, her clothes worn and faded to the same homogenous brown-green colour, loose-fitting around her skinny frame. She looks fit, athletic, poised in her dirty white trainers. She's on her toes as though she's ready to run.

She looks at me as if she knows me, but her demeanour is defensive, almost as though she's scared. She brushes her hair away from her eyes, then glances back at the double doors behind her at the end of the ward as though she's daring me to move first.

A nurse is suddenly in my face, blocking my view and asking who I'm here to visit. I lean to see around her, but the girl has gone and the double doors are settling back to their closed position.

'Elsie?' I breathe. 'What the fuck?' I brush past the nurse, ignoring her schoolteacher expression of disapproval. I run straight through the double doors and look up and down into the stairwell.

Nothing.

Back on the ward, Violet's heart monitor bleeps, providing the only evidence that she's still alive. Wires and tubes snake from different parts of her body to the machines at her bedside. Her face is squashed by the oxygen mask and her head is turned upwards, contorted as though she's frozen in pain. She looks absent. My head pounds and I squeeze my eyes closed to block out the light. I rub my temples, easing the pain radiating from the centre of my brain.

I try to picture the girl's face, but it escapes me. It was Elsie. I think. But it could have been anyone. Just half an hour ago I would have laughed at the thought of Elsie being real. Being here.

I picture Violet lying in the river.

'What now?' I say, but no one answers my question.

Chapter 45
Home - Day 10

I'm out with Mum, Dad and Lucas in the carvery on the corner of the High Street. I told Mum about the girl at the hospital, but she said it was probably just one of Violet's friends. It all feels like a dream now, like it never happened.

Lucas kicks me under the table. 'What is it, space head?'

'Sorry...'

'Worried about Violet?'

I nod. Something feels wrong but I can't pin it down. I stare at my food. My sense of control is slipping away. Confusion scratches at my resolve to contain the anxiety and my mind turns to the razor blade in my purse. It's there just for comfort. Something in case of emergency. Plan B. I won't use it. I just need to know that it's there.

'I need some air.' I stand.

'I'll come,' Lucas says, but I shake my head and Mum puts her hand on his.

'Give her a minute,' she says, giving me a nod.

I leave the restaurant without another word, not confident that I won't throw up if I open my mouth. I dodge between the tables and stumble out through the door at the back onto a paved area, almost bundling into a couple dressed for a night out. They give me a wide berth.

I sit on the pavement, unable to hold myself up and desperately trying to keep the anxiety from spiralling. It creeps up through seven to eight. I'm so close to spinning out. I *have* to contain it. I stand, try to walk, to see things, to distract myself.

As soon as I'm on my feet, my head explodes into a spin. I steady myself with both hands on the back wall of the restaurant. I scream: a long, gut-wrenching roar of defiance.

I will not pass out.

I will not let it swallow me up.

People look at me as if I'm a freak. I breathe: in for three... hold... out for five. My hands remain attached to the wall like I'm trying to stop the building from toppling onto me. I scream again: louder, more defiant, guttural. Then back to the breathing. The spin slows, and I push myself off the wall and stand unaided.

I need to go back inside.

I can't.

They'll be wondering where I am. They'll be worried.

'Fucking shit,' I say aloud. I walk to gather myself. I can't go back in. I pull out my phone and message Mum.

Me: Anxious. I need to walk.

Mum: I'll come...

Me: No, stay. I'll see you at home.

I put my phone away. The post-panic depression envelops me as I walk, and the intrusive thoughts are working overtime. I'm useless. Hillside has done nothing. I will never be free of it.

Darkness closes, pushing me down into my feet so that I can barely lift them.

I break into a zombie-jog. How far is the hospital? A mile, maybe? Two? My head clears a little and I accelerate into a run.

I'm in flight. I run hard. Endorphins battle with the anxiety. I run faster, pushing myself.

I reach the hospital and rest, catching my breath. I look up at the vast red-brick façade of the back of the building. A man in blue overalls steps out through a service door, arms clasped around bits of cardboard and plastic. The double doors swing closed behind him but rest together without clicking shut. I slip through, up some stairs and into a busy hospital corridor, the clinical smell filling my nose. I turn left and follow the signs to the wards.

I step into a lift and push the button for the fifth floor, then lean back on the cold, stainless-steel wall. My thoughts drift and stick on an image of the razor in my purse, tucked away in the inside pocket where it has always been. I haven't cut my arm since before I went into Hillside. I push the thoughts away.

I spill out of the lift and duck into a disabled toilet. I lock the door and step back against the wall, breathing heavily. After a minute, I pull my bag around in front of me and open my purse, carefully picking out the blade. I look up at the ceiling and grunt in frustration, pulling back the sleeve of my red cardigan. The scars taunt me: I'm a failure; ungrateful; selfish; a waste of NHS resources.

I let out another grunt, a plea for someone, something, *anything* to help me. My hand shakes as I hold the blade above my arm, hovering over the old scars. I clench my fist and I can see the veins in my wrist.

Someone pounds on the door. Three knocks come again. They pull me from my trance and I jerk my hand away from my arm, staring at the door, eyes wide.

'Are you OK in there?' A female voice. I stay quiet. She'll go away. After she's called twice more with no response, there's a jangle of keys and the door swings open. Seeing me motionless against the wall, the nurse frowns and looks around the cubicle as if expecting there to be someone with me. As her eyes are busy, I let my sleeve drop back down and slip the blade into my back pocket.

'Can I help you?' She looks at my bag. She is tall, six foot, maybe, with a long, grey face. The name 'Harper' is on her badge.

'I need to get to ward six.'

Nurse Harper opens the door, steps out and motions with a nod for me to follow her.

'There,' she says, pointing. 'Take a left at the end and you'll see the ward entrance. Visiting time has just finished so you might have to come back tomorrow, but you can see. You'll have to press the buzzer.'

I slip through the door of Violet's ward as a middle-aged couple is leaving. The lights on the ward are dimmed. The only sounds are the goodbye words of a family around the bed nearest me. All the other kids on the ward are reading or watching a screen with head-phones on.

Violet's bed is the last on the left. The curtain has been pulled around. I push through it. Her bed is empty and the sheets have been stripped, with clean linen neatly folded on the side of the bed, ready to be re-made. She must have been moved. My heart pounds.

Everything's OK, she's just been moved to another ward, or taken for some tests, or whatever. I scan the surfaces next to Violet's bed. They've been cleaned, cleared of her stuff. There's nothing of Violet here.

Something catches my eye on the floor and I lean down to pick it up. It's a get-well card to Violet from her grandparents. The evidence in front of me is clear, but – there has to be another explanation.

A nurse walks through the double doors at the end of the ward and looks at me with a mixture of annoyance and concern. We lock eyes and I see the whole story in her expression, her eyes, the way she's standing, the slump of her shoulders.

'She's not gone,' I say.

'Who are you?' she asks gently.

'She's not gone,' I say again.

The nurse takes a step closer to me. 'Are you a friend of Violet?'

'Where is she?'

She reaches out a hand and I stare at it, afraid to touch her, as if it would make all of this real. 'I'm sorry, love,' she says.

'But she never meant this to happen. It was an accident.'

'Why don't you come with me?' I look at her outstretched hand. It looks weathered, creased and worn from years of over-washing, like mine, but for different reasons.

I need to run. I need to get away.

I push past her and through the double doors. I go up, taking two steps at a time, accelerating until my thigh muscles burn and my lungs can no longer take in air. The number on the wall tells me I've got to the seventh floor. I go again, collapsing when I get to the eighth, the last floor before the roof exit. I lean against the wall and pull my bag from around my neck, breathing heavily.

The sign above the door says 'Service Zone'. I push through to a corridor where the lights are off, then enter a side room and flop down among stacks of freshly cleaned and folded sheets and bed covers. I cry then, and it's like an explosion of emotion that's been held back for too long. There's no one to hear me, to be unsettled by me, to think I'm a freak. So I scream out the tears and bury myself in the hospital linen.

I WAKE to the sound of washing machines and tumble dryers whirring outside the door. It's dark, but light seeps under the doorway. I look at my watch and I'm surprised that I've only been out for about twenty minutes. It feels as though I've been asleep for hours. I remember Violet and I hope for a second that it was a dream, that she's not really gone. My stomach sinks.

Where am I? My bag lies next to me and I remember the razor. I curl up on my side, hugging my knees tight to my chest and looking at the light in the gap under the door. I take a deep breath, releasing it slowly and feeling my heart begin to slow. I imagine my regular heart beats are the bleeps of Violet's life support.

I sit upright and find the blade tucked in my back pocket, then turn it over in my hand. I rub my thumb along its length for a moment. I hear Violet's words in my head and stand – then throw the blade into the bin next to the door.

I look at my phone: two missed calls from Mum. I message her that I'm OK and I'll be home later. Then I message Danny that I need to run.

I tell him to catch me up.

Retracing my steps from earlier, I burst through the service door at the back of the hospital and out into the cool evening air. It's still light. I race towards home, pushing, stretching myself.

When I get to the outskirts of town, I slow, then stop and rest for a moment, at a place where I can see Butser Hill in the distance. I tighten the strap on my bag and tie my cardigan around my waist, over my bag so that it keeps it still as I run. I tie my hair up, wiping the sweat from my face.

I wonder if Danny got my text.

At the post office I turn into the lane that leads down to my house and the foot of Butser Hill. I glide past home and through the field towards the mouth of the woods. The evening dew soaks through my trainers before I get into the trees and blisters rub on both of my feet.

The woods are empty, cool and cloaked in gloom. I'm not scared anymore; there's nothing here that scares me. Nothing left for the fear to feed on.

I get to my usual halfway point. Danny is already there, sat on a log. He stands and flicks away a cigarette, stepping towards me.

I take him in my arms, holding him close. 'She's gone,' I say. 'Violet. She's dead.'

Part Seven
Freedom

Chapter 46
Home - Day 24

Max's old estate car is a beast in dark green, with tinted windows at the back. She turns the key, and the engine whirs, splutters and kicks into life. 'Purrs like a cat,' she says, smiling.

'I guess.' I wonder whether it will move at all. It's big and tatty, and the front seats are like spongy armchairs. The smell is a musty but not unpleasant mix of dog and vintage furniture, with the hint of something sweet: pine, maybe. The dogs are nosing through the bars between the boot and the back seat.

'My foster dad is an enthusiast. He rebuilt it from two old scrapped Mark 3 Cortinas. He's working on another old one like this but smaller and a bit sporty. I'm helping him, finding my way around a Haynes Manual and a box of spanners.'

She pulls away and onto the southern road, out of town.

It's the eve of Violet's funeral and Max has been over at mine since last night. She wanted to be here first thing for her *adventure* as she called it. We spent the evening in my room, drinking Mum's cider and smoking roll-ups out the window. It was the first time we'd really hung out since Violet's death. We'd spoken but never seemed to be able to get it together to hook up. I've been to school most days. The first week I was in a daze and I barely remember being there. And these last few days I've bunked off more than I've been in.

I cried a lot last night.

Max didn't.

My tears turned to anger as I got through more cider.

We had Archie in Hillside on speakerphone until about midnight, when he got a final warning from the nurses to turn his phone off. Archie and I could hardly speak to each other without one of us sobbing. Archie hung up, then Max and I talked until about two o'clock and dropped off to sleep on my bed. Her dog, Misty, had snuggled up with BB on the sofa.

Max stamps on the brakes. The dogs stumble up against the bars in the back. She pulls into a lay-by and unclicks her seat belt, turning to face me. The dogs perk up, expectant faces at the bars. It wasn't until we were on our way to Max's car with the dogs that she finally told me her plan – her *adventure*: to break Archie out of the H-blocks, then cross the river and head up to the old oak.

'Right, Archie can't get his window restrictor off, he's tried. He's no Violet. So, he has to get out another way, out the front door.'

'You are kidding?' I say slowly.

A familiar smile appears on Max's face. 'It's OK, we have a plan.' She pulls out her phone and dials the Hillside reception. She pops chewing gum into her mouth and puts her finger to her lips.

'Hello?' she says, in a squeaky American accent, chewing her gum into the phone. 'This is Archie's father's assistant, Maxine!' she shouts. 'I'm coming over to get Archie like we agreed, but I'm stuck in this god-damn traffic so I'm running late.'

She listens. 'No, we can't lose more time, we're late already. Archie's head nurse or whatever told me that the exit drill is not necessary.' She pauses. 'Look, sweet-heart, we have a serious family crisis...' Max is sounding more desperate. With the accent and exag-gerated facial expressions, I struggle to keep from laughing.

She continues: 'That's right, and he'll be with us until next week. OK, so I will be there in... twelve minutes, according to the navigation thing. Please make sure Archie is out in the car park so I can swing by without losing any more time.' There's a pause as the other person responds.

'Thank you; you're a diamond. GPS now says ten minutes.' Max hangs up and beams at me.

'Where'd you get that voice? How long are we taking Archie for?'

'Long enough. For the funeral. And for a bit of hanging out.'

'How are we going to get him out without the nurses seeing us?'

Max leans across my lap and tugs a long brown wig out of the glovebox. Still grinning, she carefully puts it on, covering her short, scarlet-red hair. She brushes it down with her hands and fiddles with her nose ring. She uses the rear-view mirror to apply some lipstick, looks at me and pouts.

'Oh my g— Maxine!' We erupt into laughter. Max finishes off the disguise with some oversized, round, dark-rimmed glasses. 'What about me? They'll see me.'

Max nods to the back seat. 'Tinted windows. Keep your head down; the nurse won't come over to the car, anyway.' She smiles and clicks her seat belt on, and I clamber into the back seat. Before Max pulls away, she sends a ten-minute-warning text to Archie.

WE PASS the sign for the hospital. I'm breathless at being back at Hillside. Max slows and glances at me as she pulls up to the gate. She winds down her window and presses the buzzer next to the silver keypad. A disembodied metallic voice comes through the intercom to ask our business, and Max revives Maxine, the impatient American assistant.

The gate clunks and slowly opens. I slump down in the back seat, staying out of sight. Max edges forward into the car park. 'Can't see Archie,' she whispers.

'No way is this going to work.' The little faith I had in Max's plan starts to slip away. Max keeps her speed low, giving Archie time to get out of the building. It feels as if we are the getaway car in a bank job and Max is about to floor it away from a shower of bullets.

I'm excited and nervous. I peek over the window ledge as Max circles around and stops in front of the main hospital doors, engine running. No sign of anyone. The doors are about fifty feet away from us and remain closed. They are close enough that if a familiar nurse comes out with Archie, there is a chance they'll recognise Max. Just the sight of the battered old car would be enough to raise suspicion. We wait.

'Come on, Archie,' Max whispers under her breath, looking across and through the passenger window. She leans over, pulls the door handle and swings open the passenger door, ready for Archie to get in. I imagine him launching himself into the car as Max speeds away.

Finally, the hospital door opens, just as the car stalls. 'Shit,' Max croaks the word as if her throat has closed up. She turns the key and the engine whirs but doesn't start. We look towards the hospital. Archie isn't alone. Nurse Simon is with him. They walk together down the pathway towards us, Simon a step or two behind Archie, who is wide-eyed, as if the whole thing is about to go pear-shaped. Max tries the engine again. This time it nearly catches, only to fizzle and die. It sounds as though the battery is giving up.

'What do we do?' I blurt. Max ignores me and tries once more. Archie and Simon are just a few feet from the car. It fires. Max revs the engine, and I breathe a sigh of relief. 'Go! We have to go, Max, he'll see us.'

'We can't just go. Calm down: he won't see you through the tinted window and there's no way he'll recognise me.'

'You're kidding; he's not fucking stupid.'

'Shh!

Archie reaches the car. Simon opens the door and Archie gets in, his body stiff. He hugs his small overnight bag to his chest and sits facing forward, unable to look at Max.

'Hello, Archie,' Maxine says, 'your father is looking forward to seeing you.' She looks as if she's starting to enjoy herself. 'Appreciate your help, Sir.' Max leans over Archie and thanks Simon, who bends to lean into the window. I hold my breath and squeeze my body tighter behind the front passenger seat. I silently curse Max. I can *hear* the amusement in her voice.

'No problem. You take care, Archie, and I'll see you on Sunday. Remember that we are here if you need to call and you can come back earlier if you need to.' His tone is neutral and I sense an uneasiness, not his usual effusive positivity. I silently will Max to go, to put her foot down.

'Thank you again.' Max's accent is thickening and her tone verges on flirtatious. I cringe, trying to poke Max from behind her seat. She finally puts the car into gear, prompting Simon to stand back. He gives the roof a short tap with his fingers. He looks into the boot of the car as Max pulls away, a quizzical look on his face when he sees the two dogs staring back at him.

Max pulls up to the gate and we wait for it to swing open. As soon as there is enough space to get through, she puts her foot down and pulls onto the main road with the front wheels spinning. We chorus a scream of relief and excitement as she accelerates away.

~

Max parks the car a mile or so from Hillside House in a Forestry Commission car park next to the river. She nods towards the path. 'That leads to the footbridge we crossed on the way to the old oak.' She walks around to the back of the car to collect the dogs.

We step through a kissing gate and Max lets the dogs loose along the narrow pathway. She and Archie walk on, deep in conversation. I follow, happy to give them some space. The bushes either side of the path are damp from an earlier shower, and the air is fresh, washed clean by the rain.

We emerge with the dogs into a wide open space by the river. The floodplains stretch out ahead of us with the silvery watercourse carving its way through the middle. The place feels magical.

The dogs skirt the shallow edge of the water, bounding ahead. I follow Max and Archie without urgency towards the footbridge. A splash to my right catches my attention. A fish rolls over, piercing the surface of the water then sliding out of sight. 'Wow,' I say aloud, looking up for someone to share in my wonder.

I eventually step onto the footbridge to join Archie and Max. We sit with our legs hanging above the trickling water, silently taking in the view downstream.

Archie sighs. 'Good to see you guys,' he says. 'I still

can't believe it,' he adds, his voice low. 'Our little Violet.'

'She'd had enough,' Max says, her gaze fixed on the surface of the water. 'She'd been in there for too long.' She nods towards Hillside. 'They could never get her pills right. She was up and down the whole time.'

'You think she gave up?' Archie asks.

Max says, 'I think she made a decision to move past it. Not to kill herself. I don't think she meant to do that.'

'What do you mean then, Max?' I ask.

'I'm not sure. It's like she was running away.'

The only sound is the trickle of the stream under our feet. I take a deep breath. 'Like Elsie?' I say.

Max nods.

'So how'd she end up in the water?' Archie says. 'Too many pills? An accident?'

'Maybe,' Max says.

Archie slumps lower. 'She was so sweet. She deserved to be happy. It's not fair.'

'There's not much fairness going on when it comes to happiness.'

We sit in silence, watching the bubbling of the water as it rushes around the bridge supports.

The breeze has dropped and the sun warms my back. I pull off my hoodie. Black and white cows graze in bunches in the distant fields. I look downstream and cup my hands around my eyes. It's as if I'm levitating above the surface of the river, in the middle of the divide between hospital and hill, between illness and freedom, old and new.

'Shall we walk?' Archie says.

The three of us start up the side of the valley, more animated now as we follow the dogs along the wide gravel path through the trees.

'So you think Elsie's up here today?' Max asks.

I shrug. We emerge from the treeline near the top of the hill. The old oak comes into view. Up close, in daylight, it's spectacular. Its chunky lower branches sag like fat arms with elbows touching the ground to prop itself up, and the evening sun filters through the leaves to create a peaceful orange-brown glow at its edges.

'Wow. I climbed up there, in the dark,' says Archie as we get nearer.

'With nothing on,' says Max. Archie laughs. We get to the base of the tree and offload our coats and bags onto the floor, away from the scattered ash remains of our previous campfire. Our makeshift seats are still positioned around the space. I look over towards the hospital, still visible in the fading light, and I think of Violet, our time in Hillside.

Max pulls a plastic tub out of her bag with sausages to cook, a bag of rolls and ketchup.

Archie grins at her. 'You're the best, Max.'

THE GLOW of the sun slips away behind the trees just as the flames from Max's fire die down.

'Right,' Max says, pulling from her bag something that looks like a stack of mini tent poles slotted together. They turn out to be skewers, long enough to spike a sausage to cook over the fire.

'Max, you really are something else,' I say and she smiles as we rest our skewers over a log to cook the sausages above the embers.

'How's school, Charley?' Archie says.

'Settling in, doing some music with Ada and Mia for the Arena competition. I was going to mention it, Archie. Hope you don't mind me joining a rival band?'

'No, it's fine,' Archie says. 'With Mia, though? Seriously?'

'I know. It's difficult. I've not got long left before I can get out of there so I'm just trying to play the game a bit.' Max and Archie are silent. 'And there's this audition thing that's a good opportunity.'

'Who's in the group then, for the audition?' says Archie.

'Just me, Mia and Ada... and Matt.'

'Matt?' Max spits. 'Not the same Matt that assaulted you? The one that tried to *rape* you, Charley?'

'I'm keeping my distance,' I say, feeling defensive.

'Shit, Charley.'

'What have you said to Danny about the music?' Archie says.

'Nothing really. I haven't spoken to him about it.'

'I thought you and Danny were cool?' asks Max.

'I don't know, Max. I'm just taking it a day at a time.' Max and Archie both go quiet and it feels like a judgy silence.

'How long do you think you've got left in Hillside, Archie?' I ask, needing to divert the conversation away from me.

'Not sure. I've had some good sessions this week, some progress, so it could be a week or so, maybe.'

Max looks at Archie. 'Where's your PTSD rooted? Where did it come from?'

Archie contemplates for a moment as Max wipes her hands on her jeans and reaches for her rolling tobacco.

Archie says, 'It comes from when I killed my mum.'

Max and I both look at him with our mouths open, waiting for some qualification, *something* more to explain what he means.

'It was my fault, no doubt about it.' He stares into the fire, unblinking. Max and I remain silent, lost for words until Archie lifts his head. 'It was a car crash. Mum was driving. I was next to her.'

'What happened?' I ask, glancing over at Max as she finishes rolling cigarettes for all three of us.

'She pulled out of a side street in Dad's fancy fucking car with its intelligent monitoring system, advance warning technology and side impact protection airbags coming out from all fucking angles.' He pauses for breath. 'She was turning right. Truck coming the other way.' Archie's hands re-enact the manoeuvre and the crash. 'She didn't see it. She didn't see the massive fucking truck because she was talking to me, *arguing* with me.'

Max throws me a roll-up followed by a lighter. I draw on my cigarette and look into the fire, following Archie's gaze and trying, failing, to imagine what it would be like to feel responsible for the death of a parent.

'Mum got the full force in the driver's seat. She didn't stand a chance. No airbag in the world can deflect a lump of metal that big.' He looks at me again and silent tears edge down his cheeks. His angry-with-the-world demeanour is crumbling. 'Truck driver was OK, thankfully, not a scratch,' he says, taking a drag on his roll-up.

'How badly were you hurt?' I ask, my eyes prickling with tears.

'Smacked my head pretty bad and broke my left arm. Knocked me out. They put me under for a few days in the hospital while my head recovered from the trauma. The physical trauma. I nearly didn't make it, apparently. Shouldn't have made it by all accounts. Many a time I've wished I hadn't,' he adds quietly.

'I'm sorry, Archie,' I say. Max is silent, gazing at the fire and smoking her cigarette.

'I get flashbacks, you know,' he says, looking at Max, 'to the moment of impact and just before. They say it's part of the PTSD. I say it's karma.'

'Don't say that, Archie,' I whisper. 'It was an accident.'

'Accident,' he repeats, almost whispering but then becoming agitated. 'Accident. It's a funny word, don't you think? It implies that it couldn't be helped. Like, oh never mind, just one of those things.' He pauses. 'There was nothing *accidental* about it. More like a fuck-up, a distraction, a pointless argument. That's what I'd call it. It wasn't an *accident*. Actually, that's what my dad calls it too: a fuck-up on my part. That's what he reminds me of whenever I see him, particularly when the single malt comes out. My fault. If you think about it, analyse it, you'd have to agree with him.'

We are silent then. I can't find any words. The glow of the embers fades. Archie uses his skewer to flick a half-burnt stick back into the fire where the flames take it. His face lights up as he rests back on his makeshift seat.

'Shoes,' he says, throwing his cigarette butt into the fire. Max and I exchange looks.

'Shoes,' he says again, looking up and exhaling smoke. 'That's what we were arguing about. Mum didn't see why I needed to spend so much on one pair of trainers. So, I was being a total spoilt twat, wanting these stupid latest things. I can't even remember what they were.' His eyes glaze over. I look down at his feet, at the threadbare, flaking old high-top Converse that may once have been white.

They kind of made sense to me then.

Chapter 47
Home - Day 25

I wake to the sound of voices downstairs. I slip out of bed, feeling the pain in the soles of both feet from last night's walking. The trek back to the car and the drive home in the Beast had been quiet.

Archie is sat with Mum in the kitchen. He has tea and toast in front of him and they are talking like old friends. Archie is wearing red checked pyjama bottoms and a baggy old *Star Wars* T-shirt. He has his familiar bed hair, flat on one side. My groggy morning greeting is met with a similar response from Archie. I sit opposite him and grab some toast from the stack in the middle of the table while Mum gets up to make more tea.

'It's been a crazy few days,' I say to Archie. He leans back in his chair and crosses his long legs, cradling his mug of tea. He gives me a searching look and I sense he's silently challenging me again on my choices with Mia and the band. I ignore him.

Mum puts a mug of tea in front of me. 'So how long are you on home leave for, Archie?' she asks.

Archie looks at me, then back to Mum. 'Just a few days. For the funeral, and to catch up with Dad.'

'Max is picking us up,' I say. 'For the funeral.'

'Are you two going to be OK?' Mum asks, and we both nod. 'And how were things with Mia, at school?'

I tell her that it's OK and that it'll take a while to adjust. I don't want to get into this discussion now. 'I need to think about things a bit, figure out where I fit.'

After breakfast, we head out to wait for Max. As we reach the end of my garden path, we hear the grumble and splutter of the Beast. The battered old Ford comes into view, Max wearing sunglasses, her arm hanging out of her open window. She has a cigarette in her hand and a thumping tune rattles the otherwise peaceful Wednesday morning.

She pulls up and Archie and I jump in, Archie taking the front seat. I shout over the dubstep to beg for some *proper* music. Max's phone is connected to the car stereo, wires hanging below the radio and electrical tape holding it all together. 'Nice set-up, Max!' I shout.

'That's my foster dad's creation,' she shouts back, flicking the remains of her roll-up out of the window.

Archie turns the volume down as he scans the music on Max's phone.

Max lowers her voice to a normal level. 'I only asked if it was possible,' she says, 'and that was it. He was out with his wire snips and electrical tape and this is the result. Not pretty, but it works.'

I smile and relax back into the sofa-like rear seat as Archie changes the music and turns up the volume. To the sound of the Pixies, we press on to the crematorium on the outskirts of the town.

ARCHIE and I find an empty pew and shuffle along to the end. People stream into the hall. Max joins us, squeezing past me and standing with Archie. 'Loads of people,' she says, looking towards the back.

Max tuts at Archie and tightens the knot of his tie up to the top button of his white shirt, then brushes some invisible dust from the arms of his suit jacket. His eyes are glassy and he avoids my gaze.

The hall fills. 'Violet has six adoptive siblings, she told me,' I say. I recognise Violet's adoptive mum, greeting people in the central aisle. She sees me and heads over.

I'm about to introduce the others, but Violet's mum gets there first. 'This looks like Max, and Archie?' she says. 'I've heard so much about you.' Max looks surprised. Violet's mum continues, 'I heard a lot about your adventures from Violet's phone calls.' She winks at me. 'You three were a great comfort to her.' She smiles, then turns back to her task of greeting people.

The service is mercifully short, with just one hymn and two readings. It feels as if we've just got here when we are all filing out.

One of Violet's sisters said a few words, and it felt odd. As she was preparing to speak, the atmosphere was tense. The hall was pin-drop silent. The doors at the back were open and there were people spilling out into the gardens, children playing outside. She spoke of how Violet would see the best in people, never judging by how they looked. For Violet, it was about who we were. It was about understanding each other. She finished with a request that we all make a promise. A promise not to leave Violet behind, but to take her with us, in our memories and in our thoughts.

WE LEAVE by a side door and the silence from Max and Archie tells me I'm not the only one choked up. I daren't yet open my mouth for the risk of my wobbling lip turning into a full-on wail.

We cross the grass and sit on a bench by the road,

facing the crematorium. The access road in front of the building has an extravagant expanse of grass on both sides, interspersed with trees of different ages and sizes. None on the scale of the old oak.

Archie rubs a tear from his cheek.

Max looks around at the grounds. 'Who knew there was so much green and pleasant land hidden away in here?'

'Seems almost a waste,' says Archie. He sniffs. 'You could get a couple of Astroturf pitches down there.' He points at the land the other side of the crematorium building.

'Only if they didn't mind the occasional scattering of ashes at half-time,' I say, at last brave enough to speak, although my voice wobbles a little.

'Are you allowed to have fun in a place of burial?' Archie says.

People file out of the main entrance, mostly in twos. Violet's adoptive mum and dad are lined up with Violet's siblings at the exit, shaking hands with people as they appear.

Three girls of about Violet's age exchange awkward handshakes and hugs with Violet's family. They totter down the steps and stand to the side, each of them taking out their mobile phone and proceeding to tap and swipe.

I reach for my own phone in my pocket and

realise I've left it at home. Then I feel a sense of freedom. I think of Danny, and the times we've talked about 'opting out', rejecting the slavery to social media. I've not consciously dropped any of that part of my life, but it's slipped down the priority list without me really noticing. I feel an odd sense of sadness for the three girls, even though they look happy enough.

'Look,' Max says. 'Nurse Simon.' She points at him as he walks slowly out of the main door in a loose-fitting pastel suit, light shirt and a thin black tie. 'He looks like someone from a Spandau Ballet tribute band.'

'There's Lisa,' I say, 'and the witch, Camilla. Did I tell you guys about the time I saw Camilla slap Jasmine round the face?'

Archie looks at me. 'What? No.'

'Doesn't surprise me,' says Max. 'She's not right, that woman. Then again, Jasmine has got to be one of the strangest girls I met in the H-blocks. Present company excepted. Although you were without doubt the strangest boy I met in there, Archie.'

'The *only* boy,' he says.

Max smiles. 'Very odd.'

Archie shrinks down in his seat. 'Are they looking this way?' He turns his body away from the crowd of people loitering outside the crematorium. 'I need to stay out of sight. I'm supposed to be on home leave with my dad.'

Max rolls her eyes. 'No one's looking, and even if they were, we're too far away for anyone to recognise you.'

Archie on the run from Hillside brings Elsie into my thoughts. She might even be here somewhere. She's been in hiding for so long she must naturally blend in with the background.

Archie sniffs, his eyes sparkling with tears.

'Let's go,' Max says. 'I've got an idea.'

'WHERE ARE WE GOING, MAX?' Archie asks from the back of the car.

'OK,' Max says, 'promise that you won't just say no. You'll think about it? Give it a go?'

'Give what a go?' Archie moans.

'You know I said about my foster mum being an artist?'

'No,' I say, honestly recalling nothing about her being an artist.

'Yes,' says Archie.

'Well, I thought we could get something done. Something to connect us. Forever.'

Archie sits forward, a deep frown. 'For fuck's sake

Max, tell us…'

'A tattoo,' Max blurts.

'She's a tattoo artist?' I say.

Max nods. She looks at me expectantly. The lights ahead turn green and she turns her attention back to the road and pushes the car into gear.

'You have something in mind?' I ask.

'A tattoo?' Archie exclaims from the back. 'I'm not getting a tattoo.'

'Why not?' I say.

'Because… it's… I don't know. We're not old enough, are we?'

'Near enough,' Max says.

'And who's to know?' I add.

'She's done a design for the inside of our arms,' says Max. 'It's good. And it connects the three of us with Violet.'

'Where is it?' asks Archie.

I think about the scars on my arms, and how they will work with a tattoo. I'm not even sure you can tattoo over scars.

'Not here,' Max says. 'She's already created a print. We just need to head to her studio and she can do all three of us.'

'I'm in,' I say, feeling brave. 'Archie?'

Archie says nothing and slumps back in his seat as Max pulls the car into a space around the back of the high street shops.

'Her studio is here?' I ask.

'On the high street,' Max says with a smile. 'Ready?'

I nod and we both turn to look at Archie.

He says, 'I'll need to see the design first. If it's crap...'

'It's not,' says Max, and we climb out of the car.

The studio is closed when we arrive at the front door. Max knocks and her foster mum opens up. She hugs Max. She's short, a similar height to Max at around five foot three or four. She has grey hair and round rimmed glasses, tattoos up both arms. She turns to Archie and pulls him into a tight hug. I hope for a minute that she won't do the same to me but before I can step back and out of the way she does the same with me. It's uncomfortable, but not painful. 'You guys,' she says. 'I've heard so much. Come in lovelies.' She beckons us into her little studio room. The blinds are drawn, so it's dark, with a single lamp on the table next to her equipment. 'Who's first?' she says.

'Can we see the design?' Archie says, edging around the outside of the room like it's dangerous to step into Max's mum's lair.

'I'll go first,' I say. 'But...' I pull up my sleeve and show Max's mum the scars on the inside of my arm.

She gives me a warm smile. 'That's OK,' she says.

'We can work with that. You want me to use the tattoo to conceal some of them?'

'No,' I say, too quickly. 'I mean, not really. But... I don't know. I'm not trying to hide them.'

She takes my hand and runs her other hand over my scars like they're the most normal thing in the world. 'It'll be fine, my love. We will create something beautiful.' She turns to her desk to retrieve a print of her design. 'Here,' she says, holding it up for me and Archie to see. It shows an ornate-looking capital letter V, for Violet, decorated with a vine, flowers and a semi-colon at its base. The whole image would fill about half of the space between the wrist and elbow on the inner arm.

It's beautiful, and I can see that Archie likes it too. 'What's the semi-colon?' asks Archie.

'It's a symbol of overcoming mental health difficulties,' says Max. 'It's like a *to be continued* thing. A symbol for a bit of solidarity against everything the likes of us suffer, like what Violet suffered. Solidarity against suicide, depression, addiction and whatever else.'

'It inspires strength and resilience in the face of what might seem impossible,' Max's mum says.

Archie holds the print, studying it. Slowly, he begins to smile. 'I like it,' he says, and we laugh.

'Sit down then, Charley,' Max's mum says, and I take a seat.

~

WE ARE quiet as we climb Butser Hill, under a clear blue sky and in warm sunshine. At the top, we shed our outer layers and squeeze onto the viewpoint bench together, Max in the middle. I look down at my wrist, still wrapped in cling film. 'Can we take this stuff off yet?'

Max pulls up her sleeve and starts to peel back the cling film. 'Should be OK now.'

'Your mum said to leave it a couple of hours,' says Archie.

'It's been nearly that,' I say, picking at the edges of the film.

Max gets hers off first. She studies the inside of her arm. I discard my cling film and place my arm alongside Max's. Archie is slow, but eventually he joins us and we admire the three identical tattoos. 'Violet will be with us forever,' Max says.

We sit back, and I open my arm to the cool breeze, which soothes the residual pain radiating from the sensitive skin on my inner arm. The tattoo covers some of the scars, but not in a way that looks like it's meant to hide them. The design seems to flow with them, twine around them.

Archie scrutinises his tattoo. 'Didn't realise it would hurt that much,' he says.

'No pain, no gain,' says Max.

The sun is heading towards the horizon and its glare obscures the full view of the oak. Archie studies the tree, squinting and shielding his eyes, proudly telling us that it's an oak, same as the one at Hillside.

'What are you doing tomorrow, Archie?' I ask.

'Sleeping.'

'We're doing some music after school,' I say. 'A rehearsal for the audition. Will you two come in and have a listen, tell me what you think?'

'Can do,' says Archie.

'Don't get *too* excited.'

Archie glares at me, agitated. 'Come on, Charley.'

'What?'

'Why are you hanging with that sex pest and his bitch of a girlfriend?' Archie's voice wobbles.

'It's the music.'

'Who are you are still trying to impress, Charley? Be honest with yourself.'

'It's an opportunity, I can't let it go.' I stare at him, willing him to roll with it. 'Come have a listen tomorrow, please?'

He sighs heavily, and his head drops. 'For you, I will. But don't leave me alone with the sex pest. In case

I forget that I fight like a girl and I end up taking a swing.' Archie snorts and Max reminds him that *fighting like a girl* would be a step up for him.

'Point taken,' Archie says.

I look at Max. 'Will you come too?'

'Wouldn't miss it,' she says. 'Someone needs to keep an eye on Archie.'

'Thanks. Come in the back entrance to the school. The music studio is right next to the back gate. No one will notice, and even if they do, they won't know you're not just one of the students.'

The sun has dipped further now, and its rays filter through the twisted branches of the oak, casting shadows on the field in front of us.

Chapter 48
Home - Day 26

I'm early for history class so I sit in the back row, keeping the seat next to me free for Danny. My nerves nag at me. I'm not sure how he's going to react, since I hung him out to dry that day in the canteen and I've barely responded to his messages over the past few days.

He walks in and glances at me, then moves to a seat on the other side of the room. I head over to him. He clocks me and sighs. But I sit next to him anyway.

'Danny, I'm sorry,' I whisper.

'What for, Charley?' he says in a measured tone. 'The humiliating rejection in the canteen? Or for not telling me about what happened with you and Matt? Or not talking to me since you've been back? Or something else?' He looks away. I've not seen this side of

Danny. He's always so unaffected. Nothing bothers him.

'What is it you think you know about Matt?'

'Just rumours,' he says.

'What rumours?'

'It's none of my business.'

'Danny, *what* rumours?'

'Your lunchtime liaison with Matt. The rumour is he turned you down. For Mia, of all people.'

'That's not what happened,' I whisper, my face moving closer to his. I'm angry now. 'Did you not think to ask me about what happened before believing the shit doled out by Mia?' I sigh and lean back in my seat. I should just go, walk out.

'Firstly, Danny, I'm sorry about the last few days. In the canteen that day, I was an idiot. I've no excuse. I was back in the zone of trying to please the wrong people. I'm sorry.' He's silent, facing the front of the classroom. 'The last day or so I've been preoccupied with hooking up with the Hillside lot and Violet's funeral. But I should have messaged you and I'm sorry I didn't.' Still silent. 'Then this Matt thing, the stories – they're lies.' I pause. 'Matt tried to force himself on me,' I whisper. Danny's expression softens and he looks me in the eye.

I turn away. 'It's OK,' I say. 'He didn't hurt me, just shook me up a bit.'

Danny glances at the door. 'You want to get out of here?'

We bolt, to puzzled looks from around the class. We run to the music department and duck into one of the practice rooms, slumping heavily on music stools to catch our breath. Guitars are positioned around the room, some on floor-stands and some hanging from the walls.

'Tell me about Matt.'

Danny looks at the floor in silence while I go over it, again. When I'm done, like Danny, I stare at the carpet in the space between our seats. After a minute, he places his hand on mine.

'I'm sorry that happened to you,' he says quietly, 'and I'm pissed off that you didn't say anything to me. Have you told anyone? Like a teacher or the police?' I tell him about how it came out in psychology at Hillside, and the police interview.

'Why is he allowed in school, in the same space as you, his victim?'

My anger at Matt bubbles. 'I haven't seen him looking apologetic. It's like nothing happened. He's a dick.'

'He's more than just a dick; he's dangerous,' Danny says, his hand still on mine. He looks past me then, to the back wall of the room. 'I hate the thought of him getting away with that.'

'It's history, months ago now, forgotten,' I say.

He leans forward to rest his forehead on my shoulder, his cheek touching mine. I close my eyes and his touch makes my skin tingle. His eyelashes brush my cheek as he blinks and I sense him close his eyes. We stay like that for a moment, as if we're silently connecting, synchronising, until the bell sounds for the end of the morning, bringing us back to reality.

OUTSIDE, Danny and I sit together with our backs against the wall of the science department. Something has shifted. I feel closer to him, like our friendship has deepened to another level.

Mia appears in front of us with two of her crew. 'What's the deal with you two, then?'

Ada is here too. Mia scowls at Danny. 'Are you hooking up with Moon Face, Charley?'

'Mia, give it a rest,' I say, standing.

'I thought you'd seen the light.'

'I have,' I say, holding eye contact.

Mia doesn't let it go. She squares up to me then shoots Danny some daggers, which he shrugs off. Ada turns away slightly, as if shielding herself from a bomb blast.

Mia takes a step backwards. 'So, we're rehearsing later,' she says.

I back off too, trying to keep my cool. 'What time?'

'Straight after school, like I said before,' she snaps. 'We're heading over there now to meet up with Matt and get the guitars ready. Are you coming?'

I look over at Danny and raise my eyebrows.

'We don't need Moon Face,' Mia says. 'Just me, you and Ada need to head over.'

Danny shrugs again. I turn back to Mia. I'm repulsed by her, her smug look and her expectation that I'll scuttle after her as I always do.

Mia starts to turn away. 'No, you're OK,' I say. I feel a strange sensation of weightlessness for a split second.

She stops and says, 'You what?'

It's as though we are moving in slow motion. Her expression is defiant. But there's a vulnerability there too, as if my words have opened a crack in her solid exterior.

My courage wanes as Mia steps towards me. I search inside myself for something to give me strength. I glance at Danny. His eyes are on Mia and his expression is firm. Elsie's image flashes through my mind. Her independence, her resolve.

'I'm fine here with Danny,' I say, crossing my arms.

Ada looks unsure of herself, unstable for once on her seat on the fence. Danny looks amused now, and I can feel that Elsie has my back.

'I'm just saying we don't need everyone in there,' Mia says. 'Moon Face can come if you like.'

'What the fuck, Mia? That's enough: his name is Danny.'

'Yeah, whatever. Come on, Ada.' Mia turns and walks away. Ada follows, giving me a wide-eyed look as she trots after her.

'I'll see you later at rehearsal!' Mia shouts without looking around.

Danny and I sit back down. 'Screw this music thing, Danny. I can't face it. I can't face her anymore.' As I say this, the words stick in my mouth.

Danny reads my mind. 'Look, fuck it, let's just do it. It's worth it just for the band experience, but we do it for you, for us, not for them.' He pauses. 'I'll help, I'll do the sound. We just get through it, yes?'

I think for a moment. Danny's support makes the world of difference. With him, maybe I can do it. 'OK, boss.'

WHEN I REACH the music department, Matt is there already, setting up his kit. The sight of him makes me shrink with revulsion: his shaped hair perched on the top of his head, his tight school shirt accentuating his muscular physique.

My instinct is screaming at me to turn and leave, but then Mia and Ada walk in, and Ada positions herself behind the drums. She looks sombre, not her usual self. Matt glances at me and smirks as he looks away again, and I flush with anger. Mia goes to kiss him but he brushes her off as if she's an annoying fly.

On the other side of the glass inside the studio, Danny takes a seat at the sound desk. He flashes me a smile and starts fiddling with the controls. He presses the intercom button. 'Let me know when you're set up and I'll get the levels sorted,' he says to all of us. I give him an exaggerated thumbs-up, accompanied by a facial expression that's as stupid as I can manage. Ada finally cracks and laughs. I tell her that Max and Archie are coming in.

'When?' she asks. 'Now?'

'Here they are,' I say, looking through the window. In the background, Max and Archie walk towards Danny. I witness their silent greeting, their meeting Danny for the first time.

Ada watches, brightening. 'How'd they get into school?'

'Back entrance,' I say with a smile.

Archie and Danny laugh together. They both soar high above Max, Danny with his broad shoulders and straight, shaggy hair and skinny Archie with his curls.

Max gives Danny a hug, and the look on his face is perfect as he stands with her attached to him, his arms held up, not knowing where to put them. He eventually returns Max's hug and she gives me a wink through the glass and pats Danny on the arse.

Mia is still adjusting the microphone stands so I motion to Ada to come with me to meet Max and Archie. She hops off her stool, following me out of the sound room.

I introduce Ada to Archie, and he opens his arms for a hug, enveloping her. Max approaches Ada with her hand outstretched as if to shake hands formally, and I fear what she has in mind. Ada looks apprehensive but reaches out her hand. Max pulls her close for a brief hug and a theatrical release.

'Sorry about Max,' Archie says. 'She's not long been out, if you know what I mean.'

'You're still in, remember,' Max says to Archie just as a banging on the glass partition interrupts us.

'The animals are getting restless,' Danny says, looking towards Mia, who is trying to get our attention, gesturing for us to come in. 'You two had better get in there before things get messy.'

Archie peers into the sound room at Matt. 'Ah yes,'

he says, 'the sex pest.'

Mɪᴀ ᴄᴏᴜɴᴛs us in and we play through the first song without stopping. It sounds good, tight, but Matt isn't happy. He grumbles, more to himself than anyone.

Danny's voice comes over the intercom, asking Mia to turn up the volume on her bass amp.

Then Archie's voice fills the room and he leans comically over the sound desk. 'Err... cut!' he says. 'Yeah, let's cut there, it's a wrap. Err... hi. It's me. Archie. Can we just tone down that electric guitar a bit?' Matt snaps his head up. Now Archie has his attention. 'Yeah, get the sex pest to calm it down a bit.'

My jaw drops. Archie straightens into a defiant posture at the sound desk, looking straight at us. I can't help but smile at the sight of Archie playing at being a tough guy. Matt's face reddens and he starts to put his guitar down, as if he's had enough.

Mia tries to calm things down. 'Let's just go again then, Matt.' She looks over at Archie through the glass with a confused expression. Matt stares at Mia, mumbling about how we are all getting at him. Then he storms out of the room. Mia follows and they both step out into the courtyard.

'What is it with them?' Ada says.

I prop my guitar against the amplifier and we go and join the others.

'It's Matt,' I say. 'He's a nasty piece of shit.'

'Understatement,' mutters Archie. Matt and Mia are exchanging verbal blows just outside the windowed door to the courtyard.

'What's going on, Charley?' Ada says.

'Look, Ada, Matt tried something on with me.'

'Fucking hell,' Archie spits. 'Don't say it like that. He *attacked* you, he sexually *assaulted* you and tried to rape you.' He's bristling, shifting his weight from foot to foot. Ada's mouth hangs open.

'He's right,' says Danny. 'He might have raped Charley if she hadn't got away.'

Ada is speechless. Her shoulders slump and she looks over towards the increasing noise from the argument outside.

'I don't think I can do this anymore,' I say to Danny. The experience of being near Matt is too much, and the music isn't enough of a reason to put up with Mia's shit. I feel a sharp stab of doubt then, about stepping into the unknown. I have never stood alone, without Mia. Not having Mia means not having the majority of the school. Not just for now, but for the rest of the school year, and then college. I'll be alone. Danny is nodding gently. Archie is smiling. He knows that my playing in a band with Mia and Matt is a bad idea. And Max. She'll always have my back, no question.

I feel a growing anger at Matt, and Mia. Anger at myself, the constant anxiety, and putting up with it all for so many years.

Ada smiles at me softly. 'Just ditch it, Charley,' she says. 'Don't give him the satisfaction.'

'What about you?' I say.

'I'm out too. Mia is one thing, but I won't stand alongside *him*.'

I look at Matt and Mia through the door. 'You reckon she's OK?' I say to Danny and Archie. The expression on Danny's face turns from frustration to concern as he jumps up. I turn to look. Matt's arm is pulled back, hand unfurled, as if he's about to slap Mia. He has hold of her top at the neckline. I push through the door ahead of Danny. Matt has lowered his arm and is brushing Mia's top down as if he's brushing away his aggression.

I get to Matt before the others do. I aim a punch at his face, releasing months of pent-up aggression in one swing.

Matt stumbles, holds his chin and glares at me as if he can't believe I had the guts to hit him. He pulls his arm back, ready to come at me. I stand firm. Archie steps between us and lands a blow on the other side of

Matt's face. But he rolls with it, and now he's pissed off.

He spits blood onto the concrete floor. He bristles with anger; he's dangerous. Archie cradles his hand as if he's done it some damage. Matt runs at Archie, but Danny is there. He swings his fist at Matt, knocking him to the floor.

Chapter 49
Home - Day 30

At times, it feels easier to slip below the water than it does to keep swimming.

I step out with BB and we head for Butser Hill to meet Mia. After the incident at school with Matt, Archie and Danny got called in to the police station. The police didn't ask to speak to me. I guess Matt didn't want to tell them that he got beaten up by a girl. I've not spoken to Archie or Danny yet. The last I heard, they were both being held, pending interviews.

The text message from Mia came after I got home. She said that she wanted to talk to me, on my own. I suggested my house but she preferred outside, and the viewpoint bench was more of a climb than she had in mind, so we settled on meeting at the bench at the foot of Butser Hill.

The breeze in my face is warm but relentless, and the air is thin so I have to turn my head to catch my breath. Through the moisture in my eyes I see a blur of Mia, sat on the bench. BB is already jumping up at her. She pushes BB down and brushes off her jeans before turning in my direction.

'Hey,' I say in a neutral tone, not sure if this is going to be a fight or a reconciliation. I don't suppose Mia is too pleased about me lumping her boyfriend in the face.

Mia nods at me then turns back to look at the trees. I sit next to her. The woods are all but in darkness from the shadow of the hill behind us.

'Thanks,' she says, and I ask what for. 'That's not the first time Matt has been like that with me,' she says, looking me in the eye. 'I guess he didn't know that you guys could see us through the door, or he wouldn't have been so obvious. He's clever. It's like he stage manages what people see and what they don't.'

I study her profile. The skin around her mouth and chin is blotchy, with dry patches. She looks unusually flawed, imperfect.

'Has he hit you?'

'No, nothing so physical that he might leave a visible mark for someone to question.' She forces a smile and turns to me again. 'Did he do something to *you?*' Her look is steadfast, her eyes delving. 'Something Matt said made me think.' She sighs.

We are quiet then, and my mind is racing, trying to unpick what Mia is doing here, what she's trying to say, and why.

Mia says, 'He did something to me too. Not just the bullying thing and the occasional light roughing up. I can deal with that shit.'

'What did he do?'

'I knew Matt was no good,' she says. 'You did too, didn't you?' She held my eye. 'I sensed something there, but I ignored it.'

'I should have told you.'

'I wouldn't have listened,' she says. 'Mia knows best.'

'He tried to rape me. But I got away,' I say.

Mia doesn't look surprised, but her eyes are filling. Tears flow down her cheeks and she stutters an apology, spitting out sobs and trying to speak at the same time.

'Hey.' I put my hand on her arm.

She takes a deep breath to gather herself. 'I slept with him,' she says. 'He was my first. He was really lovely to me, you know? Then after that first time, every time we slept together, he got worse. All macho and aggressive, calling me a whore and then saying it was just part of the sex, to make it fun, you know?'

I nod gently but don't speak.

'The last time I went around to his place, he put some porn on his TV. The usual stuff, you know, women begging for it and men giving them what they deserve.'

I know exactly what she's talking about.

'Then he was aggressive. It wasn't rape or anything, it was just horrible. He said it was role play, but he actually hurt me.'

'Did you...'

'We had sex, but I probably wouldn't call it that. Not sure how consensual it was.'

I leave space for Mia to talk. My hands are shaking as I roll myself a cigarette.

She continued. 'I screamed like shit but that just seemed to spur him on.'

'You know that was rape, don't you?' I light my cigarette. Mia asks if I'll roll her one. I hand her mine and then roll myself another, still unable to control my trembling.

'I said "no", but it makes fuck-all difference,' she says, coughing up as she exhales. 'There's that thing, the no-means-yes thing. Universally accepted. Every scene on Pornhub. The unwritten rule.'

'Have you told anyone?'

'No.' She sounds annoyed. 'Have you?'

I nod. 'The psychologist in Hillside.' I tell Mia

about the police involvement and how I got a sense from them that he'd done something before. 'They gave him a caution.'

'If I go to the police, what would I say?'

'Tell them what happened, exactly as it was. That's all you need to do. They know the law, they can decide what to do with the information.'

Mia looks unsure. She takes a last drag on her cigarette and flicks it away. She rubs her eyes.

I turn to her. 'Did you *want* what he did?'

'No.'

'Did he try to ask you, to make sure?'

'No.'

'And, what is your gut telling you?'

'That he's a fucking...' She trails off, lowering her head. Tears continue to flow.

'You need to talk to someone.'

Mia looks me in the eye. 'Will you come with me?'

Mia's mum, Sandra, drives me home from the police station. This'll be it for Matt now, I think to myself. There's no way he'll get away with a caution again.

They let me sit with Mia in the interview room. Sandra was there too. I stayed quiet, nodding gently at Mia whenever she looked unsure. The way that she explained the details, step by step, it was clear to me that Matt had planned it. One of his sick fantasies.

When we stop outside my house, Sandra turns around in her front seat, her face lit by the white light from the new LED street lamps outside. She and my mum are a similar age. Sandra is always immaculately turned out, dressed up, make-up perfect. She thanks me for helping Mia. She has tears in her eyes.

'Mum,' Mia says gently, 'it's OK. I'm OK. Hey, Charley, I have an idea. Why don't you and Ada still go and do the audition? You can sing and get Danny and Archie to play?'

The thought of fronting the band terrifies me but, at the same time, the glimmer of possibility that we could still be in the competition is exciting.

'We can't do that, Mia, this is your baby. Anyway, it looks like Archie's mangled his hand on Matt's face and there's no way I'm taking a lead vocal.'

'Shit, really?' She stares into space for a minute then starts up again, saying that we have to do it, for her and for Ada. 'I can't do it. So you just need to grow some.' She motions to her breasts, and her mum snorts with laughter. 'Think about it. *Someone* has to do it. You're not going to make me do it after today's shit, are you?' She raises a guilt-trip eyebrow and I say I'll think it over, I'll talk to the others.

I STEP INTO THE HOUSE, mentally drained and hungry. Danny is standing in my kitchen and I automatically open my arms to hug him, like it's a reflex, oblivious to the presence of anyone else.

'Get a room.' I hear Max's voice and turn around to see her, Archie and Ada all sat at my kitchen table with Mum and Dad.

'Wow, hello.' I move to hug Archie and notice his hand in a cast. 'Oh shit, Archie. Broken?'

'The only thing I've ever punched, and my hand shatters.'

'He's a delicate boy,' Max says.

'Is it a bad break?' I say, moving around the table and greeting Max and Ada with fist bumps.

'Yes, it's bad; what break isn't bad?'

'It's a clean break,' says Max, rolling her eyes. 'You don't see Danny or Charley in a plaster cast after one slap.' We laugh.

'I didn't catch him with the same force though, eh, Archie?' says Danny.

'Respect to Charley,' says Max. 'She beat you boys to it.'

'Yeah, nice, Charley,' says Archie. 'But seriously, that fucker's head...' He looks at Mum then Dad.

'Language excused under the circumstances,' Dad says.

'That *fucker's* head,' Archie says, eyeing Dad again, 'was on its way to my face when Danny's fist flew in with a red cape and pants on the outside of its trousers. I would have ducked, of course, but better to be sure.' Archie sniggers and Max nudges him in the ribs.

'What's with Mia?' Ada asks.

'The police know everything now,' I say. When I was on my way to the station with Mia, I'd messaged Mum to fill her in. She said she'd tell the others what was happening. I tell them about the police interview, and that we're expecting them to pick up Matt. Ada looks shell-shocked.

We are quiet for a minute until Max breaks the silence. 'Carry on, Archie. You were about to tell us what happened with your Dad.'

'Yes.' Archie perks up. 'So after we saved the day and sorted out the sex pest, the police arrested *us*, would you believe? Charley managed to get away with it, despite throwing the first punch.' I smile at Archie and he continues. 'So when my dad turns up at the police station, Danny and I are in the holding cells. We were processed like criminals, not charged with anything.'

'Can they do that?' Max says.

Archie shrugs. 'Dad got there and kicked up a fuss.

Being a big-shot lawyer and all that, he knew which strings to pull. The first thing I knew was when the custody copper came in and let me out, and when I got back to the front office my dad was standing there. He was talking to this big-nob police chief, and he obviously knew him because they were talking about his kids and golf or whatever. When I came out, the chief shook my dad's hand and that was that.'

'To have family in high places,' Max says.

'After he sprung us out,' Archie continues, 'Dad dropped Danny off and took me to the hospital to get my hand seen to. We had a long wait in A&E, so we talked. First time for years we've properly talked, since Mum died.'

'Did he repent?' Max says. 'For being a bastard?'

'He blamed me. I think. But he was fucked up. We talked about what he went through when Mum died—'

'What about what *you* went through?' Max interrupts.

'I know, Max, but it's not that simple.'

Max rolls her eyes and folds her arms. Archie continues. 'His world fell apart and he couldn't hold himself together, let alone me as well. He couldn't handle it. He wasn't trying to make excuses, he was just saying what happened. He's *trying*, Max.' Archie looks down, and his voice softens. 'I want to move on and so does he.' He looks up at Max but doesn't catch her eye. 'We're going to try to start from here, you know, support each other rather than fight.' Max remains quiet. 'I'm heading back to Dad's tomorrow, so we can spend the weekend, catch up properly.'

'What about Hillside?' Max asks.

'As far as they understand, I'm out till Monday anyway.'

A ring on the doorbell – pizza. When we're settled, I float Mia's idea for the audition. 'She wants us to do it,' I say, hoping for some enthusiasm but at the same time scared shitless about being on stage.

'Did she say that?' Archie asks, passing pizza over to Danny 'I won't be much good with this,' he says, holding up his hand with its cast, a bit of pizza hanging from the end of it.

'If you can hold a bit of pizza, Archie, you can hold a guitar pick,' I say. 'And if you can hold a pick then you can still play the bass. It's your left hand that does the important stuff; the right one just needs to pluck a few root notes. And we need you to take the lead vocals. Me and Danny can back you up.'

'No fucking way. Everyone in this room knows that's got to be you.' Archie looks around for support.

Ada nods. 'It's got to be you, Charley,' she says. 'If we're going to kill it, then we need your vocal out front.'

Danny nods. 'It's the only way.'

'Shit, you know I'll be crapping it.'

'You'll kill it,' Ada says.

'Stop flapping, you moron,' Max says. 'You know you'll love it, you're a closet exhibitionist.' She smiles and I laugh.

'So, we're doing this?' I look at Archie, then Ada.

'Let's do it,' Archie says.

'Danny?'

'I'm in,' he says. 'Why not, if Mia and Ada are cool with it?'

Ada nods. 'Absolutely,' she says. 'Count me in.'

'Shit,' I say. 'We've got some work to do.'

ADA and I are the last two in the kitchen after the others have left. Mum and Dad have gone up, so I grab a couple of bottles of locally made cider from Mum's stash. We nibble on the remains of the pizza and wash it down with the scrumpy.

'Did you get the letters we sent?' Ada takes a swig from her bottle. I'd got a bunch of letters through at home from different people while I was in Hillside, but I'd asked Mum not to forward them on.

'Not read them yet, I couldn't face it. Mum has them stashed somewhere,' I say, standing.

'No, I don't mean you have to read them now...' Ada calls after me. I grab the letters from the top drawer of the dresser in the hallway and go back to the kitchen, dumping the bundle on the table.

'Quite a few,' Ada says. 'Didn't you open *any* of them?' She looks surprised as she sifts through the envelopes. I shake my head, drinking from my cider bottle. She pulls a letter out and drops it on the table in front of me. 'That's one of mine.'

I put my bottle down and pick it up, feeling a twinge of anger. 'And that one,' she says, putting another one down and continuing to sift. She finds one more and places it in front of me. I start to open one but Ada stops me, replacing the one in my hand with one from the table. 'That one first.'

'Are you pissed off with me? For not reading these? I couldn't do it, Ada. I was trying to get away from all this shit, trying to get my head straight. Every reminder of school just took me straight back there, to Mia, Katherine, Matt and everyone else that made that place unbearable.'

Ada sighs, crossing her arms and looking at the pile of letters. I put the letter back on the table, unopened. 'And me? Was I part of the problem?' she asks.

I think for a moment about the part Ada played. She'd done nothing wrong. She's the one person that mostly stuck with me. But she didn't ever say anything when Mia and the others treated me like shit, kept me out of their social circle and made plans that excluded me.

'No,' I say, 'but you didn't look out for me either.' She looks hurt. I take a swig of cider and continue. 'But that wasn't your job, so it's OK. None of this is anyone's fault. I didn't go into a psychiatric ward because of Mia, or Katherine, or anyone else. I went in there because of me. I hit the wall, and that was for millions of reasons. I was ill. I *am* ill. There's nothing you could have done that would have stopped that happening.' We are quiet again, frozen, just a few feet from each other but miles away.

'You were difficult sometimes,' Ada says, avoiding my eye.

'What do you mean?' Defensive again.

'I mean—' she looks up, '—you can be sensitive.'

'What does *that* mean?' I say, getting more agitated.

'Come on, Charley,' she says softly. 'You haven't always made it easy on yourself. You're not one for playing the game, keeping a lid on it to get by.'

'And that's bad? Anyway, that's not true. I spent the best part of five years keeping a fucking lid on it, keeping people sweet. Mia, Katherine and *you* some-times.' I lean back in my chair and turn my body away from Ada.

'It's just survival,' Ada mutters.

'Maybe I don't want to survive like that. Maybe we

shouldn't *have* to survive like that.' I look past Ada at the darkness outside and the reflection of the kitchen lights in the glass. She finishes her cider and raises the empty bottle to offer me another, then heads to Mum's stash before I can answer.

'Look,' she says as she sits back down, 'it's been tough this year. For you, I know. But also for me, and for other people. You ever wonder what it's like being openly gay in year eleven? It can be a fucking hell-hole in that place. I've had my own battles.'

I look at her and wonder for the first time if she isn't as invincible as I'd always thought. I feel selfish. I have no idea what's going on with Ada, her family or anything else. I'm so obsessed with my own feelings, my own mental illness, OCD, anxiety. Have I really no capacity for thinking about anyone else but me?

'The thing that happened to Mia, and what happened to you with Matt, has made me think. Mia is a nightmare some of the time... *most* of the time, but she's the same as us. She's trying to survive the same shit as we are, she's just doing it in a different way. Probably the wrong way.'

'I'm sorry—' I start.

'Don't say that,' Ada interrupts. 'Don't say *sorry*. This isn't about being sorry. It just is what it is. We need to move on. You already *have* moved on; you're doing brilliantly. A few more weeks of school then that's it: summer and freedom.' She swigs her cider and leans forward. 'I'm sorry, Charley.' She slumps in her chair and the way she's sitting with her legs crossed takes me back to when we were little, before life got complicated.

I smile. 'You said this wasn't about sorry. So let's move on. We've got a band competition to win.'

'Then we'll have record deals to negotiate.' Ada smiles.

'Advertising revenue to secure,' I say.

We chink bottles. 'Look, wrap these letters back up and leave them till you're ready,' she says, gathering them up. 'Who's this one from?' She laughs at the juvenile handwriting on a small, pink envelope.

'No idea,' I say, picking it up and turning it over. 'Someone under six by the looks of it.' I pull at the top and slide out a single page of a small notebook with just a few sentences written on one side. I look to see who it's from before I read it. 'Toby,' I say, puzzled. 'We used to talk on the way to school, if our paths crossed. He's sweet.'

Ada grabs it from me. 'Dear Charley,' she reads aloud, snatching her hand away when I try to retrieve it. 'Someone said at school that you were ill and if we wanted to write we could send a letter to your house.' She grins at me. 'I am sorry that you are ill and when you get back we can walk to school together if you want. From Toby. Oh, he's so sweet...' Ada melts and we both laugh.

~

AFTER ADA LEAVES, I gather up the bundle of letters and return them to the dresser upstairs. I'll tackle them another day.

As I squeeze them back in the drawer, I notice my old letters from Grannie. This is another bunch of letters I've steered away from. I've not read them since she died. She used to write to me once every couple of weeks. I wrote back most of the time, at least until halfway through secondary school, but then other things seemed to get in the way.

I pick them up and brush my hand over the top envelope, my grannie's slanted writing in blue ink. The scent of her seems to waft up from her letters and it takes me straight back to her little kitchen, where we used to talk. I plonk the bundle on the kitchen table and make myself a mug of tea. Bed can wait.

I skim through some of the letters, choosing the more recent ones. Tucked inside each envelope is a letter for me, and one for Lucas. Without fail, Grannie made sure that in every letter, she spoke to us both.

A version of Grannie comes through in her writing that is more than I remember. There's her usual matron-like tone in her encouragement to concentrate at school and keep up with the sports. Then there's her more subtle support and caring words that I must have always brushed over.

I finished my tea as I read the final paragraphs of the last letter she wrote. She ended it with the same words she'd said to me before: *Remember, Charley, you are special, and you see the good in everyone. Use this gift. Work with it. Get to know it.*

My grannie had more faith in me than I have ever had in myself. I fold up the letter and slot it back into the envelope. My OCD nudges me to retract the note and slide it in again, but I resist. I wonder whether Grannie had the same compulsions when she wrote the letter, and I imagine her sitting opposite me at the kitchen table.

'They're just symptoms,' she says. 'Side effects of a deeper sense of empathy. You just need to keep it under control. Don't let the rituals and the compulsions run your life. *You* control *them*. Not the other way around.'

'Funny side effect,' I say into the darkness, to the illusion of my grannie. 'I'd be a lot happier if I could lose this anxiety and all that goes with it.'

'You will,' she says. 'This is a learning process. The point is not to fight it, but to flow with it, control it. It's part of you. You will learn to manage it. You know this.'

I nod slowly. I do know it. I know that I can manage it.

'Yes,' my grannie says. She pushes herself to stand, holding on to the table for support. 'You know it now.'

'Stay,' I say. 'Help me with it. Show me how you control it.'

'You have everything you need. Now you just need to be kind to yourself. Allow yourself the time to learn, and to perfect your superpower.' She grins and her face seems to light up the whole room. Then she turns and heads out of the room.

'Grannie?' I call after her, but I know she's gone.

Chapter 50
Home - Day 31

At just before one o'clock, after a long morning of rehearsals, we walk into the vast audition hall at the Arena. My adrenaline is flowing. A stage fills one end, with steps up each side. Floor space the size of a football pitch has been cleared in front of the stage, for standing room. Seats cover the banks at the sides and up to a second floor of balcony seating. The roof is filled with steel framework, cable supports, banks of lights and platforms for stage crew.

I take a deep breath and look sideways at Danny, standing with his guitar slung over his shoulder. His straggly hair flops back as he tilts his head upwards and looks around at the cavernous space. He grins as he glances back at me, as cool as ever, no sign of nerves.

On the other side of me, Ada and Archie jabber excitedly to each other.

The hall is bustling with audition hopefuls. There is a band on stage, just kicking off. We watch them for a minute, rocking out with their electric guitars. They look good, professional. A panel of three are sat at a table out front, directing the audition. When the rockers leave the stage, one of the judges calls on the next band – a slow conveyor belt of wannabe stars.

'We need to register over there.' Archie points at an arrangement of tables with black covers. I slap the form Mia gave me in front of the woman at the desk and she types the reference number into a laptop.

'Band name?' she says, without looking up. I look at the others.

'Some Kind of Comfort,' Danny says. Archie shrugs and Ada nods, so we go with it.

'Contact?' the woman barks. I give my name and mobile number. 'Two o'clock audition, two songs, maximum of three minutes per song, make sure you are ready at stage left ten minutes before your time slot. A pass flops out of the printer at her feet and she hands it to me.

'Some Kind of Comfort?' I say to Danny as we meander through the groups of musicians, looking for somewhere to sit.

'It's the name of that song I've been working on. I

need you to help me finish it off. I've been working on it since you came out of Hillside that time.'

'I like it.'

The band on stage are a goth-emo outfit, destroying something by The Cure. We watch the bands pile on and off the stage, each receiving the same neutral reception from the panel of judges: a brief conflab between them, a tick in one box or other then a call of 'Next!'.

At ten minutes to two we are ready. With guitars and sticks in hands, we line up stage left. A man in headphones with a mouthpiece takes my folded pass and hustles us up onto the stage, behind the curtain. My nerves kick in. My hands start to shake and anxiety spirals. Three people come to brief us on what to do next but I'm already spinning out. Black-clad stage crew take our guitars to put in stands on the stage, just out of view of the audience and judges. Danny looks at me and he must know I'm not good. He holds my arm.

'Archie, you're going to have to sing,' Danny says, deadly serious. 'Charley, can you play if Archie sings?' I wipe sweat from my forehead and try to gather myself.

I nod. 'Archie, I'm sorry.' My voice wobbles. I'm such an idiot for freaking out again, leaving Archie to front the singing with no warning.

'It's OK, forget it, let's just do this,' Archie says.

The call comes and we are ushered on stage. We pick up and position our guitars while Ada sits behind the drum kit, adjusting the seat. All three of us out front have microphones. Archie checks I'm OK before moving to the front of the stage and taking the lead position. Danny helps Archie adjust his mic stand as he struggles with his plaster cast. I set myself up behind the microphone furthest from the front of the stage.

'When you're ready,' comes a voice from below, the middle of the three panellists, a bearded man with grey hair. 'Two songs, one after the other, no need for a big gap between them.' The two other panellists are women. One is in her fifties; she looks familiar. She has short black hair and a nose piercing. The other is younger, in her thirties, with a shaved head and heavy eye make-up.

Archie nods at them and turns to look at Ada. She beams back. Then she raises her sticks and counts us in. We hit the first note spot on together, Archie nailing the vocal. The bearded one looks up, taking an interest as Danny's guitar takes the lead. Ada's drums are tight, keeping us perfectly together. I start to relax and allow my voice to come in to support Archie, to add depth to the vocals. Archie smiles encouragement at me and as we hit the climax of the first song, we are all growing in confidence. With the final note still ringing, Ada switches her sticks, pushes out her brushes and counts us in for the second song.

Song two is slower, a ballad with heavy layered harmony, a stark contrast to the first. Archie lets me take the vocal lead from the back, adding his harmony. I sense we have engaged the three judges. By the close of the second song they are talking and nodding, then the bearded man calls 'Next!'.

Off stage, at the bottom of the steps, we look at each other, shell-shocked and ears ringing. It was all over so quickly. We barely had time to register what we were doing.

'I'm so sorry, Archie,' I say, 'I totally fucking freaked, I'm sorry. You really killed it.'

'*We* really killed it, Charley. I think we got that spot on.' Archie beams as we step away from the stage.

'Fantastic vocals,' Danny says. 'You and Archie really came together. That felt good; I've dreamed of that for years.' We are all buzzing as we sit and re-live the audition.

Ada and I shuffle closer to each other as Archie and Danny head towards the bar: Danny with his confident, loping gait and characteristic stoop. Archie is more jittery, light on his feet. 'Peas in a pod,' Ada says.

'You reckon?' I say, surprised. 'Chalk and cheese, more like.'

'Same height, both a bit gangly, both with long hair.

I don't know Archie so well, but there's something similar about them.'

'I guess.' I'm not convinced. 'Archie is great; he's been such a rock for me in Hillside. But Danny... He's a whole different kind of rock.' I grin at Ada and feel my cheeks flush. Ada snorts with laughter and sways into me.

'Thought as much. I can see you two together. He worships you.'

'Do you think so?'

'Without a doubt.'

I look around. It feels good to be in such a magical space full of musicians. My thoughts drift to Mia, and then to the conversation I had with Ada last night. 'You should speak to Mia,' I say.

'Can't seem to bring myself to.'

We are quiet for a minute and I look over to the stage. Two girls with guitars are competently delivering a folky number.

'What happened up there?' Ada nods at the stage.

'Usual thing: bit of pressure and I spin out.'

'You came through, though; you were OK, and we smashed it.'

'I guess. I thought it was going to be a bad one, but I managed to hold it together. Thanks to you lot.'

'You'll get there.' She smiles.

Where is 'there' that I'm trying to get to? What is

my new normal, my equilibrium? 'I'm much better. I don't think I'll ever be without the anxiety and the shit that goes with it. I'll always have my battles, but I've learnt a lot in Hillside.' I pause. 'And we all have our battles, eh? Mine are just my own special ones.'

Ada smiles. 'You are indeed a special one.' She pauses. 'That was so awesome up there.' She grins up at the stage. 'Be great if we get it.'

'It's a long shot,' I say, looking around the Arena at the number of people all hoping for the same thing.

'YOUR ATTENTION, PLEASE.' A voice comes over the PA system, echoing around the Arena. There is an increase in bustle. The announcer hushes the audience and we stand up. My nerves are shredded, my mouth is dry. The Arena has filled up as all the bands from two days of auditions have filtered back to hear the results.

'If you are one of the two winning bands that we call out, please head over to the desk with your registration number.' A buzz ripples through the arena.

'Oh, spit it out,' Archie says, jiggling nervously. Danny is calm and I lean into him a bit for support. He links his arm with mine and pulls me close. Archie links with my other arm and Ada completes the chain as the nerves flow between us.

'So,' the voice returns, 'can the band Dragon Fly please go to the registration desk.' We hear a cheer from a section of the audience at the other side of the Arena. 'Well done to Dragon Fly,' the announcer repeats. 'OK, so the second and final band to make it through is one we saw here this afternoon.' We jolt to attention, looking wide-eyed at each other. I tighten my grip on Danny and Archie's arms. 'Can the band Some Kind of Comfort ...' I hear no more as all four of us screech and jump into the air. We break our chain and embrace in pairs and then settle into a group hug. We calm down enough to hear the tail end of the announcer's instructions and then, walking on air, we bound towards the registration desk.

'Oh my God...' Archie says. 'This is unreal.'

'No way...' I say, unable to take in what's happening and physically bouncing off the two boys as we walk.

'It was never in doubt,' Danny says with a grin, he and Ada both looking cool. The PA system crackles again and the announcer reveals the headliner for the Arena Festival for whom we will be the supporting act.

'Susie Chapman,' he shouts to muted applause.

'Who?' I say to Danny.

'Susie Chapman. She's good: one of the top folk-country singer-songwriters around at the moment. I've got loads of her stuff at home.'

'Never heard of her,' says Archie.

'Nor me,' says Ada.

Danny rolls his eyes. 'She's *really* good.'

The woman at the registration desk smiles up at us. 'Some Kind of Comfort?'

'Yes!' Danny grins at the poor woman. I leave him to it and step back, looking at the stage. I imagine myself there, with a heaving crowd packed to the rafters. I think about my freak-out, all the people that will be in the audience, and I think maybe we should get Archie to lead the vocals. I can't let them down like that again.

Chapter 51
Home - Day 33

Tonight is the dinner for the band competition winners at the Arena, a pre-gig celebration before the main show tomorrow. We get to bring our families and dine in the balcony restaurant that overlooks the main stage. There are two bands on through the evening, but no one I've heard of. I'm weirdly nervous at the thought of everyone being in the same place at the same time: my friends from home, Max and Archie, all the parents, and my family.

In the shower, warm water massages the back of my neck. I pick up Dad's shaving foam and a disposable razor. The touch of the blade on the soft skin under my arm throws me back. Pressure builds behind my eyes. I feel dizzy and have to steady myself with a hand on the shower wall. I move from four to seven on the anxiety scale. I slam the razor onto the floor of the shower and rinse myself down. With my eyes still closed, I slip to the floor, squatting in the warm spray.

I stretch my right arm out and look at the scars on the inside, mostly turned white apart from the newest one, from just before I went into Hillside, still a deep red colour. I pick up the razor, blinking water from my eyes to see its single blade. I press the head against the corner of the shower door until the orange plastic gives way and I can slip the blade out. It falls out onto the shower tray and I stare at it for a moment, then push it around with my finger.

'Fuck it,' I say aloud, kicking the razor away, and the water carries it back towards me like a magnet. 'Fuck you! Fuck everything!' I stand up, wiping the mix of tears and water from my face on my way back to my room.

'Hey, pop star,' Max says, perched on a stool at the bar with a pint in her hand. The balcony bar is the full width of the Arena, with a VIP guest area that overlooks the stage and Arena floor. I smile at Max. She jumps off her stool and greets Mum and Dad with unexpected hugs, then turns to Lucas. He scowls and she settles for a fist bump.

'They've got a table.' Max points, grinning. 'Archie

and Danny are there, with their carers. I'll come over in a minute.' The restaurant is loud with conversation, and the air is humid, difficult to breathe.

Max puts a hand on my arm. 'Hey,' she says. 'Are you OK?'

I smile and nod. But I'm not sure yet. I'm not sure what's going to happen out on that stage when it comes to the crunch. Maintaining my smile, I turn and head for the others.

'Hey, Charley,' Danny says as we get to the table. He introduces me to his mum and his soft Sheffield accent is more pronounced than normal. Danny's mum holds on to my hands and studies my face, her eyes sparkling. She's shorter than me, under five feet, with long, dark hair that hangs over the front of her shoulders. She exchanges a smile with Danny and gives me a hug.

I sit opposite Danny and his mum. Danny says, 'You look great. Are you doing OK?' I want to say that I'm up at a level six or seven, that I'm crapping it at the thought of being on stage and that it's becoming clear that I can't hack it in the real world, outside of Hillside.

'Yeah, I'm fine.' I sigh. 'It's been a weird couple of days.'

Archie sees us and introduces his dad, who looks like an older, better-dressed version of him. They look relaxed together. Danny's sister Katie homes in on

Lucas, persuading him to share his earphones and let her join in with the game on his phone.

Ada arrives then, with her mum, sparking another round of introductions that also brings Max over to sit down so that we can order food.

I lean back and watch for a moment. Dad is animated, like he always is when he's with new people. He's talking to Archie's dad about work. There's a look of pride on Archie's face as he watches his dad talking.

Mum's wearing one of her flowing, knee-length dresses over jeans with her faithful old Dr Martens boots. She and Danny's mum talk about Sheffield and laugh together. I even hear a hint of a Yorkshire accent from Mum. Danny jumps into their conversation from time to time, explaining something or clarifying as if he's mediating an important meeting.

Down the table, Archie and Max are in an animated exchange. Archie has his hand on Max's shoulder and their bodies are square-on, their faces just inches apart. It's odd, as if they are arguing but smiling at the same time. Archie turns his head slightly and they lean in to a kiss. I stare, eyes wide and mouth open.

Max smiles at me. 'You are so slow, Charley,' she says, then laughs. Archie puts his arm around her shoulder, both of them now grinning at me. Danny and

Ada join Max and Archie's laughter, drowning me out as I insist in vain that I'd known all along.

'I couldn't resist the serial-killer suit trousers, and those flaky white Converse!' Max shouts above the background noise. Archie lifts his leg so we can see his new white trainers, and then leans over and kisses Max on the cheek.

'Shall we see what this band look like?' I say to Danny and Ada as the noise of the crowd in the Arena sounds as if it's reaching a peak. 'While this lot are finishing off their food.' I nod towards our parents, who remain deep in conversation.

As soon as we push through the double doors to the Arena balcony, the buzz in the air is palpable. The Arena is heaving. People cram every corner and every seat. The main floor area is packed tight, with faces looking up to the stage where the lead singer is adjusting her microphone.

'Fantastic view from here!' Archie shouts into my ear. I smile and nod at him, as the drummer counts them in for their final song. The volume is almost painful when the two electric guitars kick in at the same time as the rhythm section. The crowd on the

Arena floor heaves and pulsates as a single, homogenous mass.

I look across at the faces of my friends, and I bet that Danny, Archie and Ada are thinking the same as me – tomorrow it will be us, up there on this stage. At the end of the song, the band file off the stage. Ada throws an arm around my shoulder and plants a kiss on my temple. 'It's going to be awesome,' she says.

'I can't think about it. You don't think it's going to be this rammed, do you?'

'What, with the biggest country star of the decade playing? No, it'll be empty, Charley.'

'Shit.'

Chapter 52

Home - Day 34

I hang back with Dad while Max and Lucas press ahead with the two dogs to the top of the hill. Lucas looks animated, all hand gestures and eye contact with Max.

Dad links arms with me. 'Lucas is on a roll.'

'About time someone gave Max a run for her money,' I say.

'He missed having you around when you were in Hillside. He's come out of himself since you've been home.'

'He's crazy about Danny.'

I sense Dad glancing at me, but I leave him hanging. 'He could have a worse role model,' he says.

Max keeps slipping on the steep section of the hill and Lucas helps to pull her up.

'What is it?' Dad asks.

I laugh. Dad has this intuitive understanding of my feelings. 'I can't stop thinking about Violet.'

Dad is quiet for a moment. 'Give it time,' he says.

'I've felt stronger since Hillside, but...'

Dad waits for me to finish.

'Especially since the Arena last night, I can't seem to shake these dark thoughts again. It feels as if it's only a matter of time before the darkness find a way in. I wonder what's the point...'

'Don't talk like that,' Dad snaps.

'I don't mean... I just... I'm scared, that's all.'

'I know,' Dad says. 'Life is scary. I'm scared too.' He links tighter with me and pulls me in. 'And I've got these flipping polar bears to deal with.' We laugh, and then continue to walk in silence, puffing as we hit the steep section.

'I can't do this thing tonight,' I say.

I've already told the others that there's no chance of me doing the main gig. They'll be better off not having to deal with me freaking out. Archie and Danny gave me a load of shit before eventually backing off. Ada didn't say much, but she was disappointed for sure. They'll thank me in the end.

'Don't they need you?' Dad says, and I can tell he's trying to hide his disappointment.

'They'll be OK. Archie's got an awesome lead vocal in him.'

'Do they know you're not doing it?'

'Yes. They're already at the Arena, getting ready and getting nervous, I expect. Especially Archie.' I smile.

'Well...' Dad says slowly. 'If you're sure.'

'Whenever I think about it, I start shaking. They're better without me when I'm like this.'

Dad is quiet. At the top of the hill, BB and Misty are sniffing out a rabbit hole. Max is sat on the viewpoint bench with Lucas, looking over the fields. I sit next to Lucas. Dad turns to take in the view, standing behind us. It's overcast, and the old oak is partially obscured in shadow. It looks bedraggled, as if it's been battered in a storm.

Lucas nudges me. 'You're not going back, are you?'

'Where?'

'Hillside.'

'Not if I can help it.'

'What if you *can't* help it?'

'Lucas, what's up? I'm not going back.'

'You seemed good, but now you seem bad again. Like you were before.'

I sling my arm around his shoulder, surprising myself at how mild the OCD feelings are. With Lucas, I think because of his age, it's harder. But it's like the balance has tipped, and the fear of contamination and germs is no longer as strong as the desire to move on, to be a sister to Lucas. 'It's not as easy as I hoped it might be. It's going to be a constant battle.'

'More battle scars?'

'No. I won't do that. I've got the tools, Lucas, I just need to keep on keeping on.'

'Just keep swimming...' Lucas smiles. After a moment he says, 'Why aren't you doing it, then?'

'What?'

'The Arena. Just keep on keeping on, you said.'

'I know,' I say, looking up at the darkening sky. 'One step at a time, I guess.'

My phone pings. Message from Mum that Mia is looking for me.

'Mia is coming up,' I say.

'Here? Now?' Dad says.

'Yes. She's at the house. She's on her way.'

'Are you OK with that?'

'Sure.' I feel surprisingly little animosity towards Mia. Max remains quiet. Lucas is mucking about with the dogs.

Dad gives me a wink. 'I'll head back with Lucas and BB; leave you kids to it.'

Lucas gets up and starts towards Dad, but I grab his hand and pull him into a hug. The warmth and love I feel washes away any sense of nagging anxiety. 'Don't worry. I'm not going anywhere.'

He smiles at me. 'Just keep on keeping on.'

MAX THROWS another stick for Misty, sending her scampering down the hill and back again for the fourth time. Neither her nor Max show any signs of tiring.

'Here it comes,' Max says, watching Mia winding her way towards us up the hill.

I look at Max. 'Be nice.'

'Always.' She smiles at me. 'If she has a dig, I can't promise I won't take her down.'

As Mia reaches us, Max stands.

'You can stay, Max,' Mia says as she sits next to me on the bench. Max sits back down, next to Mia.

'What's up?' I say to Mia. 'I'm not sure you've ever called around at my house before.'

'You might be right. There are a lot of things I haven't done before that maybe I should have.'

'I'll say,' says Max.

Mia takes a breath. 'Look, I just wanted to say that the police have been in touch.' My heart pounds. Maybe they've let him go and he's out there somewhere.

'They're holding him. They've charged him.'

'What charge?'

'Several. Based on your and my statements, they are charging him with rape, attempted rape and sexual assault.' Mia's words hang in the air and I'm surprised at the relief I feel. The sun is dipping towards the tree-line on the horizon and it feels like closure. Max is looking at me, still protective.

I think about what this will mean. I feel a sense of validation – as if I needed him to be charged before I could accept that what he did was wrong.

'It's going to be tough,' I say.

'Tough for both of us,' Mia says.

'Thanks for coming up to tell me.'

Mia says nothing but looks out over the fields. 'Danny messaged me yesterday,' she says.

'What?' I say, surprised that Danny would message Mia without mentioning it to me.

Mia reads my surprise. 'It's OK. It seems he just wanted to say thanks.'

'For what?'

'I think for the band competition thing, and giving you guys the chance to have a go at it.' She pauses a moment, then says, 'I'm sorry, Charley. I was horrible to Danny. He's a good guy.'

'He is,' I say.

Mia looks around. 'Where are they? Ada and Danny?'

'At the Arena.'

She looks at her watch. 'Why aren't *you* there?'

'Not this time.'

She jumps up. 'Oh, fuck off, Charley. We're going. Now.' She grabs my arm and I allow her to pull me up.

Max jumps up too. 'I actually agree with Mia, which is an odd phrase coming from me. Let's go. I'll drive.'

Max shouts for Misty, and Mia starts down the hill. I look at my watch. Nearly eight o'clock. There's no way we'll get there in time: they'll be on stage in a few minutes. Just below my watch, the wisps of vine from the tattoo are visible and I turn my arm to look at it. Violet's capital 'V' stares back at me, with the semi-colon of solidarity. I feel a surge of adrenaline. Then the thought of standing on that stage transforms from fear through excitement to determination.

'Let's do it!' I run arm in arm with Max down the hill to catch up with Mia.

MAX's CAR screeches to a stop in the town square, across from the entrance to the Arena. Two minutes past eight.

I jump out, then poke my head back into the car. 'Will you get Lucas, and Mum and Dad?'

'Yes. Go! We'll see you in there.'

I fly across the town square, my bag behind me like

a cape. I elbow my way through the queues outside the Arena.

'Charley?' A familiar voice comes from just behind me. I look around. It's Katherine in a short skirt and breast-hugging top with two other girls, each of them chaperoned by a boy I don't recognise. Sweat pours off my face and I stare speechless at her, my fists clenched as tight as my jaw.

'Nice outfit,' she says looking me up and down, reminding me that I'm not dressed to be on stage, in my mucky trainers, sweat-soaked dress, and mum's old cardigan.

'Back of the queue, then.' She flicks her eyes backwards. 'We've all been here for ages so don't think you can just push to the front.' She smirks. I try to relax my muscles. I look at them, thinking how little I care for what any of them think or say. I feel pity for Katherine. I don't know what went on between her and Matt, but I can't believe it was anything good. I turn to the security guard and pull my backstage pass from my bag. He waves me through and I don't look back.

I pile through the door of the dressing room. It's empty. I head for stage left, rounding the corner at speed and almost colliding with the three of them at the bottom of the steps to the stage. They just stare at me, their mouths open. 'Sorry,' I blurt, out of breath and dripping with sweat. 'I'm sorry, I'm OK. I'm OK this time and I'm sorry.'

'Forget it,' Archie says. 'Can you sing?'

'Fuck yes, too right I can sing. If it's OK with you?' I look at Archie, feeling manic and ready for anything. He's so calm, almost serene. He smiles at me and it's like he's seeing me for the first time. Danny touches my arm, probably trying to figure out if I've finally lost it, or finally come home.

I hold his gaze. 'Let's do this.'

The compere introduces us as the local band, the second of the two winners of a local competition. At the edge of the stage, I kick off my trainers and strip off my cardigan, dumping it to the side. I cool off in my sleeveless black dress. I glance with some degree of pride at my tattoo. My scars are visible too, but I don't care. They are battle scars, like Lucas says. I'm ready.

'Put your hands together, for your very own local band: Some Kind of Comfort!'

I BOUNCE across the stage with the others. The boards feel sticky under my bare feet and the smell of dry ice fills my nostrils. I get to the microphone and squint in the lights. The noise of the crowd is deafening and it takes my breath away for a moment. The Arena heaves with bodies, there to see Susie Chapman but welcoming the four of us as if we are the next best thing. To the left and right of the stage are massive screens, and I can see a thirty-foot version of myself at the microphone stand. The camera moves to show Ada settling at the drums. I'm transfixed. The atmosphere is charged.

I put up my hand, shielding my eyes from the lights. There is a swarm of faces in the standing section, cameras flashing. Above and around them, the packed seated sections rise from the Arena floor far up into the ceiling. The heat from the lights is intense and sweat is dripping off me. I adjust the microphone position, my guitar hanging freely over my shoulder.

In the white stage lights, Archie looks pale, wide-eyed. He peers through his chin-length curly fringe. Even Danny's usual coolness is being tested. He flusters, getting his guitar strap over his head. Ada grins as she makes herself at home in her throne behind the drums, settling and then spinning her drumsticks between her fingers.

'Hello,' I say into the microphone, my voice reedy and small in my head but booming across the Arena through the sound system. I wipe the sweat from my forehead with the back of my hand and squint to see the crowd. There is a slight delay after I speak into the microphone before the audience responds. When it comes, the wall of sound almost physically knocks me off my wobbly legs.

'Thank you,' I say, then give Ada a nod. She's grinning as she knocks her drumsticks together to count us in.

The opening synchronous harmony is pitch-perfect, kicking in on the first note. The sound of the guitars and vocals is crisp and powerful through the stage monitors. Then comes the pulsing of the crowd, packed in tight and jumping in time with the music. The quality of the sound system, with our instruments and our music, brings tears to my eyes. It ripples through the Arena with such force and presence that I forget for a moment that the sound is ours. Archie's and Danny's voices fill the Arena.

Be cool. I glance up again at the big screen to my left and see my magnified face. On the VIP balcony above the Arena floor, Max is jumping and punching the air, bouncing between my dad and Archie's dad. I catch Archie's eye and direct it towards them. He reaches his hand into the air and gives a thumbs-up to his dad.

A hush comes over the Arena as we start the second song. There is a palpable latent energy. I take a moment to breathe it in, the hairs on my arms and the back of my neck standing on end.

My nerves have gone, and we play through the

next two songs with confidence. When the last chord rings out, I look at the others and all three grin back at me.

'That song,' I breathe into the microphone, my confidence sky high, 'is called "No More". I wrote it for us girls.' A cheer pulses through the Arena like a Mexican wave. I let the noise of the crowd subside. 'And for the boys too,' I say, turning to Archie and Danny, and up to Ada with a nod for her to get ready to count in our last song. 'We all need to step it up; we all need to say let's not do this anymore.' Cheers and whistles ripple through the crowd. I look up at the VIP area and smile. Mum is screaming and clapping her hands above her head.

'This is our last one,' I say, sweat dripping off my lips and on to the microphone as I start to strum the four-chord sequence of the song. 'This is a new song,' I say when the crowd quietens down again. 'This song has some special meaning for us because it's about a journey we've been on. A journey on which a close friend of ours, Violet, faltered, and she didn't make it.' I pause. 'We're going to try a mash-up, a version with a break in the middle that brings in one of Violet's favourite songs, an Ed Sheeran tune.' A cheer goes up.

'This is named after the band; this is "Some Kind of Comfort".' As I finish my words, Ada counts us in with four confident clicks of her drumsticks. She drives the tempo hard. It's tight and the *feel* is good. The song drops in the middle as we morph into 'Supermarket Flowers', and with just the sound of my finger-picked guitar and lone vocal, the crowd is silent. The air is charged.

Max takes advantage of the hush and screams out to Archie. 'We love you, Archie, show us your arse...' The undeniable sound of Max's voice is greeted with cheers and whistles around the Arena.

Archie rises to the heckle, stepping towards his microphone. 'We love you, Max,' he says then turns to give the crowd a special arse wiggle. Cheers and whistles increase and Max's second heckle is drowned by the noise. We take that as a cue to kick back in. We pick up the tension and start to build to the chorus when the voice of Susie Chapman drifts in. The crowd erupts and for a second I can't catch my breath.

Susie walks on stage with a microphone. She has caught on to the words of the song and is right with me as we launch back into the final chorus, full on and to a heaving mass of jumping people on the Arena floor. The whole place comes alive. The final chord sounds, with a crash on the cymbals, and I step back up to the microphone at the front, picking the outro section on my guitar and repeating the words of the chorus one last time. Susie joins me in a hug and I turn back to the microphone. 'Thank you,' I say, out of breath. 'You really have made our year.'

We walk off stage, my ears ringing and all of us with fixed smiles from ear to ear. Danny gets off stage first and stands facing me. He smiles as I skip towards him. I step up to him and our eyes lock. He puts his arms around my waist and leans towards me. I lean forward and take his face in my hands, and we kiss.

A cheer from Ada and Archie behind us breaks the spell and Danny lifts me slightly off the floor as we laugh.

I turn to the others just as Ada launches herself at me. 'My god, that was something else,' she says, hugging me.

'You were awesome,' I say. Max runs onto the backstage area. She ducks between two of the security crew at the top of the steps who try and fail to get hold of her. They start to give chase but stop when Archie and I wave, signalling that she's with us. Max turns back to them and makes like she's been roughed up unnecessarily before facing us with a beaming grin, arms out for a three-way hug.

'What the fuck?' Max shouts above the noise. 'What just happened out there? When did you guys get that good?' She stands in the middle of our circle, turning between us and grinning like a baby. 'Come on,' she says, lifting her arms in the air and beckoning us to her with her fingers. 'Come and give some love to your manager, and remember this moment, remember who it was that got you here.' She beams and the rest of us grab her and lift her up. She screams and laughs as we spin her around. Eventually we all collapse in a dizzy, euphoric heap on the backstage floor.

Chapter 53
Home - Day 35

By the time I finally flop onto my bed, a beaming smile fixed on my face, I have aches and pains in muscles I never knew I had. My heels feel bruised, my calf muscles tight.

Dad must have heard me come in because he slips into my room and lies on his back next to me.

'You are amazing, you know that?'

I smile. 'Yeah, I guess I am.' Dad elbows me in the ribs. 'Thanks, Dad.'

'What for?'

'For what you and Mum have done, to get me through.'

'Felt like it was touch and go there for a while.'

'Tell me about it.'

'*Are* you through?'

'I'm on my way.'

We are quiet for a minute. Dad is so still I wonder if he's dropping off to sleep when he says, 'Turns out the polar bears weren't so bad.'

'No way?' I smile. 'Careful, Dad. You can't trust them.'

'We apprehended their leader.'

'Not the vicious, merciless killer of the ice caps?'

'Pebbles.'

'What?'

'Her name is Pebbles.'

'She doesn't sound very ruthless.'

'We talked it out. She had them all de-fuse their vests and lay down their arms.'

'Legs.'

'What?'

'Polar bears don't have arms, Dad.' I grin. 'They must have laid down their legs.'

Dad laughs. 'Hearts and minds, that's what it's all about. Winning hearts and minds.'

'Well done, Commander.'

'Thanks. But, er...'

'What?'

'I'm afraid you know too much.' Dad gives me his evil maniac expression and launches into a tickle fight. I squeal and laugh, defenceless and beaten by the element of surprise.

I WAKE with warm sunshine on the back of my neck.

Memories of last night diffuse into my consciousness. I smile, then turn over and squint at the sun leaking around my blind, dripping light across my bedroom carpet.

I pull myself up to a sitting position on the side of my bed and look down at my arm where the sleeve of my night shirt has rolled up. I run my fingers over the scars, and the tattoo. Violet's capital 'V' feels slightly raised where the skin of my arm still has some healing to do after the work of the tattoo needle. The scar tissue further up my arm is smooth to the touch.

Mum calls up the stairs, 'Charley? Your friends are here, are you up?'

My phone pings.

'Coming,' I shout, pulling my sleeve back down and looking at my phone. Danny's message asks if I'm up for a run, and that he'll give me a ten-minute head start.

Still in my pyjamas, I head downstairs. I almost lose my footing and stumble comically into the kitchen, where the smell of hot toast and coffee wafts over me. I smile at the comforting sounds and sights of Sunday morning breakfast.

No one saw my comedy entrance.

Mum and Dad are talking to Max and Archie over toast and jam. Ada is with Lucas, in his familiar position with his headphones around his neck and a laptop in front of him.

Mum looks up. 'Here she is, the star of the show.' She jumps up to give me a hug.

I smile. 'I'm still buzzing.' Dad gives me a smile over Mum's shoulder and I sit in the chair that he pulls out for me, between him and Lucas. Lucas closes his laptop and covertly brushes some crumbs onto the floor for BB, sparking a snap of a memory of my own attempts to avoid food in Hillside. The thought quickly fades.

I swipe on my phone to find one of the selfies I took on stage; I show Lucas. I lean my head against his as we look at the pictures together. He gives me a quizzical look then turns back to the phone.

'OMFG,' he says, causing Dad to snap at him to drop the F. 'That is a great picture.' Lucas covertly mouths OMFG again in my direction.

We flick through the rest of my photos and some of Lucas's while we eat breakfast. Lucas's phone is passed around the table and Archie says that we look like proper rock stars, with the lights and smoke.

I message Danny that I'm not up for a run, but that we are heading up the hill with something to plant for Violet, and that we should meet up there after breakfast. Dad picked up the sapling from the garden centre first thing this morning. Mum thought we'd have to ask someone's permission before planting a tree up on the hill but Dad persuaded her that no one was likely to object.

'We should head up to the hill,' I say. The others agree and I make a move to go and get dressed.

Mum calls me. I stop at the door and look back. 'I'm proud of you,' she says, tearful. 'Not just the music. I mean, that's amazing, you know, but, everything.'

Archie and Max are sat just out of Mum's view and they look at me, making fake sad faces.

'Thanks, Mum. Tell those two to stop taking the piss.' I smile. Archie and Max turn to Mum with innocent faces before cracking up again. I smile to myself and scramble up the stairs.

LUCAS RUNS AHEAD of us with the dogs. Archie and Max lag behind looking like a couple of rejects from the military, Max with her camouflage jacket and spade slung over one shoulder, Archie in his long army-green coat, carrying the young sapling in its pot. Ada and I link arms and catch up with Lucas, plodding along with his head down.

'What's up, Lucas?' I say as we come alongside him.

Lucas frowns. 'Were you scared? On stage in front of all those people? There's no way I'd do that.'

'I'd have said the same thing a few days ago. But then something kicked in, and when you get that confidence, you have to just do it. It's the best feeling.'

'I can't do it,' he mumbles.

'Your drumming's really coming on though, Lucas, and good drummers are hard to find. The heartbeat of the band.' I glance at Ada. 'You can hang at the back like Ada does; you don't have to be in the limelight.'

'Lydia says I'm rubbish.'

'Who's Lydia?'

'At school.'

'What does she know? Lucas, look at me.' I stop on the hill and turn him towards me. 'I've heard your drumming, you're amazing, you can do *anything* that you put your mind to, OK?' He nods at me and we continue walking. 'Don't let them get to you, Lucas. I'm here, and I'll look out for you, OK?'

'And who's looking out for you?' Lucas says. I glance back down the hill at Archie and Max slowly edging towards us, deep in conversation.

'Not Laurel and Hardy, that's for sure,' I say.

'Who?' Lucas says.

'*You'll* look out for me.' I beam at him.

Ada links her arm with mine again. 'And me,' she says. 'I'll look out for both of you. And maybe I can show you a few things on the drums, Lucas. We can do some together?'

'Really?' Lucas smiles.

'Yeah, it'll be fun.' Ada ruffles his hair.

At the top of Butser Hill, Danny is sat on the bench. I can just make out that he's wearing blue checked pyjama trousers and a matching top. Lucas sees him and breaks into a run, reaching the top ahead of us.

'Nice pyjamas,' I say.

'Thanks. Nice wellies,' he replies, pointing at Mum's pink boots. Lucas looks Danny up and down and raises an eyebrow at his pyjamas. 'I got lost on the way to the bathroom,' Danny says in defence then stands, greeting me with a kiss.

'Ah, for fudge sake, Charley,' Lucas says, watching Danny and I embrace, then turning away and shooting off after the dogs.

We kiss again and then turn with Ada and watch Max and Archie struggling up the hill, taking it in turns to drag each other by the arm.

'I see you have the comedy army escort.' Danny laughs as Max and Archie make it up the final section. 'Is that what you're planting for Violet?'

'Yep,' I say, scanning the summit for a good spot. Ada sits on the bench and Danny pulls me close.

'Get a room, will you,' Max huffs as she gets to the top, breathing heavily and parking the spade up against the bench, turning to check out the view.

Archie groans as he relieves himself of the weight of the little tree. He turns to Danny, checking out his pyjamas. 'Did you sleep up here?' he teases.

I point over at a spot on the hill that's a little out of the way of the main path and has good space around it. 'What about there?' I say. 'There's plenty of space and there's a view out to the west.'

'Violet would like that view,' says Max. She grabs the spade. 'Let's do it.'

We head over and Archie places the pot down in a spot that's perfect. The baby tree already looks at home.

'What kind is it?' Danny asks.

Archie takes in a comedy gasp as if he can't believe that Danny doesn't know what kind of tree it is. Max laughs and rolls up her sleeves ready to dig, her tattoo on display. 'You've done it now, Danny. No lectures please, Archie.'

'Oak,' says Archie as he looks at Danny while gently cradling the leaves in his hand.

I offer to take over from Max for a bit, but she

waves me away. 'This one's mine to dig. You and Archie grab the tree.'

Max finishes the hole. Archie holds the tree as I ease off its pot and we guide it into place. Max stamps the loose earth back into place and we stand back to admire the little Oak.

'What now?' Archie says. 'I feel like we need to salute or something?'

We laugh, then look out over the fields towards the mature oak in the distance. Max strains to see. 'What's that?'

'Can you see something?' Archie asks.

'Yeah, something... Archie,' Max says, 'have you get your bird-watching things on you?'

'If you call them by their proper name, then yes I have.'

'Pass them over, stalker-geek,' Max says. Archie slides his binoculars from the inside pocket of his jacket and hands them to Max. She lifts them to her eyes. 'Nothing,' she says.

'You seeing the mysterious Elsie again?' says Archie.

Max grins. 'She was there. She is everywhere. You just have to open your eyes, Archie.'

Danny peers through the binoculars. He shakes his head and shrugs. 'Nothing,' he says.

Ada looks at Max and laughs. 'You Hillside girls are something else.'

'Girls?' Archie says. 'Why am I always one of the girls?'

'It's a compliment, Archie,' I say.

'I guess,' he says. 'I can be one of the girls.'

'Me too,' says Danny.

I take a deep breath, returning Danny's smile. 'I love this view,' I say.

The End

Thank you!

I hope you enjoyed *Some Kind of Comfort*.

If you can spare a minute to leave a short review or just a rating on your preferred store, then I'd be very grateful. Thanks!

To join my Reader Club, where you can keep up to date on forthcoming publications, news and freebies to go with my books – including a free eBook prequel to the Interland Series called *The Reader* – please visit my website: www.garyclarkauthor.co.uk.

The *Interland* series books can be found here:
THE GIVEN (Interland Book #1)
INTERLAND (Interland Book #2)
THE DARK (Interland Book #3)

Acknowledgments

Whilst not the first book I published, *Some Kind of Comfort* is the first book I wrote. It has a strong personal connection for me, and that reason alone is probably why it took me so long to release it. Even now, after a million drafts, edits, rewrites and re-structures, I feel it could do with another round or two. But, hey, it's time to let it go, set it free to spread its wings and find its own way in the world.

A writer's first novel might be a bit like a band's first album – the one that's influenced by experiences over the early years of the band, and is then passionately splurged out in the recording studio. It might not be the most refined set of tracks, but it's raw, and it encapsulates the heart and soul of the band like nothing else that comes after.

Charley's story is my first album, something I worked on for years, taking me away from my family and into a dark room while I figured out how to write, and how to do justice to her journey. Her story is an important one. There are many like Charley around the world who suffer, many in silence, without the help they need and deserve. Once her story gripped me by the throat, I couldn't get free until it was down on paper.

So, thank you to my family for looking out for me as I struggled in the grip of this story; supported me as I learned to write, working through writing courses at Faber and Curtis Brown; and, picked me up after my tantrums when I ripped up chapters and declared how useless I was, and that I'd never be able to write. Jude, Ella, Evan, Ash – we got there in the end!

Thank you too to my friends who read early drafts and were kind enough to be constructive in their feedback without putting me off! Not one of you said (not aloud, anyway), "Err, yeah... maybe you might want to find another vocation..." – thanks to, Andrea, Lee, Geoff, Hannah and Dave.

Finally, Ella, you are one amazing individual. So generous of thought, kind and selfless – you have such empathy and intuition. Your bravery, openness, and dedication to the plight of others who suffer, whilst trying to navigate your own personal challenges, is staggering, and is what inspired and shaped this book. This might be *my* first album, but you rock!

About the Author

Gary graduated from the University of Surrey in the UK with a degree in Engineering, embarking on a career that has taken him all over the world from the Far East to the Americas. He is a graduate of the Faber Academy and Curtis Brown creative writing programmes. Now a father of three, he has settled with his family close to where he grew up on the edge of the South Downs in Sussex, where he indulges his love of books, and passion for writing.

I'd love to hear from you so feel free to contact me on the email address here.

Author email: gary@garyclarkauthor.co.uk

Or visit my website: www.garyclarkauthor.co.uk

Sources of information and support

Current at the time of publication (2022)

In the UK:

National Health Service

https://www.nhs.uk/mental-health

Mental Health UK

https://mentalhealth-uk.org

For information, support and contacts for mental health charities in England, Wales, Scotland and Northern Ireland, including rethink.org.

Mental Health Foundation

https://www.mentalhealth.org.uk

MIND

https://www.mind.org.uk

Mental health charity

Telephone: 0300 123 3393 (9am-6pm Monday to Friday) or text 86463

The Samaritans

https://www.samaritans.org

Telephone: 116 123 (24 hours a day, free to call)

Time To Change

https://www.time-to-change.org.uk

Resources and support for mental health.

In the US:

Healthline

https://www.healthline.com/mental-health

Mental health resources

National Suicide Prevention Lifeline

The Lifeline is a free, confidential crisis service that is available 24/7.

Call 1-800-273-TALK (8255)

En español 1-888-628-9454

Mental Health First Aid

https://www.mentalhealthfirstaid.org/mental-health-resources

Mental Health America

https://www.mhanational.org

Freedom from Fear

http://www.freedomfromfear.org
Mental health/anxiety disorder charity

S.A.F.E. Alternatives

Information about self-injury and about starting treatment.
S.A.F.E information line: 1-800-DONT CUT (366-8288)

Other sources

CheckPoint

https://checkpointorg.com/global
International support with local websites and emergency contact numbers.

United for Global Mental Health

https://unitedgmh.org/mental-health-support

World Health Organisation

Mental Health: https://www.who.int/health-topics/
mental-health#tab=tab_1